## Was Daniel right about her?

Was her life nothing more than a fight for the sake of fighting?

"I can't apologize for what I am. I've made a lot of headlines in my day, crashed a lot of barriers...and I like it," Dallas admitted. "I like knowing there's nothing I can't do, no frontier too dangerous to explore."

"Except one," Daniel said softly. "You're still single, aren't you? And let me guess—no long-term affairs, no live-in lovers, in fact no emotional commitments of any kind."

Dallas didn't know what to say. There was nothing she *could* say. She felt opened, touched, exposed in a very vulnerable way, because as much as she would have liked to deny it, her only fear was commitment to another person. Love, and all it implied, was still an unexplored frontier to her, and she knew it would always remain so.

# Books by Rebecca Flanders

These books may be available at your local bookseller.

Don't miss any of our special offers. Write to us at the following address for information on our newest releases.

Harlequin Reader Service
P.O. Box 52040, Phoenix, AZ 85072-2040
Canadian address: P.O. Box 2800, Postal Station A,
5170 Yonge St., Willowdale, Ont. M2N 6J3

# The Last Frontier
## REBECCA FLANDERS

*Harlequin Books*

TORONTO • NEW YORK • LONDON
AMSTERDAM • PARIS • SYDNEY • HAMBURG
STOCKHOLM • ATHENS • TOKYO • MILAN

Published November 1985

First printing September 1985

ISBN 0-373-16128-X

# Chapter One

"You want me to go *where*?" Dallas McCabe lighted a cigarette and spared her producer a brief, puzzled glance that contained not so much alarm as disinterest. "South America?"

Simon Armstrong suppressed a sigh of long-suffering patience—a trait he had acquired in spite of Dallas, not because of her—and tried again. "South *Carolina*," he corrected. "The Appalachian Mountains—actually, a place called Burrowsville."

But he was competing both with the enthusiasm in the crowded bar and the closing moments of Dallas McCabe's "Spotlight," and he once again lost her attention. Simon sighed, ordered another round and sat back to wait for the credits.

The two coworkers were celebrating the broadcast of the documentary that had taken seven weeks to film, by watching the program at Darien's, the workingman's bar where most of the research and interviews had taken place. Dallas, the common man's heroine, had once again been elevated to the status of superwoman with the exposé she had done on unfair union practices within the automobile industry, and the excitement level inside this Detroit pub was high.

Simon should have known better than to make his pitch tonight, but he had held out some vague hope that by catching her off guard he would have a better chance.

He had no cause for complaint, Simon knew. In the past five years Dallas McCabe had taken "Spotlight" from a little-known local production to network syndication to the highest-rated prime-time news show in the country. The mere sight of the "Spotlight" van was enough to send crooked politicians, underworld criminals and negligent corporate heads scurrying for cover. Dallas McCabe could not walk down the streets of any major city in America without receiving slaps on the back, hand-pumping congratulations and heartfelt testimonials of admiration and gratitude from nine out of ten passersby.

But not all the lives Dallas touched were affected so positively, and her reputation as a militant champion of justice had not been achieved without making a few enemies along the way. And that was exactly what Simon wanted to talk to her about tonight...if he ever got the chance.

From the screen over the bar a camera pulled back on Dallas sitting behind a news desk, composed and cool in a gray-tweed jacket and a silk blouse that added just the right touch of femininity without fragility. Her blond-streaked hair, cut in a short, practical style that somehow did not appear boyish, framed a face that was high-cheeked and smooth-complected, and her eyes were the shade of blue that the camera loved. Her well-modulated tones floated out over the room: "Until next week, this is Dallas McCabe for 'Spotlight.' Good night." And then chaos broke loose.

Applause and cheers rose up, the swelling crowd of men grew around Dallas, slapping her on the back, ordering another round, rehashing the show, offering congratulations. "Give 'em hell, Dallas!" "That's our woman!" "You show 'em how it's done, lady!" "And if they give you any guff, you just send them out to Darien's; we'll show them a thing or two about making cars, won't we, boys?" There was a rebel yell or two, some playful scuffling, and Dallas shouted back, "I couldn't have done it without you boys! Here's to you!" She lifted her shot glass in a toast and downed her fourth tequila in a single swallow. Another cheer rose up.

It went on for two more rounds, and it never ceased to amaze Simon the way that woman could dispose of tequila—even though he had been there the night she had won thirty-seven hundred dollars by doubling the pot for every shot after the fifth one. She had drunk the ex-champion under the table, and when she got up, she didn't even stagger. That was the stuff legends were made of.

But there was one thing about Dallas's admirers: They were respectful of her privacy, even a crowd of hard-drinking, rough-talking assembly-line workers like this one. When they began to wander back to their own tables with final grins of thanks and encouragement, Dallas signaled for another drink and straightened her arms against the bar, leaning back on the stool with a smile of satisfaction. "We did it, Simon," she said simply, magnanimously inviting him to share the victory. "This'll keep those boys in the Labor Department stirred up for a while." She took out another cigarette and struck a match on the edge of the bar. She squinted a little as she brought the flame up, her words muffled by the cigarette in her mouth. "So what's this about Mulesville?"

"Burrowsville," corrected Simon patiently. "And you've already got plenty of people besides the Labor Department stirred up, which is exactly why I think we're due for a change of pace."

"What kind of change of pace?" Dallas inquired with modified interest. She shook out the flame and gave the bartender a smile as he brought her another tequila.

"Human interest, ecological preservation, natural resources..." Simon tried to dress it up, but already she was looking skeptical. "Look, it's a great story. Trust me. Besides," he added, picking up his beer so that he wouldn't have to meet her eyes, "it's a good chance for you to get out of town for a little while."

For a moment Dallas stared at him, not comprehending, and then she shrugged and lifted her glass. "Oh, that."

In the past five years she had covered everything from baby smuggling to racketeering; she had been in dives and sleazy alleyways and corners of the subway system where men were killed for train fare. She had climbed to the top of a ten-story building under construction to report on the use of faulty materials, with a fifty-mile-an-hour wind threatening to topple her with every step. She had covered the invasion of Grenada and given her report with bullets zinging over her head. She had conducted a blackout interview with a notorious mobster while two hefty men stood just outside of camera range, machine guns pointed at her chest. A few threatening phone calls weren't about to make her turn tail and run.

"Oh, that!" Simon reiterated incredulously, and then glanced around nervously, lowering his voice to a hiss. "It just happens to be your life we're talking about!"

Dallas tried to subdue her exasperation. Simon was one of her best friends in the world and a hell of a producer, but he did have a tendency to be a mother hen sometimes. "Look," she said patiently, "I know I've stepped on a few toes with this union thing, but it's nothing I can't handle. Don't you see that's all the more reason for me to stay and do a follow-up? This is the worst time in the world for me to be traipsing off to South Dakota—"

"Carolina," Simon interrupted. "South *Carolina*." He was quickly running out of patience. "Just hear me out, will you? Will you just do me one favor and hear me out?"

Dallas, figuring the quickest end to the discussion would be to let him have his say, shrugged and lifted her glass again.

"This story was made for you," Simon began his well-rehearsed sales pitch. "The underdog fighting the system, the little guy trying to live his own life under the pressure of bureaucratic insensitivity... Then you throw in the natural-resources element, the environmental protection slant."

"And so what does this have to do with South Brownsville?" interjected Dallas, trying to get him to the point.

"Burrowsville, South Carolina," he corrected, not even bothering to show his impatience this time. "And Daniel Masters is what it has to do with."

"Who's he?" Dallas inquired without much interest. A hockey game had started, and she had twenty dollars riding on it. She sipped her tequila and pretended to listen to Simon, but her eyes were on the television screen.

"That guy who wrote all the books on going back to nature. You know, the professor at M.I.T. who one day just packed up and moved to the mountains, dedicated his life to preserving the culture and the national resources of the Appalachians. He's written five books on folklore and wilderness living, and the critics say they're classics. But he never comes out of the mountains—a real mystery man. Only, now, the government claims the land he's living on belongs to it, and it's trying to evict him. Hell, honey, you could make this into a real cause célèbre, and people would eat it up—besides the fact that you'd be the first one to lure him out of the woodwork, so to speak."

"Oh, come on, Simon," Dallas distracted herself from the hockey game long enough to say. "I'm a street reporter, not a mountain goat. What business have I got out in the Ozarks?"

"Appalachians."

"Whatever. Unearthing some crusty old hermit—"

"Professor. An honest-to-God professor of modern engineering and the author of five, count them, *five* best-selling books." Simon was becoming agitated. "Barbara Walters could make a two-hour show out of that. Why can't you find something to say about the man for thirty minutes? One segment, half a show, that's all I ask. Okay, fifteen minutes," he capitulated. "Look, you go up there, spend a little time checking out the place, talk to him, put together a story, send a camera crew in. What's it going to take? A couple of days? A week?"

"It'll take me that long to find the place," Dallas muttered, and then shouted, "Way to go!" as a score was made.

Simon ran a hand nervously through his thinning hair. He liked to tell people it had been thick and lustrous before he started working with Dallas. "Think of it as a vacation," he persuaded. "A chance to get out of the city, away from the pressures—fresh air and sunshine and communing with nature."

Dallas turned back to him, polite but adamant. "I *like* the city," she said. "I like the smog, the pollution, the crime. It's my life. Fresh air gives me asthma and I'm allergic to the sun. If I want a vacation, I'll go to Lake Erie, not some godforsaken Rocky Mountain—"

"Appalachian," he groaned. "*Appalachian* Mountains."

"And the only kind of nature I'm interested in communing with," she finished firmly, "is the kind that's hanging on the rack at Allen's Furriers."

An expression of bleak determination came over Simon's face. "Dallas," he said simply, "I somehow get the impression that you're not giving this project the full benefit of your serious consideration."

Dallas looked at him, her face softening with an attempt at understanding. She knew that Simon's somewhat-less-than-eloquent plea for the story had little to do with its journalistic merit or even with a genuine interest in the cause of this nature lover in the Adirondacks or the Andes or wherever. He had been nervous about the union piece from the beginning, and from the beginning there had been trouble. Little things at first—equipment had been tampered with, canisters of film exposed, and the van had been vandalized. Then, their best source had disappeared off the face of the earth, and Simon was sure foul play had been involved. Dallas, though admittedly disturbed, thought it was just as likely that the source had been bought off, or simply had got cold feet and decided to run. It wouldn't be the first time something like that had happened in the middle of a story.

Then the threats had started. At work, at home, Dallas received two or three phone calls daily, suggesting that she drop the story and promising dire consequences if she did not. The police had tapped both lines, but so far there were no results. And yesterday a huge wreath of roses, the kind most commonly seen at grave sites, had been delivered to the studio with a note that read: "These may come in handy if you decide to air that story."

That had really frightened Simon. Of course, there was no way to kill the story a mere twenty-four hours before airtime, and for the first time, Dallas had cause to be grateful for the bureaucracy of television production that had prevailed over Simon's better judgment.

It wasn't that Dallas was not somewhat alarmed herself. But if she had been the type of woman who frightened easily, she never would have made it this far in this business. She lived with danger daily; it came with the territory, and she had learned long ago the truth of the old adage: "The only thing you have to fear is fear itself." She would weather this storm, as she had so many others, and would most likely emerge none the worse for wear.

"Look, Simon," she said gently, "I know what you're trying to do, and I think it's sweet. But I'm a big girl; I can take care of myself. The last thing I'm going to do is let a bunch of low-life thugs drive me off my own territory. Besides——'' she lifted a shoulder with a negligent air that she hoped would impart confidence ''—it's over now. The story was broadcast; the truth is out. What can they do to me now?''

Simon smothered a groan and drained the last of his beer. He supposed he had more admiration for Dallas McCabe than for any woman—or man, for that matter—in the world, but she was without a doubt the craziest person he had ever met.

She was sexy, feminine and as sharp as a razor. She was just as much at home pitching pennies on a ghetto street corner as she was at a White House luncheon, and she had never yet failed to walk away from either event the winner. There probably wasn't a red-blooded male over thirteen in the entire country who wasn't in love with her, but the only thing Dallas was in love with was her work.

Oh, there were men in her life, and plenty of them, but her affairs were always very discreet and very short-lived. It would take a superhero to get involved on a long-term basis with a woman like Dallas, and there just weren't too many of those left. Simon knew she had been married once, but he was one of the few people who knew it. Sometimes he wondered if the failed marriage had made her the way she was, or whether the marriage had failed because of the way she was. Sometimes he wished she *were* married; that might just be what it would take to calm her down. Then again, probably not.

Simon set his empty glass on the bar with a thud. ''These people have long memories, lady. And you know perfectly well it's not over—''

"Do you want another?" she interrupted, glancing at his mug, and Simon shook his head. Dallas debated for a moment, then lifted her hand for the check, deciding to call it a night. She wanted to get home and call Senator Bailey; he had promised to watch the show, and she wanted to talk to him while it was still fresh in his mind, to volunteer any further information he needed for the congressional investigation that was just now getting under way. Simon was right. It wasn't over, and she intended to follow this story through every step of the way.

Simon started to take out money, but Dallas reached for her wallet. "No way," she said. "This one's on me." She owed him something for all his concern, and he hadn't wanted to come to the pub to watch the show, anyway.

"Your money's no good here, Dallas." The bartender lifted both hands, with a grin of refusal, when she pulled out some bills. "On the house."

Dallas flashed him one of those smiles that had won a thousand hearts, and tucked her wallet back into the hip pocket of her jeans as she stood. She no longer carried a purse. Besides the fact that it was an unnecessary piece of luggage to keep up with on assignment, it was, in her opinion, an open invitation to muggers. Not that being mugged was any big deal to her; one mugging a month was par for the course, with or without a purse. The last mugger, she remembered with a twinge of amusement, had actually sent her wallet back—money and credit cards intact—when he opened it and discovered who it was he had robbed. There were a few fringe benefits that came with being a celebrity.

"One last time, Dallas," Simon said as they stepped out into the heavy air of the Detroit night. "Get out of town for a while. Let this thing cool off. You've got to—"

"Do my job," Dallas finished for him. The night sounds and the street sounds were a rhythmic background for her footsteps on the cracked pavement. They were as much a part of her as were the scents of greasy food and pollution, the flash of neon and the hostile faces of street gangs. It was in her blood, the city and its life. This was where she belonged, she thought with a touch of impatience, where the action was—covering hard news, fighting crime and corruption, not wandering around in the mountains with some old mad scientist. What was Simon trying to do to her?

"Look," she said firmly, her final word on the subject, "I'm sure your little story about the life and times of Bougainvillea—" Simon didn't even try to correct her this time "—is just fine, but you can get anyone to cover it. I'm going to hang around here, at least until the investigation gets well under way. You're really making a lot of fuss about nothing," she added, gesturing toward her red Datsun, which stood, hub-caps still intact, under the shade of a burned-out light across the street. "These people are all bluster and blunder. Nobody's really going to do anything to me. Don't you know that if I thought there was really any danger, I'd be volunteering for mountain duty quicker than you could blink an eye? But it's stupid. You can't let these people scare you."

Simon stopped and looked at her as they stepped off the curb. His expression was severe, but his tone was far less convincing. "I could order you to go, you know. I'm still the producer of this show."

"And I'm still the star," she retorted. "I can have you fired." Then she grinned, linking her arm through his as she urged him across the street toward her car. "Come on, Simon, don't be such a—"

It sounded like a ten-megaton nuclear explosion. Dallas heard the roar and saw the light, and the force of the expanding hot air was so great that it literally knocked them both off their feet. Then Dallas wasn't aware of anything else until she was hugging the sidewalk, smoky debris and ashes raining down on her, excited voices from the gathering crowd dancing in her ears, and she lifted her head slowly to the yellow-white fireball that had once been her car.

Another thirty seconds, and that car would not have been empty.

Dallas might have been stubborn, impulsive and fashioned with nerves of steel, but she was no fool. It sometimes took a while, but she eventually got the message. And the message she got that night was: These people aren't kidding.

It was a long time that she lay there, stomach-down on the sidewalk, listening to the sound of Simon's terrified gasping beside her and the chattering voices of the growing crowd, watching her car go up in flames while sirens grew ever nearer. Then she turned her head, looked at Simon's white, dirt-streaked face, and she said simply, "Appalachians, did you say?"

## Chapter Two

Burrowsville, South Carolina, was not on the map. That, somehow, did not surprise Dallas. What did surprise her was that places such as Burrowsville could actually exist in this day and age, and that people really lived there.

Armed with directions from the research department, Dallas rented a car at the airport and set out on the three-and-a-half-hour drive to Murdock, which, her secretary assured her, was no more than ten miles away from Burrowsville. All along the road she saw them—towns, villages and sleepy little settlements stuck out in the middle of nowhere, tucked into a curve in the road or perched upon the rise of a hillside, and it never failed to amaze her. Pretty, whitewashed buildings, stately antebellum homes with driveways lined with marigolds and pansies...a service station here, a restaurant there, and then miles and miles of nothing but rolling meadow. What did these people do, she wondered, shaking her head in dim incredulity. How did they support themselves, how did they entertain themselves, and what in the world could ever persuade a person to live way out here? New York, Detroit, Chicago—the entire heartbeat of the civilized world—were thousands of miles away. A trip to the airport would be an all-day affair. Why in the world did they do it?

To another person, the pastoral beauty of Indian summer in the mountains would have been the absorbing fascination on that long drive into nowhere, but Dallas, unused to the wonders of nature, was not about to be impressed with them now. Her reporter's mind was busy dissecting and analyzing this piece of Americana hitherto unknown by her, and the hours passed quickly. She almost wished she had time to stop and do some interviews—not that she thought there was a story here, she assured herself quickly, but it would be nice to satisfy her own curiosity.

The police had been able to discover nothing about the firebomb in her car, and that was another thing that didn't surprise Dallas. Her next story, she had resolved grimly, was going to focus intently on corruption within the Detroit Police Department, and she even had had a proposal on the story ready for Simon the next morning, for a Dallas was a firm believer in the philosophy of getting right back on the horse after a fall. Simon had heard her out patiently for fifteen minutes, then calmly presented her with a round-trip ticket to Greenville, South Carolina.

"Take as long as you need with Masters," he invited magnanimously. "I'm giving you the month off. If you want to take a couple of weeks and do a feature, great. If you want to finish up with him in a few days and spend the rest of the time in Rio or Vegas or the Bahamas, that's fine, too." He could see the protest beginning to form on her lips, and he continued implacably, "But one thing's for certain: If you show your face in this city before the middle of October, I swear to God you'll never work in front of a camera again.''

Dallas began a tirade of furious, sputtering challenges. To say she had completely recovered from last night's fright would have been absurd, but Dallas dealt with fear, just as she did with everything, head-on, examining it and analyzing it and challenging it in the light of day. She had never run from anything in her life; she was not, as she told Simon in no uncertain terms, about to begin now.

Once again, Simon endured her expostulations patiently, with a calmness and a bland intractability in his eyes that made Dallas uneasy. And when she paused for breath, he merely reached into one of the several neat stacks of papers on his desk, pulled out a single sheet and handed it to her. It was a memo to the executive producers, recommending that Dallas McCabe be promoted to the production staff.

"Don't look so shocked, Dallas," he said smiling benignly. "You've worked hard for it. You've earned it; it's long overdue."

Dallas stared at him, speechless first with fury, then with the horrible understanding that he was serious— deadly serious. If he had threatened to fire her again she only would have laughed at him. Her contract was explicit, and the network wouldn't have heard of it. But promote her...that he could do. He could take her off the streets, put her behind a desk with a handful of budget sheets and a file cabinet full of program plans, and the only time she would ever see the work she loved would be in weekly planning meetings. He would do it. He really would.

Dallas replaced the memo carefully on his desk, swallowing hard. There was a small white bandage on

Simon's forehead and a scrape on his cheek from the close encounter with concrete he had had the night before, and Dallas winced a little with guilt for that. He was right, of course, and he had been from the beginning—the union story was dangerous and she had been playing with fire. But that was her job, and that did not make what he was doing now right.

"Simon," she began, keeping her voice very reasonable, "I know you were frightened by what happened last night—"

For just a moment anger snapped in Simon's eyes, and he said, "Frightened? Hell, yes, I was frightened. And so were you, young lady, don't you try to deny it! But that's not what this is all about." He pushed away from the desk and walked over to the window, separating the blinds to look out for a moment on a sooty Detroit morning. He spoke with his back to her. "It's about being reasonable and about reacting appropriately to a given situation."

He turned then, his eyes very serious. "I've got two things to say to you, Dallas," he said. "The first is as a friend—a father, if you will—and the second is as a boss. As a friend...Dallas, you have a real problem reacting appropriately to any situation. You see, you don't react at all—you *act*. You've got to take matters into your own hands; you've got to have that control; you simply can't accept the fact that there are some things you just can't do anything about. Your way of dealing with any unpleasant situation—whether it's something that frightens you or threatens you or makes you angry, or something that simply puzzles you—is to grab it by the horns and wrestle it to the ground and pin it until it cries 'uncle.' You're not happy unless you're fighting something, controlling something, making sure the game is played by your rules. You simply will not learn the value of a tactical retreat, a backing off and a biding of your time, and that sometimes the best thing you can do is just to go with the flow and let things develop at their own pace. I'm not certain that's a healthy way of life, Dallas,'' he said soberly.

Dallas lowered her eyes to his desk to hide, at first, a surge of outrage, and then to hide the sudden and disconcerting flicker of recognition his words had brought. She was the best on-camera investigative reporter in the business; she had made a name for herself using exactly the tactics he deplored; she had righted injustices and uncovered corruption that no one else dared challenge, and no one—no one—had criticized her methods or her work before. But deep inside, what he said struck a nerve, and it unsettled her. Maybe he was right. Even now, as scared as she was, she dealt with her fear by doubling the attack, not by making a sensible decision to back off. And maybe that wasn't the smartest thing to do; maybe that wasn't how reporters lived to a ripe old age anchoring the evening news, but that was the way she led her life. How could he expect her to change now?

"You sound like an est instructor," she grumbled, still not meeting Simon's eyes.

Simon drew himself back into his professional pose. "As your boss," he said firmly, "I want you to know that the network backs me a hundred percent on this. We can't have reporters who make more headlines than they cover. We're canning the story until it cools off."

Dallas's eyes flew to him now, and, mute with shock and horror, she saw that this time he wasn't bluffing.

And, damn it, she knew he was right. The minute a reporter started making the news, she lost her effectiveness, and she was furious with her own impotence over a situation she couldn't control. Still... Burrowsville.

"Look," she tried to persuade, compelled to give it one last shot, "you can't get a story together on this short notice. You take your time getting things set up with What's-His-Name, the hermit, and I'll start nosing around the police department, and I promise, whenever you get the go-ahead, I'll drop everything and rush right out to Appalachia."

Simon smiled benevolently. "We've been working on arrangements for the past month. Everything's all set. Your plane leaves in the morning."

Dallas glared at him. "The past *month*? Without even telling me?"

"I told you," replied Simon mildly. "Last night. Think of it as a challenge," encouraged Simon cheerfully, ushering her to the door. "Capitol Hill, the Securities and Exchange Commission, the AFL-CIO and now Burrowsville, South Carolina. You'll do great, Dallas. It'll open up a whole new world for you."

There was nothing more she could do.

*Burrowsville, here I come.*

DALLAS MCCABE HAD MADE HER REPUTATION by always being willing to do the story no one else would touch. No problem was too complicated, no injustice too small, no scope too limited for Dallas McCabe to investigate—just as there was no story too big, no corruption too widespread, no institution too powerful for her to take on. Simon knew that, and he was banking on it. Of course, he simply could have ordered her to take a leave of absence or a vacation, and given the ultimatums, Dallas would have been forced to comply. But that would have been a mischanneling of the raw energy left over from the union incident, and Simon was too shrewd a producer to waste his reporters that way. He wanted to present Dallas with a challenge, and for a reporter like her the only challenge left was in a project like the Masters's story. As much as she might hate it, as much as she might protest and grumble and declare that her talents were being squandered on a backwoods story that any cub reporter could have covered, she would not refuse to do it. She had a reputation to maintain.

So, at four o'clock in the afternoon, Dallas made inquiries of a Murdock service-station attendant, who not only confirmed the existence of the town of Burrowsville, but was actually able to give her fairly uncomplicated directions. The fact that those directions included such landmarks as a burned-out barn, a billboard that a storm had blown down last winter, and such statements as "Turn left at the lily pond on your right" and "Go past the crooked stop sign to the pasture with old man Harding's Black Angus" did not faze Dallas in the least. She had negotiated the wartorn streets of Beirut; she could certainly find her way across the hills of South Carolina.

Fifteen miles and one hour later, having corrected only two wrong turns—the lily pond had no liles, and the Black Angus had apparently gone in to supper— Dallas parked her car in front of a small weathered building with a sign above it that announced: "Burrowsville Gen'l Merchandise and U.S. Post Office." That and two other buildings seemed to comprise the entire town.

Dallas, who told herself that eight years of reporting the highs and lows of the human condition should have prepared her for anything, tried not to look around with too much dismay. After all, it was much as she had expected, wasn't it?

No. No one, outside of the set designer on a movie about the Great Depression, could have expected this.

Dallas got out of the car, ran her fingers through her wind-tousled hair, straightened the hem of her sweater around her denimed hips, and took a deep breath. *Why,* she wondered again, *would anyone want to live like this?*

That, she supposed, as she squared her shoulders and marched toward the ramshackle store, was exactly what she had been sent here to find out.

The inside of the building was a scene Norman Rockwell had never painted...and for very good reasons, Dallas reflected as she pushed her sunglasses up into her hair and looked around curiously. Lighted by bare-bulb overhead fixtures, it was dim and dusty, a veritable cornucopia of mismatched paraphernalia. Leaning shelves were crowded with canned goods, fishing lures, overalls, saw blades and diet soda. There were barrels of penny nails and stacks of chicken wire against the walls, wood stoves, kerosene lanterns, canvas tents and fishing poles arranged in a random display. Tin washtubs, water dippers and iron cookware were hung on pegs above the wall shelves, as well as an assortment of wicker baskets and a patchwork quilt or two. In one sweeping glance Dallas could see that the place contained everything from foodstuffs to underwear, and it was almost too much for the mind to absorb.

There were three men in the store. One, a hefty man of about sixty, in the typical farmer's blue overalls, with a leathery brown face and strong workman's hands, was examining a collection of insecticides. Another, scarecrow-thin and of indeterminate age, wearing a blue cap with the word "Bass" embroidered in yellow letters on it, was leaning against the counter and grinning companionably at her. The man behind the counter had a gray face and alert blue eyes, and it was he who spoke first.

"Help you, miss?"

Dallas smiled the smile that had won her a hundred interviews, and strolled toward the counter. "I sure hope so. I'm looking for a man named Daniel Masters. Do you know him?"

"The writer fella?" A slow, pleased grin spread over the proprietor's face. "Sure do. Everybody knows him. Made this part of the world famous, that he did." And then his gaze sharpened on her. "What do you want with him?"

"What's the matter with you, Cal?" The sound of a voice at her elbow startled Dallas, and she turned to find the man in overalls peering at her with delighted curiosity growing rapidly into certain recognition. "Don't you ever watch the TV? Don't you know who this lady is? Why, it's Houston—"

"Dallas," corrected Dallas politely, and the man nodded in cheerful agreement.

"Dallas..." He snapped his fingers impatiently, trying to recall the name.

"McCabe," supplied Dallas, and again he nodded in agreement.

"That's it, all right," he declared. "Why, the wife and me, we never miss you Sunday night. Right after preaching, we settle down in front of the TV."

"Sure, I see it now," declared the man behind the counter, pleased. "By dog, if it don't look just like her, too. Can you imagine that! Just wait till I tell Lucy. How about that, Willis." He nudged the counter leaner with his elbow. "We've got a surefire celebrity right here in our own store!"

The skinny man with the Bass cap nodded enthusiastically and just kept grinning at her.

"Hey!" said Cal, the counter man, with sudden understanding. "I'll bet you're here to do a show on Masters, right?"

"You gonna put him on the TV?" inquired the farmer, and then he guffawed. "Good luck, is all I can say! Do you know one of them fancy New York publishers was down to see him last year, and he turned 'im away with a shotgun, way I heard—"

"'Tweren't no shotgun, Luke," objected Cal. "It was a four-by-four."

"I heard shotgun," argued Luke a trifle belligerently, "and I heard it from a man that was there."

*Great,* thought Dallas, trying not to shrink under the mental image of wild mountain men with shotguns and four-by-fours. *Simon, I love you.*

"Do you know—" Cal interrupted the argument with a sudden snap of his fingers "—I should've known something was up!" He turned away from the counter to a collection of small letter boxes behind him—apparently, the post office. "Masters got a letter not more'n a month ago from Detroit. A telegram, too. Didn't think nothing about it at the time, but he don't get much mail, don't you know."

He presented the two envelopes to Dallas with a persuasive smile. "Maybe, long as you're heading up to see him, you wouldn't mind taking these along and saving me a trip."

Dallas glanced at the letter, first with curiosity, then with dismay. The "Spotlight" logo was plainly prominent, and it didn't take much guessing to assume the telegram was from the same source. Simon's "arrangements" for the interview, no doubt—unopened, unread. *Thanks a lot, Simon. You're right on top of things, aren't you?*

"Sure thing." Dallas forced a smile and tucked the envelopes into her pocket. No point in crying over spilled milk now, and she would have to do Simon's job as well as her own. "Now, if you'll just tell me where to find him." She found herself growing more and more anxious to get this job out of the way.

"Well, that won't be no problem," replied Cal, and he looked to Luke for an affirmative nod. The man in the Bass cap grinned at all three of them affably. "You just follow the old Indian trail, can't be no more than twelve-fourteen miles up the mountain; his is the first place you come to."

"Great," Dallas said with some enthusiasm. In all probability, she could go over there tonight, introduce herself, make arrangements for an interview tomorrow, have the camera crew in by the next day, and put South Carolina well behind her before the end of the week. No problem. "Now, just how do I find this Indian trail road?"

"Nothing to it," declared Cal, obviously just as pleased as he could be to help. "Here, I'll draw you a map." He rummaged under the counter and came up with a brown paper sack and a stubby pencil. "You just go out of town about three miles, turn right across from the old cotton mill, follow that road till the pavement ends—oh, about three-quarters of a mile, wouldn't you say, Luke?'' He was making neat marks on the paper that Dallas was certain she would have no trouble at all deciphering. ''Then the dirt road winds around for another mile or so; just follow it till it ends, and there she is.'' He punctuated the map with a cross mark. ''Course, I'm not too sure how I'd feel about leaving my car there for any length of time,'' he confessed, looking out the window to where the rented Chrysler was parked. ''Some of the old boys, you know, they feel like anything left alone is theirs for the taking. Tell you what, though, I'd be glad to ride out there in the morning with you and bring your car back here. Keep a good eye on it for you.''

While impressed by his neighborly spirit, Dallas hardly thought that would be necessary. She was used to leaving her car parked in the worst areas of Detroit; she wasn't going to worry about it for a few hours in the deserted sections of backwoods South Carolina. At least, she thought grimly, nothing could happen to this car that would in any way top what had happened to her last one.

''Thanks,'' she said, folding up the map, ''but I won't be gone that long. And I'd really kind of like to get out there tonight—''

''Ain't no point in starting out tonight,'' interrupted Luke, somewhat alarmed, and Cal echoed his sentiments with a low hoot.

''Lord, no, you don't want to start up that trail with dark coming on,'' he agreed. ''Why, you get off the path and you're wandering into virgin land, some places I don't reckon has ever been explored by white man. All Indian land, don't you know, as far back as you can go up in them hills. Except for a few settlers here and there."

"Besides," concurred Luke, "it'll take you the best part of the day to hike it. Gets pretty rough once you cross Knee-High Ridge."

"Wait a minute," Dallas said. Slowly, very slowly, understanding was beginning to dawn. "Do you mean to tell me that I have to *walk* up that mountain? I can't drive?"

Luke looked at her peculiarly, as though he were surmising that for a hotshot TV celebrity she wasn't, after all, very smart. "Lord, no, miss. The old Indian trail ain't nothing but a footpath. You couldn't even get a wagon up there. What use would the Indians have for a wagon trail? Course, if you had a mule..."

"Oh, hush up, Luke, she ain't got no mule." Cal looked at Dallas with some concern. "Say, you weren't figuring on going up there alone, were you, miss?"

Luke gave him a disparaging look. "What're you talking about, Cal? This here's Dallas McCabe. She ain't afraid of a few old grizzly bears!"

Dallas's voice sounded rather small, but very controlled, as she said, "Would you happen to have a telephone I can use?"

Cal nodded in the direction of the door, to a dusty black wall phone, circa 1940, and Dallas approached it with determination jutting out her jaw and grimness in her eyes. The studio accepted her collect call, and she caught Simon just as he was going out the door.

"Are you *crazy*?" she hissed into the receiver, aware of three pairs of attentive eyes on her back.

"Dallas?" His voice sounded as though it were fighting its way up a tunnel. "Is that you?"

"Who else would it be?" She was having difficulty keeping her voice to a low growl. "How many times did you try to contact Masters?" she demanded.

There was a long hesitation. "Why, we followed the usual procedure..." His voice was drowned out by a crackle of static. "An explanatory letter and a follow-up telegram notifying him of your arrival—"

"You dolt-head! He never received either of them! He doesn't have any idea I'm coming, and it's a fifteen mile *walk*—"

"Fourteen," corrected Luke behind her.

"*Walk*, do you hear me?" ranted Dallas, undeterred. "Up a *mountain*. And he doesn't have any idea I'm coming! He never even consented to an interview! I'm turning right around and—"

"Could you speak up, babe? We've got a hell of a bad connection here."

*"Coming home!"* she practically shouted, then quickly cast a reassuring smile at the three men who were perusing her. She continued pleasantly, "Nice try, Simon, but you blew it this time. I'm not a cross-country hiker, and I'm not going to walk in cold—especially fourteen-miles worth of walking—on an interview. I'll—"

"Where're you calling from anyway? Ole Rocky Top? I'm catching about every other word. But I'm glad you got there okay and I'm glad you called. We've got the story slotted in to air November first—several months before Masters's court case, which should be perfect—but we've got a problem with the camera crew. We can't get one up there until the fifteenth, so you might have to do your prelim and come back for the filming. Sorry to break up your vacation that way, but this story is starting out to be bigger than we thought. It's making the major papers already, and we're budgeting some big promos..." His voice faded out into static again.

Dallas stared in blatant incredulity at the dirty-green wall that backed the ancient telephone. How was it he couldn't hear her, but managed to make sure she heard every strong-arm tactic he had to offer? "Now you wait just a minute, Simon," she said loudly, disregarding her interested bystanders. "I told you—"

"I knew you wouldn't let me down, Dallas." His voice took on that fatherly note of affectionate pride, and Dallas must have known right then that she was lost. "And don't think I don't appreciate it. I know you hated this story, but you're still a pro, and nothing's going to stop you, is it?" Just as Dallas was beginning to wonder suspiciously just how much of her objections he *had* heard, another rattle of static caused her to wince and hold the receiver away from her ear. The last she heard was "Going to be dynamite, I know. And unless we hear from you, we'll have a crew in Burrowsville the fifteenth. Take ca—" And then the line went dead.

Dallas stood there for a long time, grimly debating whether to turn and throw the silent telephone receiver through the window or whether to smile and accept defeat gracefully, like the "pro" she was. Damn it, she decided irritably, at last returning the receiver to its hook with an anticlimactic click, Simon knew she couldn't hold up against the old we-need-the-story-badly-and-we're-all-depending-on-you routine. Simon, like his namesake Legree, had a bagful of dirty tricks, and he wasn't afraid to use a single one of them.

She had, of course, two choices. She could turn right around tonight and head back to Detroit, only, no doubt, to be sent right back to Burrowsville as soon as the snafu about the letters of introduction was cleared up—or she could square her shoulders and put on her hiking shoes, proving to Simon what an idiotic excuse for an assignment this was, and giving him no leeway to accuse her of shirking her duty when she came back empty-handed. It was an awful lot to go through to prove a point, but in the long run it would probably be more efficient than trying to convince Simon verbally. Besides, the worst that could happen was that Masters would shoot her and she would have a legitimate excuse never to return to this miserable little godforsaken hamlet again.

Deliberately, she wiped her dusty hands on her jeans and turned with a smile to her anxiously waiting audience. "Could any of you boys recommend a nice hotel?" she inquired sweetly.

# Chapter Three

Bleary-eyed and disgruntled at seven forty-five the next morning, Dallas stood beside her rented car and listened to Cal's generous last-minute instructions. "You just stay on the footpath," he advised, "and you won't have no trouble atall. Lot's of hill folk use it, you know, when they come down to town for supplies and such, and once in a while we get a tourist bird-watching or plant gathering, so it's worn down and easy to follow. Pleasant little walk, at that, and you picked a good day for it, not too hot." He squinted at the pink-striped sky and amended, "Might get some weather later on, though, so I wouldn't waste any time sightseeing."

Dallas restrained herself from assuring him, quite acidly, that sightseeing was the last thing she had come here to do. She shivered and shoved her hands deeper into the pockets of her down vest and tried to share Cal's benevolent view of the "good day." "If the trail is well-used," she said hopefully, "maybe along the way I'll meet somebody with a horse."

Cal chuckled and spat a stream of tobacco juice on the ground. "Not likely, Miss Dallas. Most folks've already laid in winter supplies, and the only tourist around is you. Nope,'' he decided, leaning back with his hands in his pockets to survey the winding trail again, ''the only thing you're likely to meet along the way is a furry-tailed rabbit or two, maybe a deer if you're not too loud.''

Cautiously, Dallas turned her eyes toward the beginning of the footpath that wound into the woods just beyond a narrow ravine and across a shallow stream. She forced herself to ask the question that had been preying on her mind since last night. ''What about...larger animals?''

He looked momentarily confused, then dismissed it with a shrug and another spit onto the ground. ''Now don't you pay no attention to old Luke. Them bear and cougar are more ascared of you than you be of them, and like as not'll run the other way before you even spot 'em.'' Then he chuckled. ''Matter o'fact, the only time you got to be scared is when they don't run. That means something's wrong. You remember that, Miss Dallas, and you'll be just fine.''

He turned to get back into the car. ''We'll take real good care of your car now, don't you worry. And you remember to just go on up to the Wilkins place when you get back and ask to use the phone; I'll come right to the door to pick you up.''

Dallas cast a longing glance toward the roof of the Wilkins place, visible through the treetops, not fifty yards back the way they had come. There was still time to back out.

But she wasn't going to do it. Not in front of this man who thought she had given God personal advice on how to create the world, and not for the satisfaction of seeing Simon's smirking face. Okay, two days, three at the most, out of her life...what was it going to cost her? A nice little walk in the country couldn't do her any harm, and she could even look on it as something of an adventure.

She gave Cal a brave smile and a cheery wave, thanked him for his help, hitched the backpack more securely on her shoulders, and set off with less than surefooted grace down the slippery, pine-needle-covered ravine. She heard the car start, the tires crunch on the dirt road, and then nothing but her own foot-steps as she set determinedly out on the trail.

Cal had insisted upon selling her the backpack this morning, as well as a pair of sturdy hiking shoes and some camper's provisions for lunch. She had thought at the time that, if nothing else, she had probably brought him more business than he had seen in a month, but as soon as she started on the trail, she was grateful for his suggestions. The cowboy boots she had worn down were stylish but hardly practical, and the last thing she needed to keep up with while hiking fourteen miles was a overnight bag. She had trans-ferred into the backpack two changes of clothes, a carton of cigarettes, and—just in case she was gone longer than she planned—a bottle of tequila. There was still room left over for half a dozen candy bars, a canteen of water and some very uninteresting-looking packets of dried food that Cal had insisted she take. She was, she thought, prepared for anything.

Like most Americans, Dallas considered herself in pretty good shape. She was hardly ever more than five pounds overweight, and she solved that in a matter of days with crash dieting. She jogged whenever she wasn't too tired or too busy, if it wasn't too hot or too cold, and sometimes she got as far as two blocks be-fore she was distracted by a fan or a street acquaintance and allowed herself to be talked into going into the nearest café for lunch or a quick drink. She smoked too much, but she did make a concentrated effort to cut down—every January first from sunup to noon.

Consequently, Dallas gave no thought to pacing herself. She tackled the hilly terrain with the same aggressive, ground-eating stride that she would have taken on Michigan Avenue, working off some of her distaste for this assignment by getting on with it quickly. In five minutes she was sweating; in ten, she was panting. When fifteen minutes had passed, she decided it was time to stop and have a cigarette.

By the third cigarette break Dallas began to realize this little jaunt was quite different from a lunchtime stroll along the riverfront. For one thing, it was a lot quieter. For another, Dallas realized in amazement as she paused, gasping, to look back at the distance she had covered, she was traveling straight uphill. Every muscle in her body was quivering, and her lungs ached with each cold inhalation of air. The backpack felt ten pounds heavier than it had when she started. And worst of all, an incredulous glance at her watch showed she had barely been traveling an hour.

With a groan, Dallas slipped the backpack off her shoulders and, careful of the tequila, lowered it to the ground. Then she stood there in the middle of the stubbly footpath, with nothing but vegetation as far as she could see, hands on her knees, trying to breath deeply, cursing the day she had ever heard of Simon and "Spotlight" news. The only thing that kept her from turning around at the moment was the outrage she would feel at having put her body through this torture for nothing.

Thus committed, Dallas's attitude toward this assignment took on the air of a vendetta. She *would* make it to the top of this mountain. And once she got there, she would, by all that was holy, get a story out of Daniel Masters, if she had to sit on his chest and beat it out of him. Dallas McCabe would not be broken. Not by union mobsters, not by Simon Armstrong, not by her stubbornly protesting muscles, not by the entire range of Appalachian Mountains, and, most certainly, not by a redneck recluse.

Daniel Masters. Her eyes narrowed dangerously as she focused her thoughts on the man behind her misery. A recluse, was he? Publicity-shy? Well, he had best be prepared to get over that little quirk, and quickly, because after all this trouble, Dallas McCabe was not going to be turned away on a whim. And she could positively guarantee, as she stood in the midst of an empty forest, sweating like a pig and gasping for breath, that from this moment onward Daniel Masters's life would never be the same.

She dug into her backpack for the folder on Masters prepared by the research department—which until now she had not had the least inclination to read—and took out her canteen and a candy bar as well. A drink of the tepid, stale-smelling water did nothing to fortify her spirits, but the chocolate helped to erase the taste, and with a final, determined breath, she swung the backpack onto her shoulders and trudged onward, reading as she walked.

Daniel Masters, thirty-six years old, born in St. Louis, Missouri. In addition to his professorial duties at M.I.T. he had headed up the research and development department at a respected electrical-engineering firm, and was known for his contribution to the microcomputer. Dallas had no trouble categorizing him: one of those unstable computer personalities, all wrapped up in bits and bytes, who suddenly reached circuit overload, freaked out and moved to the mountains. Typical stress burnout, she decided with a thread of disdain. If they did feature stories on every high-powered intellectual who had a nervous breakdown, they wouldn't have time to cover the news. And, as a woman who daily faced down the terrors of the streets of Detroit, she had little respect for a man who couldn't hold his own against a bunch of computer chips.

Masters's first book, *The Life and Lore of Appalachia*, had received moderate attention from regional reviewers when it was first published. His second book, *Mountain Song*, had apparently chronicled his adventures in the wilderness and had brought the first book back into prominence. These were followed, over the next two years, by two more nonfiction works about survival in the wilderness, ancient lore and legend, and the balance of nature—all subjects that Dallas found less than riveting, but that the public apparently loved. His most recent work, *Wildflower: A Novel*, had been on the *Times* best-seller list for eighteen weeks and had received enthusiastic literary acclaim. Unfortunately, Dallas had missed that one, too.

The man was prolific, she had to give him that. But then, sitting up here in a cabin on top of the world, what else did he have to do but write? Daniel Masters knew a good thing when he saw it, that much was obvious—how to make a fortune in three easy steps. And after Dallas gave him all the free publicity he could use, he would probably sweep down from the mountaintop and retire to his tax-sheltered condo in the Bahamas, where he would no doubt make a second fortune writing books on how to make a million before age forty. *And that's the way of the world, folks,* Dallas thought bitterly as she forced herself to put one foot in front of the other. *Some people spend their lives carving success out of a rock with a teaspoon, while others trip all over it wherever they go.*

To her amazement and annoyance, that brief biography, and an even briefer summary of Masters's land-dispute case, was all the research department had managed to dig up. It was typical of a slipshod story thrown together at the last minute, nothing more than a manufactured excuse for a feature. And from this she was supposed to make a half-hour television interview. "I'll get you for this, Simon," she muttered, and thrust the papers over her shoulder and into her open backpack. "If it's the last thing I do, I swear I'll get you."

By late afternoon her shoulders felt as if they were splitting at the seams and her spine threatened to go right through her skull if she took one more step. The backpack, which had seemed so efficient and manageable this morning, now weighed a ton. Groaning, she stopped to slip it off her shoulders.

Dallas could practically feel the steam rise from her overheated body to meet the cool, damp air that surrounded her. Even her eyes were blurred with fatigue and perspiration, and she thought, very close to despair, *How much farther? How much farther can it possibly be?* But a deeper question nagged at her, one she would not consciously even put into words, and that was, *How much farther could she go on?*

The sound of water was closer now; the under-growth, in concurrence, was a bit more lush and thick, giving the forest an even darker, stiller atmosphere. Glancing up through the shadows of the close-growing pines, Dallas discovered to her dismay that there was more than one reason for the lack of sunlight. The puffy white clouds that she had glimpsed intermit-tently all morning had lost their innocence and had gathered to a slate-gray blanket overhead that seemed close enough to touch and was dropping closer every minute. The wind had begun to pick up, too, and car-ried with it the very definite smell of rain.

"Great," she muttered, thrusting her hands into her pockets in an unconscious stance of self-defense and looking around her. But no amount of bravado would protect her from the inexorable forces of nature, and the best she could hope for was to try to outwalk it. The very thought of picking up that backpack again was almost more than she could stand.

"All right," Dallas decided with a breath, looking down at the sturdy orange backpack. "Obviously, something has got to go."

Groaning with every movement, she got down on her knees and began to search through the contents. Jeans, sweaters, underwear... The reporter in her would not let her part with her notebook or the Mas-ters file, and the addict in her could not consider leav-ing behind the carton of cigarettes, which hardly weighed enough to matter anyway. At last it came down to the fifth of tequila, which weighed almost more than everything else in the backpack put to-gether, and the four remaining candy bars. She solved one problem by eating two candy bars without cere-mony, but still she was left staring regretfully at the tequila bottle, which she had every reason to believe would become her most valuable possession before the day was over.

But she didn't really have much choice. She uncapped the bottle, took a generous swig in last salute, and then, wincing and gasping against the eye-watering influx of alcohol into her system, she tossed the bottle into the bushes. And then she froze.

The bushes had begun to move.

There was no mistake about it: a purposeful rustling, a pause, a huge movement that shook the leaves of the undergrowth frantically, stopped, then proceeded again. Something was coming out of the woods toward her. And it wasn't human.

For a moment Dallas was frozen with fear, the tripping, thundering roar of her heart making breathing impossible, the perspiration on her forehead and her neck and in her armpits turning abruptly icy. *Bears. Cougars. Mountain lions. Wolves.* Dear God, what did she know about wild animals? She would be torn to pieces.

Another movement from the bushes sent a rush of adrenaline through her, and cold breath returned to her lungs in a gasp. Blindly, never taking her eyes off the increasingly purposeful movement of the bushes, she groped around on the ground until her fingers encountered a thick, long branch that would serve as a weapon.

Slowly, Dallas got to her feet, facing the movements of her adversary, gripping the club in both hands like a baseball bat. Her eyes were wide, her chest heaving with gasps for breath she no longer seemed to be able to control, and the rattling of the bushes was magnified tenfold over the roar of her heart in her ears as the enemy moved ever closer. "Holy Mary, Mother of God," Dallas whispered, and squeezed her eyes shut, gripping the club even tighter.

The animal broke through.

Dallas swung blindly, and the rotten wood broke into five separate pieces with the whoosh of air. The force of the missed blow knocked her off balance and onto the ground, where she sat, holding a four-inch stub of broken branch and staring straight into the startled eyes of a raccoon.

The moment the two terrified adversaries locked stares seemed eternal, but it was hardly longer than a heartbeat. Dallas scrambled to her feet, grabbing the backpack, at the same moment the surprised forest creature darted across her path toward an opposite tree. Dallas set off again along the trail at a somewhat-increased pace than she had kept before, her heart thudding in her ears, her feet barely touching the ground.

*Someday,* she thought dimly, *I'll laugh at this.* But right at that moment she was too busy putting distance between herself and unknown danger to laugh about anything.

It began to rain. And then it began to pour. The solid earth beneath the carpet of pine needles dissolved like confectioners' sugar and sucked at her boots, slowing her progress. Cold rain dripped off her hair and trickled down her neck, soaking her shirt, despite her waterproof vest. Great drops of water sprang off the canopy of overhead branches and splashed in her face, and terrible noises came from the encroaching undergrowth on either side as rain met earth. She was slapped by branches, tripped by vines, torn by brambles, and the foggy, rain-induced twilight that penetrated the forest made visibility almost zero. She had given up cursing Simon and Masters and even herself. She had only enough energy to put one foot in front of the other.

And then the unthinkable happened. The trail, which had grown ever narrower with each step, abruptly forked. Dallas stopped and stared. Cal had said nothing about a divided trail. He couldn't possibly have mentioned it; she was certain she would have remembered. But would she have? How much attention had she really been paying last night, so embroiled was she in her own fury and determination for vengeance.

But it didn't matter now. Dallas stood there with cold rain plopping on her head and dripping down the back of her neck, and she knew she had to make a choice. One fork of the branch, narrow and overgrown, curved off to the left and led heaven-knew-where. The other choice, though not in much better condition, moved straight ahead, where it was overtaken completely after a few yards by a thick tangle of vines and bushes. "Just keep going," Cal had said, "straight up that trail...can't miss it."

"All right," Dallas muttered, pushing back a handful of her soaked hair. "Straight ahead." Where, no doubt, the trail would emerge clear and visible again, on the other side of the copse. If not, she could always turn around and go back. She plunged into the undergrowth.

Dallas took two, perhaps three, stumbling, tugging steps, fighting against the vines that wound themselves about her ankles and the thorny twigs that tore at her clothes. She tried not to think about all the creatures that might be hiding in that tangle, ready to snap and snarl and leap out with bared claws. She clenched her teeth and squared her shoulders and pushed determinedly on until suddenly she wasn't walking anymore. She was falling.

Her heels dug into slippery clay, her splayed hands grasped at blades of grass and scrawny twigs that slipped right through her fingers, and the seat of her jeans made a perfect pattern in the mud as she slid downward unimpeded, landing at last, with a primal scream of sheer shock, chest-deep in icy water.

For a moment Dallas sat there, sputtering and gasping, convinced by the numbness of her limbs and the shortness of her breath that she was mortally wounded or on the verge of drowning, at the very least. But the swirling of cold water around her soon restored a measure of coherency, and with another yelp of pure discomfort and disgust, she staggered to her feet.

The stream in which she had landed was not deep—barely to her knees when she stood—and hardly over six feet wide, but the current was strong and the bank was sheer. Forcing life into her paralyzed muscles, fighting against the dead weight of her backpack and her soaked clothing, she struggled to the sharp drop of the bank. She got a handhold on a protruding root, another on an overhanging sapling, which looked as though it would give up the ghost at the slightest provocation, and pulled herself precariously up. Her numb feet slipped and slid on the slick mud; her hands threatened to loose their hold. She was panting and moaning like an animal now, as with every bit of determination she had, she pulled herself upward and caught hold of a clump of grass.

Crawling and sithering, in danger of tumbling backward into the stream with every movement, she maneuvered herself by inches up the embankment, where at last she collapsed, facedown in the mud and weeds, rain pommeling her back, and the sound of rushing water and her own agonized breathing filling her ears.

When at last she opened her eyes in preparation to push herself up onto her knees, she found herself staring at a large pair of sturdy, mud-encrusted boots. Her eyes went slowly upward, over a pair of denim-covered legs, across the hem of a wet black poncho, until she found herself looking directly into both barrels of a shotgun.

Dallas slowly, ever so cautiously, pulled herself upward. The gun did not waver. Her eyes went carefully above gun level to the scowling, black-bearded face above it, and her smile was as weak as her voice. "Mr. Masters, I presume."

# Chapter Four

The gun swiveled slowly to one side as he extended a hand to help her up, and that was when Dallas realized, to her enormous relief, that the weapon had not been pointed at her at all. He was merely holding it at the waist-level hunter's stance while he walked, and her nose had happened to get in the way. Puffing out her gratitude in a huge sigh, Dallas grabbed his wrist as his hand closed firmly around her forearm, and she pulled herself to her feet.

"Who are you?" he demanded, not entirely without hostility.

He was without a doubt the largest man Dallas had ever met, and she had spent half her life with teamsters, football players, and pro wrestlers. Perhaps it was only his stance, as he loomed there in the midst of the lashing elements, with a gun in his hand and a glare in his eyes, that put her in mind of the rulers of Olympus, but he was definitely big: six four at the least, with shoulders broad enough to block Dallas's view of the surrounding countryside, legs like tree trunks and hands as strong as a lumberjack's, wild black hair, well below his collar and tousled by the rain, a strong, square, bearded face and scowling eyes that could have been any color from hazel to black, but now reflected nothing more than aggravated wariness. *Pure, unadulterated Neanderthal,* observed Dallas with as much dispassion as possible. He probably even had hair on his back. All in all, the prospect of a meaningful, or even coherent, interview with this specimen did not hold much promise. And that was even presupposing he didn't push her off the mountain before she asked the first question.

*Way to go, Simon,* Dallas thought. *You rescue me from a bunch of union mobsters so I can be murdered by a wild mountain man and buried in the hills, where no one will ever find my body. You sure know how to keep your reporters in line.*

Dallas forced another smile, blinking at the rain that dripped persistently from her plastered-down bangs into her eyes, and she said pleasantly, "I'm Dallas McCabe." The smile, and her courage, faded beneath his unrelenting stare, and she added in a somewhat smaller voice, "I guess I didn't catch you on a good day."

The rain was increasing its force now, pounding on the earth and the overhanging leaves, making the stream behind them sound like an ocean. His eyes narrowed further against its power. "Are you lost?"

"That depends," responded Dallas, shivering with a new onslaught of misery, wet and cold, "on where I am. Are you Daniel Masters?"

Now he was definitely cautious. "I am. What do you want with me?"

There could hardly have been a more inauspicious moment in which to announce her intentions, and Dallas had no idea of doing so while her bad-tempered quarry stood in the pouring rain holding a shotgun.

She unzipped her vest and reached into the inside pocket for her damp letters of introduction. She handed them to him with another forced smile. "I brought your mail," she offered.

He hesitated, studying her, then took the envelopes. He glanced at them briefly, and to Dallas's enormous relief, his face almost relaxed into a smile. "Since when can Cal afford special-delivery service?" he said, but he did not wait for an answer. He tucked the letters into his pocket beneath the wet poncho and bent to retrieve the large burlap sack he had dropped to the ground when he reached to help her up. "Come on," he said with a jerk of his head. "My place is just over the hill."

"Best news I've heard all day," Dallas muttered as he swung the sack over his shoulder and started up the hill against the driving rain.

"Why didn't you take the bridge?" he tossed over his shoulder as an afterthought.

Dallas stared blankly at the black expanse of his back. "What bridge?" she shouted back over the noise of the rain.

He merely shook his head in helpless exasperation for the apparent stupidity of flatlanders, and gestured toward her left.

Dallas suddenly realized where the other fork in the trail had led.

The ferociously increasing rain and the demanding uphill climb precluded further conversation, even had Dallas been desirous of it. With the end of her journey so close, the sheer depth of her exhaustion overcame her, and it was all she could do to keep her eyes upon the steadily plodding footsteps in front of her. She was dimly aware of the swaying overhead limbs, the sucking mud, the slapping branches that Daniel Masters pushed inexorably aside, but mostly all she felt was her aching lungs, her screaming muscles, and the cold-to-the-bone misery of being soaked through. Nothing else had any real meaning to her until she looked up to see a wisp of smoke coming through the stack-rock chimney just ahead.

Through the twilight-gray curtain of rain the log cabin looked sturdy and secure. Its roof sloped sharply over a narrow front porch; the steps leading up to it were nothing but flat rocks of graduating sizes. Vaguely she was aware of a couple of outbuildings and a split-rail corral, but mostly she concentrated on that curl of smoke from the chimney and the warmth it implied as she fought her way, gasping and stumbling, across the cleared area of stubble and mud toward the steps.

On the porch, Daniel paused to dump his sack and remove his mud-encrusted boots. From chin to toe, from neck to heel, Dallas was covered with the slime of thick, red clay. The waterproof vest had offered some protection, but most of her was soaked. She hardly thought taking off her boots would do much to protect the inside of the cabin from mud and rain, but because her host was doing so and she was too tired to protest, she bent to untie her boots and pull them off. Her frozen toes screamed in protest.

Without a word of invitation, or even a backward glance at Dallas, Daniel lifted the wood-and-leather latch and strode inside. Dallas, shivering, followed him, her wet socks leaving squishy footprints on the hardwood floor.

Dallas was too tired to give more than a cursory inspection to her surroundings as she closed the door against the blowing rain behind her. It was a single room, containing a bed, table, chairs, shelves and other clutter. Against the front wall, atop a stone hearth, was an old-fashioned Franklin stove, toward which she gravitated instinctively. There was a typewriter on the table, and on the typewriter was the biggest, blackest, ugliest looking bird Dallas had ever seen. It was a testament to her exhaustion that she didn't even blink once in surprise. After all she had encountered today, it seemed only natural that her last stop should be an Abe Lincoln log cabin presided over by a remnant from an Edgar Allen Poe poem who stared at her with unblinking, beady eyes and looked as though it were at any minute prepared to squawk, "Nevermore!"

Neither did it surprise her when Daniel Masters greeted the bird by its only possible name. "Well, Lenore, how the hell did you sneak in here? I thought we had a deal: daytime, you act like a bird; nighttime, you can pretend you're a house pet." As he spoke he was placing his rifle on the hooks designed to hold it over the fireplace, stripping off his rain cape and hanging it on a peg by the door. He didn't even glance around as the bird answered him with a series of irritated, raucous squawks. "Hm." He shook his long dark hair like a dog, scattering water droplets everywhere, and continued his scolding conversation with the bird. "Don't expect sympathy from me, you underdeveloped pterodactyl. I just came out of that storm, remember? A little water never hurt anybody."

Through another paroxysm of shivers, Dallas watched the bird lift itself from the typewriter and sail across the room, making a perfect two-point landing on Daniel's shoulder. Daniel brushed it away irritably. "Go away, you brat, before you find yourself sitting in a wet tree with the rest of your kin."

Lenore gave one last squawk of protest and fluttered to perch on top of the window frame, where she could observe the goings-on of her master undisturbed.

Combing back his wet hair with his fingers, Daniel Masters began to unbutton his damp flannel shirt, never once glancing in the direction of his shivering houseguest. Incredibly, he seemed to have forgotten all about her. The shirt came off and was tossed over a ladder-back chair, and he stood in water-splotched jeans, socks and a tight-fitting, long-sleeved, woven-cotten undershirt of the type worn by skiers and other outdoor sportsmen. Without hesitation, he reached down and stripped that over his head, too.

Though Dallas generally preferred her men—like everything else in her life—a bit more on the manageable side, she could not help but be impressed by this giant's physique. His shoulders were rock-hard, triceps carved in precise relief between corded neck and bulging biceps. His chest was as broad as a mountain, pectorals firm and well-developed, not a rib or a ripple of fat showing down the contours of his torso toward a firm waist. He did not, after all, have hair on his back, but the dark, straight pattern of it along his chest was like a finely woven silken web that tapered intriguingly as it neared his jeans.

His fingers went unselfconsciously now to those jeans, unsnapping, unzipping, and though Dallas would not deny a certain detached curiosity about the remainder of that overdeveloped physique, her gut instincts told her that this might not be the best time to have her curiosity satisfied. She cleared her throat purposefully, catching his attention. "Excuse me."

He paused with perhaps two inches of white flesh showing between waist and jeans, and his expression, when he jerked his head around, was definitely startled. And then, incredibly, as he registered her presence, an uncertain but unmistakable flush of color began to creep its way up his neck. If Dallas had had even a quarter of the energy necessary to do so, she would have laughed out loud.

Quickly, he tugged the jeans up again and refastened them. "Sorry," he mumbled, and his eyes were uncomfortable as he looked at her. "Guess I'm too used to living alone." He looked at her for another moment and then decided, with uncanny powers of observation, "You're wet."

Quickly in charge again, he turned to a shelf and extracted from it a threadbare towel, a washcloth and a flannel shirt of the type he had just taken off. "The things in your backpack are probably soaked," he said, pressing the bundle into her hands. "I'll stoke up the stove in a minute and we'll try to dry them. Meanwhile, you should get out of those wet clothes." He hesitated, obviously considering that problem. "I'll change on the porch," he decided. "Just throw your dirty clothes outside when you're done." Then, grabbing a bundle of fresh clothes for himself, he left her with only the inscrutable Lenore for companionship.

*Not exactly a raving welcome,* Dallas decided philosophically, *but not a bad start. At least he didn't throw you out into the rain—not yet, anyway.*

Deciding to take advantage of his hospitality while it lasted, Dallas stripped off her soaked and filthy clothing as quickly as her aching muscles would allow, huddling close to the stove all the while. Its meager heat did little to penetrate the chill that puckered her skin and seemed to go right through to her deepest tissues, and she thought grimly, *Hypothermia. Pneumonia. A person could die of a head cold way up here in the middle of nowhere, and it would serve you right, Simon.*

She found a pitcher of water on a small table near the bed, and, dampening the washcloth, did her best to scrub away the mud from her hands and face. Then, with the towel wrapped around her hair and dressed in the soft, though not overly warm, flannel shirt that almost reached to her knees, she scooped up her soiled clothing and opened the front door.

Daniel was waiting for her, relatively dry next to the wall, dressed in fresh jeans and a buttoned but untucked cotton shirt. His jeans were hanging over the porch rail, where they caught the full force of water dripping from the eaves, and without a word, he took her clothes and arranged them in like manner. "They'll be clean in an hour," he told her and gestured her back inside. "Now let's see what we can do about getting the rest of your things dried out. Old Cal must be going soft in the head," he muttered, "sending a woman up here in the middle of a storm."

Dallas bristled. "It wasn't raining when I left," she informed him. "And my being a woman has nothing to do with it. As for Cal…"

But the creak of metal as he opened the stove door drowned out her voice, and Dallas thought it was just as well. It would probably be more effective if she waited until her teeth stopped chattering to introduce herself, anyway.

He piled two fat logs on top of the radiant coals inside the stove, stirred a few sparks to life with a poker, then closed the door and got to his feet. "That should do it," he declared with satisfaction, brushing off his hands. "Just spread your things out on the hearth; they'll dry in no time. Do you have people up on the mountain here? Where are you planning to stay tonight? I know you didn't come all the way up here just to bring me these."

As he spoke, he was extracting the two water-splotched envelopes from the pocket of the shirt he had discarded, and Dallas correctly surmised that to answer his questions at this point would be redundant. She busied herself by kneeling beside the hearth, quietly and quickly unfolding her damp clothing from the backpack and spreading it before the stove. She cast furtive, unobtrusive glances at him as he opened first the letter and then the telegram. She watched his face darken as he read, and then grow completely implacable. She watched him crumple both sheets in one huge fist, and then he looked at her.

What might have once passed for friendliness in his manner was now completely gone. His eyes were blank, his lips tight. He said expressionlessly, "Dallas McCabe."

Dallas got to her feet, the wretched condition of her overused body momentarily forgotten as she called upon her last resources of strength for a final defense. "I'm sorry about the mix-up, Mr. Masters," she said. "Obviously, those letters were supposed to get here before I did." She gave him one of her most endearing smiles. "This is really very embarrassing, but I hope you'll—"

"I don't give interviews," he said flatly. His eyes were cold as he glanced toward the rain-sheeted window and then back to her again. "It's too late for you to go back down tonight. You're welcome to supper and a place to sleep, but that's all. I want you off my property and well on your way off this mountain by sunrise tomorrow."

And with that, he grabbed his rain-slicked poncho and stalked out of the cabin.

Dallas released a pent-up breath, smoothed her palms on the soft flannel covering her hips, and looked around the cabin a little uncertainly. Her eyes landed upon the vulturelike countenance of the bird, and she lifted her shoulders slightly in self-defense. "Well," she murmured, "I think it's going pretty well so far, don't you?"

But the forced optimism collapsed into weariness as she lowered herself by groaning inches back onto the floor, searching for a cigarette. The pack she had opened an hour before had sustained water damage, and, never one to waste commodities, Dallas shook out the remaining damp, crushed cigarettes and arranged them in a neat row along the hearth to dry. He didn't do interviews, huh? So, big surprise. This morning it would have been enough to report to Simon that Daniel Masters himself had put an end to this insane assignment, but Dallas's competitive instincts had been aroused during that body-slaying journey up the mountain, and she had no intention of letting Simon, or Daniel Masters, off the hook that easily now. The only trouble was that, right at this moment, she was too tired to do anything at all about it.

She found a dry package of cigarettes midway through the carton and opened it with fingers that shook with fatigue. Her lighter was too water-logged to be of much use, and she searched around the cabin for a match, her temper deteriorating by the minute.

Daniel Masters seemed to collect everything but matches. The open shelves were lined with row upon row of colorful foodstuffs in clear glass jars, books with torn covers and well-turned pages, bowls and jars that held everything from buttons to nails. The drawers in the nightstand held pencils, paper and five typewriter ribbons. Even the rafters were occupied, she noticed, strung with rows of dried weeds and what looked like bunches of onions, and lined with colorful clay bowls that contained who-knew-what. Finally, she ran her hand along the top of the mantel and discovered a box of rifle ammunition, a paperback book, and—at last—a tin box that, when opened, yielded a dozen boxes of kitchen matches.

"Eureka," Dallas mumbled. She struck a match on the mantel, popped a cigarette into her mouth, and was just about to light it when the door whooshed open with a gust of wind and rain.

"Not in here you don't, lady," Daniel Masters commanded sternly.

He strode inside, having once again left his boots on the porch, and lowered the burlap sack he had been carrying when Dallas first met him onto the table with a thud. She could only imagine what kind of disgusting dead game it contained. "Air pollution is one of the things I came up here to get away from," he said. He pulled off his black slicker and hung it again on the hook by the door. "If you want to smoke, go outside."

Dallas, staring at the torrential rains that pressed against the window in one continual flood, opened her mouth for an incredulous protest. But all she got out was a yelp as the match began to burn her fingers, and she shook it out quickly, scowling at him. What else could she expect from a bleeding-heart naturalist? One whose conservative values, she thought as her eyes narrowed suspiciously upon the sack on the table, apparently did not extend to wildlife preservation. What poor dumb creature had he slaughtered in cold blood to satisfy his macho caveman instincts? Rabbit? Squirrel? Fowl?

Daniel took down a huge iron pot from its hook on the wall and filled it with water from a wooden bucket. He strode over to the stove, jerked the cover off of one of the burners, and set the pot down on the fire with a thud. Then he turned on her. "What the hell is the idea," he demanded, "sending a reporter all the way down here from Detroit to come barging into my house, invading my privacy, announcing that you're going to do a half-hour television show—television, of all things—without so much as a please or thank you! You could have been shot for trespassing, do you know that? Didn't it ever occur to you people to wait for an invitation?"

Dallas held on to her temper as well as she could. Carefully, she returned the cigarette to its package, keeping her face impassive. "I explained to you about the letters, Mr. Masters."

He turned away with an impatient hiss. "I'm not interested in letters. I want to know what you're doing here." He lifted a huge bowl of vegetables from the counter, and the glance that scraped across her as he turned was both damning and filled with derision. "A woman, for God's sake,'' he muttered in disgust. He set the bowl on the table with a great deal more force than was necessary. "That's all I need."

Dallas's fragile control was beginning to fray. "I don't think my gender has anything to do with—''

"Look at you." He gestured abruptly, his dark eyes fighting with a mixture of anger and contempt. "Half-drowned, covered with scrapes and bruises—you'd still be lost in the woods if I hadn't happened along! They couldn't settle for just sending a woman up here, they had to send an incompetent one. What kind of slipshod outfit do you work for, anyway?" He picked up a knife and sliced a carrot neatly in two, the thud of the blow drowning out his remaining muttered words.

Dallas seethed. *Misogynist,* she thought. *Ignorant backwoods bigot. Bunny killer. I'm going to tear you limb from limb in front of a prime-time network audience. When I get through with you, every skeleton in your closet is going to be dancing jigs, and there won't be a rock left for you to hide under.*

Instead, she said sweetly, "Do you have something against women, Mr. Masters?" As she spoke, she bent, at great personal expense, to lift her water-splotched notepad and pen, poised to note his answer.

His look was long and cool and not the least bit intimidated. His eyes, Dallas noticed, were brown. And with a knife the size of a meat cleaver in his hand, he looked even bigger than he had before. "I have," he responded evenly, "something against manipulation. I am not for sale, Miss McCabe, not to *Life* magazine, not to the 'Today' show, and most certainly not to—'' he gave an impatient turn of his wrist that dismissed Dallas and all like her in a single motion "—whatever the name of your outfit is."

Dallas's ears pricked up with the mention of her competitors and she thought Simon must have been onto something after all. But that was too little too late for whatever remained of Dallas's diplomatic spirit, and the look she leveled at him had brought several U.S. congressmen to their knees. "You are news, Mr. Masters," she said coldly. "God knows why, but somebody out there thinks something about you is worth telling and, by God, I'm going to be the one to do the telling." Her eyes crackled with the low, restrained fury that was only the lightning flashes before the storm; her hand clenched on the notepad, and with every word her voice grew lower, more deliberate. Masters paused in his energetic chopping of vegetables to look up at her.

"Before I'm done with you," she continued tightly, "every man, woman and child in America will know everything about you from what you have for breakfast to the size of your socks, and if there's anything interesting in between they'll know that, too. If you stole a candy bar when you were six, if you ever cheated on an exam, if your grandmother was a Republican... Got any old girl friends you'd rather forget, Mr. Masters?" she demanded, eyes glittering. "Any income-tax returns that weren't quite accurate? History of arrests, misdemeanors, traffic tickets?" As she spoke, she moved toward him until nothing but the table separated them. On this she braced her arms, leaning forward belligerently, her eyes glittering, her voice rising. "Because nothing about you is private anymore, Mr. Masters, have you got that? I was sent here to get a story—nobody told me what *kind* of story. And I'm not leaving here until I have something to put on the air, if I have to turn over every slime-encrusted rock on this mountain to get it!''

Had Dallas been less furious, exhausted and frustrated, and perhaps just a bit wiser—especially considering the way his hand tightened about the heavy wood handle of the knife—she would have lost no time putting the width of the room between them. But as it was, she only stood there, practically nose-to-nose with him, her chin thrust out stubbornly, her eyes glowering, and his shoulder muscles bunched as though in preparation for combat.

"Now you listen to me, *Ms* McCabe," he spat furiously. "Nobody comes into my home and threatens *me*! Especially some loud-mouthed, strutting little peahen with a superman complex and not enough sense to get out of the rain!" Dallas gasped her outrage but he continued, eyes narrowing, voice rising, "You can take your nasty little innuendos and your half-formed journalistic instincts and your damned TV cameras and go right back down that mountain the way you came before I *throw* you out!"

"Do you think I wanted to come here?" Dallas shouted back, all semblance of control completely gone now. "Do you think climbing fourteen miles up some godforsaken mountain in the middle of nowhere to interview some backwoods hermit with a circuit burned out is my idea of a fun day? Well, think again, mister! I've got work to do out there, important work, and all you and your little land-squabble case are doing is getting in my way! Hell, I wish you would throw me off the mountain—at least then I'd have a story!"

They stood there, poised for combat, jutting chins and flashing eyes only inches from each other, and the electricity that snapped between them was thick enough to buzz. And then he opened his mouth for the final blow and released only a breath that fanned across her heated cheek with the scent of cinammon and cloves. Slowly the tension relaxed from his shoulders and his rock-hard facial muscles; the fury in his eyes faded into rueful amusement, and he said mildly, "Well, I certainly am glad we got that off our chests." He picked up the knife again and resumed his work. "Do you like garlic?"

Dallas stared at him. When she didn't answer, he shrugged and chopped the garlic anyway.

Daniel glanced up at her as he pushed the chopped vegetables to one side and began to peel potatoes with sure, deft strokes. His expression was still pleasant, his voice only minimally curious. "How did you find me, anyway? I gave Cal strict instructions not to let anybody else up."

Dallas straightened up, relaxing marginally, but keeping her wary gaze upon him at all times. "He liked me," she responded without compromise.

One corner of his lips twisted into a quick, wry expression of disbelief. "Must've been a new experience for you," he murmured.

*All right,* Dallas thought. *War rages; battlefield changes.*

She wandered back over to the hearth with as much grace as her cramped muscles would allow, placed her cigarettes on the mantel, and unwrapped her hair from the towel, drying it casually with her fingers in the warmth of the stove. "What did you bag for dinner?'' she inquired, with an easy nod toward the sack on the table.

He did not glance up. "Are you a sportsman, Miss McCabe?"

She shrugged disinterestedly. "Actually, the only way I've thought hunting could be sportsmanlike would be one-on-one, animal and man, in hand-to-hand combat. But I suppose that's all part of the life up here, isn't it? Getting back to nature, living off the land, raping the forests, exterminating the wildlife..."

He put down the knife, opened the sack and reached inside. Before Dallas could do as much as flinch, he said, "Catch," and tossed an apple at her.

Dallas caught the apple against her chest, startled. She stared at him.

"I don't hunt, Miss McCabe," he said, blank-faced. "And nobody lives off the land anymore, thanks to three hundred years of civilization before us. What wildlife is left up here needs every break it can get, and I'm not so helpless that I have to kill to keep from going hungry."

*Great,* thought Dallas, turning over the fruit in her hands. *From macho caveman to Johnny Appleseed in one easy step.* She polished the apple on her shirt, hiding her disbelief. "So, what's the gun for?" she asked conversationally. "Do you always carry a shotgun to gather apples?"

To her very great surprise, he only chuckled, shaking his head as he gathered two handfuls of vegetables and carried them to the pot of boiling water. He made three trips from table to stove without answering, and then, when the last of the vegetables were boiling and the pot was covered, he looked at her.

"Look," he said plainly, and his expression revealed nothing but weariness with the entire matter, "we got off to a bad start. I've had a hell of a day, and so, I take it, have you. I brought you out of the rain; I've offered you shelter, clothing and food; all I ask in return is that you get off my back, okay? I've already told you there's not going to be any interview, so there's no point in your wasting your time. Let's just eat, sleep, and tomorrow morning get you on your way again, all right? And no more yelling; it scares the bird."

Dallas glanced toward the window, where Lenore, still perched as implacably as ever, looked far more interested than scared, and then back to the man who stood only a foot or so away from her. In the grainy fading light of the cabin and even at this distance, he looked less like an enraged grizzly bear and a bit more like a rather rumpled teddy. His hair was beginning to dry and to curl up at the ends in soft, loose waves. His eyes looked more tired than threatening, and he smelled of garlic. No man who smelled of garlic could be all bad.

The adrenaline fizzled out of her, like a faucet that had been left on full bore too long and had finally exhausted its supply. Suddenly, Simon's story, her own personal outrage, and even her professional integrity seemed a lot less important than the almost overwhelming need to curl up someplace warm and close her eyes. *And let's face it,* she chided herself wearily, *the man's got a point. You did barge in here unannounced and uninvited—Simon's fault, not yours— and he did take you out of the storm and give you dry clothes and offer you a meal and a place to sleep, and then you come on to him like a hit man for the CIA.*

*It's a wonder he doesn't use that shotgun on you, and he could hardly be blamed for it, either.*

Dallas lifted her shoulders in an uncomfortable gesture of concession. "All right," she said, sighing, too tired to argue about it even if she had wanted to. "I owe you an apology. Usually, only crooked politicians and cutthroat mobsters get the first-class Dallas McCabe treatment, and—" she managed a wry smile "—at first glance, you don't look like either. I guess a truce is in order and...thanks for the hospitality."

He smiled. Dallas had never noticed before how nice a bearded man's smile could look. Or maybe it was just the exhaustion playing tricks on her eyes. "Better," he said.

He took the box of matches from the mantel and lighted two glass-globed candles, one on the table and another on the mantelpiece. Between them they gave off a surprising amount of cozy, yellow-cast light.

"Don't you have any electricity at all?" Dallas inquired curiously, combing her almost-dry hair with her fingers. Fortunately, her hairstyle never required much attention, and it would fall into place naturally as soon as it was completely dry.

Daniel took a glass jar filled with dried beans from a shelf, shaking his head. "Too much trouble."

That Dallas did not pretend to understand. "More trouble than trekking down that mountain to buy candles every few weeks?"

He laughed softly, shaking his head as he spilled a generous portion of beans into the boiling vegetables. "I don't buy candles; I make them. I make or grow almost everything I use up here."

That was far too complicated a subject for Dallas to pursue at the moment. So, the man made candles. Interesting, but hardly material for a feature-length story. With a scowl of irritation at herself, she dragged her mind out of its reporter mode and tried to think of something non-interrogatory to say.

Daniel saved her the trouble. "This will be done in about twenty minutes." He replaced the cover on the pot and cast her a glance of shielded amusement. "I guess you're starved; you don't look much like the cross-country hiker type to me."

Dallas pressed her hand to the small of her back and gingerly stretched a little. "Very observant. And thanks for the offer, but I'm really too tired to eat. However—" she glanced at him hopefully "—I wouldn't turn down a drink if you were to force it into my hand."

He turned toward the pantry. "I've got some sweet cider."

She thought wistfully of the discarded tequila. "Actually, I had something a little stronger in mind."

He opened the pantry door, and Dallas looked around for a place to sit down and pretend to be a polite guest. She wished she had the energy to walk out onto the porch and smoke a cigarette. There were several ladder-backed chairs, a big cushioned rocking chair, which she knew instinctively was reserved for the master of the house, and a long, low deacon's bench that looked attractively uncomfortable. The next best option was the bed, built big to accommodate his long frame, covered with a colorful patchwork quilt and two huge, fluffy pillows. Cautiously, wincing with every movement, Dallas sat on the edge. She practically tumbled backward the moment her full weight rested on her thighs. Like a water bed, the frame was built up somewhat higher than the mattress and the support system had a definite sag in it. Quickly Dallas floundered to her feet, guiltily smoothing out the wrinkles in Daniel Masters's formerly neat quilt, and there was an undertone of laughter in his voice as he came up behind her.

"That's all right. Sit down. I guess that is the only other comfortable seat in the house. Here—" he offered her a pottery cup "—try this."

Dallas accepted the cup and gratefully eased herself down onto the soft bed, curling her feet beneath her, propping a pillow between her shoulders and the wall. The mattress made a crinkling sound when she moved. "Nice bed," she offered a little uncertainly. "What kind is it?"

"Rope bed. The kind the old pioneers used to make. The tick is filled with straw, but the pillows are feather."

She lifted an eyebrow. "You made it?"

"Um-hm. No trick to it at all. Everything but the rope and the sheeting came right off the mountain."

*So, big deal,* Dallas thought. *It's a lot easier just to open a catalog and order.* She lifted the cup and took a generous swallow of the clear liquid.

It had the bite of pure ethyl alcohol, but went down as smoothly as twelve-year-old Scotch. It hit her stomach like a miniature fireball and left her eyes watering and her skin flaming. She sat up straight and gasped for breath.

"What—" she managed, when she could finally speak. She restrained the urge to fan her burning mouth with her hand.

Daniel Masters's eyes were twinkling. "White lightning," he replied. "Pure corn whisky, one hundred proof."

Dallas eyed the innocent-looking liquid with new respect, which was shared by Masters as she glanced at him. "Did you..." She had to clear her throat to get the hoarseness out. "Did you make this, too?"

He laughed, shaking his head as he returned to check the dinner on the stove. "No way. Real moonshining is almost a lost art around here. There are only one or two good stills left—I mean the genuine article, like you're drinking now, not that cheap garbage that'll kill you if you're not careful—and the fellows who run them are just too old or too tired to do much more than set aside a few jars for friends. Luckily—" he grinned at her as he wrapped his hand in a towel and lifted the cover off the pot "—I have a friend."

He had a nice grin. It made his burly face look almost handsome—sexy even. Or maybe it was just the moonshine.

Dallas took another sip, a bit more cautiously this time, and it *was* smooth. Extremely. The cabin was filled with the warm rich scent of onions and legumes, and Dallas even felt the small sharp stirrings of an apetite. She was beginning to feel much better. "Why don't the old men teach other people how to make it?" she wanted to know. It seemed a pity to let such a fine art die.

He shrugged. "Mostly because nobody wants to learn, I suppose."

"Why not?" Dallas was certain that if it were she who had gone into self-imposed exile upon the mountaintop, the making of moonshine would be the first thing she would want to learn.

Daniel stirred the mixture in the pot and recovered it. "It's hard work, for one thing," he answered. "It's dangerous, time consuming and even expensive, to do it right. Not to mention illegal.''

''There's that, I suppose,'' Dallas murmured, and took another sip. Better than tequila, the hot liquid penetrated her aching muscles and eased the hideous day right out of her mind. As a matter of fact, in a few more sips, she was certain she would be quite drunk.

''It's used a lot like medicine up here,'' Daniel said, turning from the stove to take down some pottery plates and silverware, ''as a base for cough syrups and tonics and just plain old pain-killer. It's hardly ever drunk just for the fun of it. Too valuable.''

''Hm. I can imagine.'' The rhythm of the rain against the windows was soothing and cozy, the lamplight warm and the dinner smells enticing. She was beginning to understand why Simon spent every vacation in that rustic cabin he had on Lake Michigan. This rural life could have a certain appeal, she supposed, under the right circumstances, and providing one didn't stay too long. Tonight, with the storm raging outside and the cup of liquid magic in her hands, Dallas had no complaints.

It was too bad that Daniel Masters had turned out to be everything she had expected. The possibility of being stranded overnight in this cozy little cabin on top of Mt. Nowhere could have had definite appeal if her companion had been a little more...suitable. If only he weren't so big, and so, well, hairy. She might have been able to overlook his mean temper and narrow mind and his crazy ideas, and she supposed, if one looked at them in exactly the right light, his eyes might even have been described as sexy, but all that hair, and those muscles...overkill, she decided. Definitely overkill. Not her type at all.

It was a pity.

Daniel straigtened up from laying the plates, looking at her across the table with a peculiar amusement tugging at his mouth. "Lady, I'd go easy on that stuff if I were you," he advised. "I didn't mean for you to drink the whole cup. It'll put you out quicker than a light if you're not used to it, especially in the shape you're in."

"Ha," Dallas scoffed, a little thick-tongued. "I can drink you or any other man under the table any day of the week and twice on Sundays."

To prove her point, Dallas tossed down the last swallow, carefully set the cup on the bedside table, and gave him a triumphant smile. Then her smile began to fade, her eyes drifted slowly closed, and she fell face-forward on the bed, completely unconscious.

# Chapter Five

Dallas was dreaming that she was lying in a hammock in a bubble underneath the sea; the sound of the ocean whispered and receded around her, and a breeze from some unknown origin gently rocked her. It was very restful.

Suddenly a tremendous crash shattered her peaceful nirvana, and Dallas sat bolt upright in bed, blinking like an owl in the unfamiliar surroundings and muttering incoherent expletives no owl would have ever vocalized.

"So, you're awake." Daniel Masters straightened up from gathering the collection of cookware he had just dropped noisily, his voice mild and his expression pleasant. "Good morning." He set the pots and pans on the work counter with another ear-splitting clatter, and Dallas scowled at him.

Whatever momentary disorientation she might briefly have felt was quickly dispelled, not only by her grim, bleary-eyed view of her surroundings, but by the incredible soreness of her body. Every muscle she possessed seemed to have knotted overnight, and all Dallas really wanted to do was to sink back into the soft bed, lie very still, and try to forget once again where she was.

It was still raining, so hard that Dallas could not tell if day had dawned. She strongly suspected it was still the middle of the night. The candle lamps were still burning, but they seemed far less cheerful than they had previously. The entire room, as a matter of fact, looked nothing more than depressing—dark and cluttered and makeshift, all wood and straw and clay, like a scene from a 1930s' nightmare. Dallas could not prevent a moan of sheer misery as she pushed back her hair and squinted at her watch.

"What time is it?" she mumbled.

"At least an hour after sun up, maybe more." His voice was unbearably cheerful, his movements precise and energetic as he cracked some eggs into a bowl and began to scramble them. "There's no need for clocks around here. What's the matter; did your watch stop?"

"Not waterproof," she muttered, shaking it. There hardly seemed to be a point in investing in expensive watches only to have them stolen once or twice a month.

"At any rate, it's long past time you were up." He moved to the stove and something began to sizzle in a skillet. "I've already done most of the morning chores."

"Good for you." Dallas pushed back the warm covers and gingerly swung her legs over the side of the bed, wincing as her feet struck the cold wood floor. That, for the moment, was the limit of her energy.

Daniel glanced at her. "You really look like hell in the mornings, don't you?"

Dallas could not muster a retort.

Masters himself looked fit and refreshed this morning. His hair was dry and silky, and the way it curled in dark uneven lengths around his neck and collar line, shading his forehead and drifting over his temples, might even have been considered attractive by some. The tan shirt he wore tucked into bleached jeans was loose-fitting and collarless, with dropped shoulder seams and full sleeves, making him look even broader through the chest and arms than he already was. On his feet he wore soft leather moccasins, and his jeans were beltless. His eyes were clear and his step was easy; he was the very picture of healthy male competence.

With a great effort, Dallas pushed herself off the bed, wincing with every movement. She looked around the room once, then twice. There were two doors. One, she remembered last night, led to some sort of pantry; the other led outside. "Where's the bathroom?" she asked, as politely as she could manage at this hour of the morning.

"That depends." Daniel was applying his full energies to the beating of some sort of batter in a large bowl. "If you just want to wash your face and comb your hair, feel free to use that washstand right over there." He nodded in the direction of a small chest that held a pitcher and a mirror. "If not—" a grin fought for possession of his mouth and he directed his full attention to the vigorous whipping motions he was making with a wooden spoon in the bowl "—the outhouse is about fifty yards away, directly behind the cabin. You can't miss it." The grin won out as he glanced at her. "It has a little crescent moon cut out of the door."

Dallas allowed no expression whatsoever to cross her face. She was distinctly aware of the pounding rain that pelleted the roof and washed against the windows. He was enjoying this, the sadist. Whatever small rapport she might have allowed him last night completely vanished and she inquired deliberately, "What if I want to take a shower?"

"Do what I did," he suggested. "The soap is on the washstand and the water is coming right out of the sky."

Dallas allowed herself one muttered and very imaginative oath, snatched her cigarettes and a pack of matches from the mantel, and stalked toward the door.

"Take my coat," Daniel offered, moving to the stove.

Dallas glared at him for one very unsatisfactory moment, then snatched his poncho off the hook and slammed the door hard behind her.

It was not a pleasant rain; it was cold and hard and miserable. Neither was it a pleasant trek through mud and weeds to what Daniel had referred to as the outhouse, even though Dallas had had the foresight to put on her boots. When she returned, she huddled on the porch against the door, finally got a cigarette lighted against the wind and dampness, and stood there smoking and shivering and brooding over the stupidity that would lead any man to want to live like this. Outhouses. Mud. Candles and wood-burning stoves. Straw mattresses. Well, she had to admit, the bed had been nice, but hardly worth all the other sacrifices. She wondered without much real interest where Masters himself had slept last night. She hoped he was at least smart enough not to make any wisecracks about moonshine this morning.

On her necessary trip, she had vaguely noticed a couple of other outbuildings, but now had a chance to study them with more interest. Neither was particularly large, but one, inside the fenced-off area, might have been a barn; she heard a low mooing from inside, which testified to the presence of a cow. Next to the barn was a lean-to that, judging from the muted sounds she heard over the rain, probably contained chickens. The other building was tall and narrow, and she had no earthly idea what its purpose was. But she was somewhat cheered by the fact that a barn that contained cows might easily contain horses as well, and a horse would certainly make her trip back much easier.

That was when the full impact of the weather first struck her. It was raining. He had said one night of shelter, and then she must be on her way. Surely he wouldn't send her down the mountain in this torrent? But, worse, how much longer could she possibly stay cooped up here?

Dallas looked uneasily from the driving rain to the sturdy little cabin at her back and decided that, of the two evils, the grueling journey back down the mountain was definitely the worse. Besides, she still had a story to get.

She took a final deep draw on her cigarette, tossed it out into the rain, and pushed open the door, resolved to be as nice to Daniel Masters as she possibly could.

"Boots," warned Daniel before she had taken the first step across the threshold.

Biting back her temper, Dallas removed her boots, took off the poncho and shook out the clinging rain drops, then hung it neatly on the hook as she closed the door. The pleasant smile she had painted at great expense upon her face quickly became real as the warmth and the intoxicating breakfast smells swept over her. A sharp pang of hunger gripped her as she remembered how little she had eaten the day before.

"Coffee!" she exclaimed, going toward the table eagerly. "And bacon!" She could not resist a sly glance at Daniel as he set the platters on the table. "So, you're not a complete health-food nut, after all."

His look was blank. "Am I supposed to be?"

Dallas had no intention of picking a fight with him while all that wonderful food was sitting on the table, just waiting to be devoured. She inquired instead, slipping into her chair, "Where did you get the bacon?" One thing this house definitely did not contain was a refrigerator, and she had not exactly noticed an all-night market on her way up the mountain.

"From the smokehouse," Daniel replied, pulling out his chair. "That tall building across the way there. I bought the coffee, though." He shrugged, lifting his mug to his lips. "Some habits die hard."

Dallas paused in the process of scraping a healthy serving of bacon onto her plate. "Is it safe?" she inquired hesitantly. "I mean—aren't you worried about botulism and things?"

He laughed and speared a three-inch stack of pancakes with his fork. "Safe enough. I've been eating that same hog since last winter and haven't poisoned myself yet." He transferred three more stacks of pancakes to his plate, and Dallas delicately replaced all but a single slice of bacon on the platter.

After only a few bites, however, Dallas forgot all about food poisoning and whatever other sanitary dangers might lurk within the depths of what he called the smokehouse. Dallas had never realized before that, like most people, she had never really tasted fresh food. The scrambled eggs were less than an hour from the nest and flavored with the redolence of sugar-cured bacon, which, once she had tasted it, had her quickly reaching for the last three slices. The buttermilk pancakes were made with the apples Daniel had gathered yesterday, and the butter tasted like fresh cream. The syrup had a tangy, woodsy taste that was addictive. Daniel told her it was sorghum syrup and, of course, he had made it himself. There was also an assortment of preserved fruits and jams—strawberry, blackberry, boysenberry, pears, peaches and apples—as well as wild-clover honey, and, of course, Dallas had to try them all. One thing was certain: Daniel Masters didn't suffer in the food department for his life-style. A week of this, and no crash diet in the world would be able to save Dallas's figure.

At last, so replete that her eyes were heavy and the last thought in her mind was the possibility of walking anywhere, Dallas sat back and sipped her coffee, sighing, "That was wonderful."

Daniel helped himself to what remained of the pancakes and eggs, and divided the last of the coffee between their two mugs. There was a glint of amusement in his eyes as he murmured, "I'm glad to know I can do *something* right."

Dallas winced. "Look, I know I was pretty rough on you last night..."

"But we have a truce," he finished for her. He pushed a forkful of pancakes into his mouth and watched her thoughtfully. "You're a pretty tough lady, aren't you?" he commented after a moment.

Dallas sipped her coffee, not losing eye contact. Did this mean he was going to test her toughness by tossing her out into the rain, to find her way back to town on her own? "When I have to be," she admitted cautiously.

"Well," he replied cryptically, finishing off his coffee, "let's hope you don't have to be while you're up here, because I really don't think you're as tough as you think you are."

Dallas kept her face impassive, but her reporter's mind was working quickly. "Is that what this is all about?" she inquired mildly, gesturing. "This return-to-nature bit—a kind of self-test, to see how tough you are?"

Dallas did not know what she had expected, but it was not the musing half-smile that touched his lips. "I never thought about it that way," he admitted, and he stood, gathering up the plates and utensils. "That would be a pretty insane test, wouldn't it? Because up here, if you fail, you die."

Dallas lifted an eyebrow mildly, but decided to forgo a comment on the state of his sanity. Instead, she replied, drawing him out in the best Dallas McCabe fashion, "Aren't you taking this whole thing a bit too seriously? It can't really be a matter of life and death, you know. It's not as though you're stranded at the South Pole; civilization is only a few miles away."

"Sure," he agreed, and came back for the coffee cups. Dallas parted with hers reluctantly. His dark eyes were shrewd. "And it only took you how long to get up here from so-called civilization?"

Dallas flushed a little, beginning to get his point.

"The nearest neighbor," Daniel continued easily, stacking the dishes in a tin washtub, "is five miles away. We keep a pretty close watch on each other, but in the end, what it really comes down to is every man for himself. You could die of an infected hangnail up here before anybody knew about it."

Dallas's disbelief was patent, and he lifted his shoulders negligently as he took a kettle of boiling water from the stove and poured it over the dishes. "Of course, that kind of thing hardly ever happens, because you don't live up here if you haven't got sense enough to take care of yourself. But if you get sick— pneumonia, say, or appendicitis—or have a bad accident, the nearest doctor is half a day's ride down the mountain and then fifty miles beyond that, over in Murphey. And there are other things. Floods in the spring and fall. We get snowed in; all there is to see you through the winter is what you put up the fall before. It wouldn't be hard literally to starve between the first snowfall and the last, not to mention freezing if the wood's not cured right or you didn't cut enough. Yeah," he finished in a thoughtful drawl, scooping up two fingerfuls of what looked like soft soap from a jar on the counter, and plopping it into the dishwater, "I think I'd call it a matter of life or death."

Dallas looked around uneasily, and failing to find what she was searching for, demanded, "Don't you even have a two-way radio?"

His back was to her, his hands immersed in the scalding water, and his glossy black hair caught the light as he shook his head. "I have one, out in the barn somewhere." Unexpectedly, he flashed a quick half-grin at her. "Like you, I was a little scared when I first came up here. We're so used to being taken care of, you know. When something goes wrong, you call someone—police, fire department, ambulance, plumber. Help is only a seven-digit number away. I wasn't ready to cut the umbilical cord to civilization just like that, but I didn't have any choice.'' The dishes, washed and rinsed, were stacked neatly on the counter to await drying. This he accomplished with a few deft swipes of the dish towel as he talked. ''I'm in a hollow, believe it or not, and can't get a radio signal in or out. I had to go cold turkey when I cut my ties, and let me tell you, it was pretty terrifying, the first winter I spent up here alone.''

Dallas tried to digest all this. No telephone. No radio. Very little chance that the next face you saw might be human. But it was entirely too much to absorb. She couldn't imagine that kind of isolation, and she refused to acknowledge that, right at this moment, she was a victim of it.

''Well, it's your own fault,'' Dallas said, for some reason, irritable. She took out a cigarette, started to put it in her mouth, and remembered just in time. She debated whether or not it was worth going back out in the cold and damp for. ''Nobody forces you—or anybody else—to live up here.''

''That's right. It's our choice.'' He put away the last dish and turned to look at her, drying his hands. ''Real life.''

*Real life,* Dallas thought derisively. A lot he knew about real life. He probably hadn't heard a news broadcast or read a paper in five years. Bridges collapsing from shoddy materials. Teachers being raped at knife point in their own classrooms. Cocaine-addict pilots crashing planes into the sides of mountains.

Chemical spills killing tens of thousands of people. That was real life, and that was where Dallas belonged, trying to do something about it, not stuck up here in this water-logged cabin, listening to some self-righteous nature buff bemoan the hardships of not having a radio.

Dallas decided to have the cigarette after all, and pushed her chair away from the table with a loud scrape. "Whatever turns you on, I guess," she commented in passing.

Daniel said, very softly, "What the hell are you doing here, lady?"

Dallas stopped and looked back at him. They were only a couple of feet apart in the small room, and every detail of his expression was clear. His eyes were deep and intense; his stance, as he leaned against the counter with his weight upon his palms, patient and at ease. His shirt, Dallas noticed, was fastened with ties instead of buttons, and he hadn't bothered to close the laces this morning. The narrow triangle of bare chest that was revealed held Dallas's attention for the few seconds that passed before she could gather her thoughts to respond. She thought irrelevantly how much like a pirate he looked with his dark hair and flowing shirt and that artfully masculine path of bare chest.

Dallas answered, somewhat impatiently dragging her mind back to the matter at hand, "You know that. I'm with 'Spotlight' news and I'm here to do a story."

He shook his head with a small, rather rude hiss of laughter and pushed away from the counter. "You couldn't care less about my story. I'd be very much surprised if you had the faintest idea what the story was even supposed to be about. You're not interested in what's going on here, you have nothing but comtempt for my life-style, and to get right to the root of the matter, you don't even like me.'' As he spoke, he opened the pantry door, took down a huge pottery bowl from a shelf, and went into the pantry. When he emerged, the bowl was filled with flour, his face marked with nothing more than mild curiosity. ''Not that it matters much at this point, but what gives?''

Dallas could hardly argue the irrefutable truth. She replied instead, unconcerned, ''So we're even. You don't like me, either.'' She started for the porch again, then hesitated, turning back to him with a small frown of curiosity. ''Have *Life* and 'Today' really contacted you about an interview?''

He set the bowl on the counter. ''So have *Time*, *Newsweek*, and about every talk show in the country over the past two years. I thought everyone had pretty much gotten the message by now.''

Dallas could not help shaking her head in confusion and wonder. As far as she was concerned, there *was* no story here, but could the rest of the industry be wrong? What were they seeing that she was not?

A moment ago she would have been willing, with very little persuasion, to forget about ever trying to get an interview out of this joker. In the face of world hunger, widespread corruption, the threat of nuclear destruction and social disintegration, what could he possibly have to say that would be of any interest to her viewers? But her competitive instincts were aroused now, and she decided that the cigarette could wait a few more minutes.

She watched him uncover yet another clay jar and carelessly pour a white mixture into a bowl. ''So why,'' she wanted to know, ''are you so dead set against in-

terviews, anyway? What have you got to hide? Or,''
she suggested shrewdly as the obvious began to dawn
on her, ''are you just holding out for the best offer?
Why do a free interview when one of the glossies
would pay six figures for it, right? Or there may even
be another book in this. Okay, I can't blame you for
that.'' She shrugged. ''Nobody ever got rich giving
stuff away, I guess.''

He narrowed a look on her that was not comfortable. It was the kind of look one might give a person
who was making impolite noises at a formal dinner
party. There was a twinge of disgust in his tone as he
said, ''You're a cynical bitch, aren't you?''

With short, tight movements, he began to transfer
flour from the big bowl to the smaller one by double
handfuls. Dallas thought he had said all he was going
to say and decided to reconsider her approach while
having that long-postponed cigarette. But just as she
turned for the door, he spoke again, abruptly.

''Do you have any idea how much money I made
last year?''

Dallas turned back slowly. Now this was getting interesting. ''No,'' she admitted carefully. ''But I'd like
to.''

He gave another unpleasant snort of laughter, vigorously breaking eggs into the flour mixture. ''I just
bet you would.'' He glanced at her, and his eyes had a
glint to them that was definitely not friendly. ''Well,
I'm not going to tell you,'' he announced, as though
that decision should surprise her. ''I will, however, tell
you what I spent: two hundred and forty-three dollars, and that includes a new typewriter. I'm not interested in money, Miss McCabe,'' he said flatly,

turning back to the concoction he was mixing in the bowl. "I don't have much use for it."

Dallas was thinking with lascivious delight about the last man who had said that to her: a successful evangelist who had ended up serving time for fraud and income tax evasion. But one look at Daniel Masters's strong, square back all but convinced her that the comparison would prove to be nothing but a dead end. If Daniel Masters said he wasn't interested in money, that was more than likely the case. Why else would he live like this? And who cared, anyway?

*Life* magazine, *Time*...

Dallas said, "You still didn't answer my question. About why you won't give interviews."

He turned, his gaze steady and demanding. "And you didn't answer mine."

For a moment it looked like a standoff. Dallas was aware, for not the first time, of a power within this man that had nothing to do with his size. There weren't many people, male or female, who could face down Dallas McCabe, and she suddenly wasn't particularly anxious to get into a battle of wills with this man. It was silly, anyway. She shrugged a little and tapped the cigarette against her palm. "Okay, you're right," she relented. "I don't think there's much of a story here, and even if there was, I'm not the reporter for it. I was sent as punishment, if you want to know the truth, and I frankly think my talents would be put to better use if I were assigned to cover the national Sausage Stuffers Convention in Cincinnati. But I'm only a working girl and I do what I'm told." She spread her hands in a gesture of concession. "Now, your turn. What have you got against the public's right to know?"

For a moment she thought he wouldn't answer. He turned to pick up a pitcher of milk and sloshed a generous amount into the bowl, stirring the mixture with several wide, circular strokes of the wooden spoon before replying, "I'm trying to preserve the way of life up here, not exploit it." His voice was tight. "All the hell we need is a bunch of reporters and TV cameras and crazy tourists invading the place. There's little enough left as it is. Why can't you people just leave things alone?"

There was a venom to the accusation that Dallas thought was totally unwarranted—and worse, it stung. This was not the first time, by any means, that her choice of profession had been challenged by a potential target of her skill, but it was the first time Dallas had ever let it bother her, or had even listened. Perhaps it was because this time she knew there was a grain of truth to his defense against invasion of privacy. Daniel Masters was not a corporate giant, a politician, a charismatic celebrity influencing the destiny of millions. He had done nothing wrong. He was just a man who wanted to live his life in peace, and he had every right in the world to object to having his simple mountain hideaway turned into a fishbowl. Daniel Masters was right; Dallas was wrong.

*So what,* Dallas thought in irritation. She had never liked this story from the beginning. It hadn't been her idea. And if there was one thing in the world Dallas McCabe disliked more than being wrong, no one had found out what it was yet.

But none of this showed on her face as she replied coolly, "I don't make the news, Mr. Masters." And she went outside to smoke her cigarette.

Dallas felt like a street criminal as she stood on the porch, leaning against the cabin, with one foot propped on the wall behind her, smoking all alone. What was with this guy, anyway? Did he really believe half that self-righteous malarky he spouted, or was it all some kind of scam to grab publicity for his next book—or maybe to prejudice the courts in his favor over the land dispute? But if it was publicity he wanted, why was he turning down a chance at "Spotlight"? Why wasn't he grabbing all the free press he could?

No, all the evidence pointed to the fact that he was just another die-hard nature freak who had taken Thoreau a little too seriously. Or maybe her original assessment was correct, and he was simply crazy. Lots of people went into seclusion after a nervous breakdown, and the eccentricities of the genius genre were not to be discounted. He might even be one of those weird survivalists who barricaded themselves against the terrors of technology with paranoia and with foxholes dug into the sides of hills. And even though Dallas had to admit a certain personal curiosity as to just what was behind the obscure behaviour of Daniel Masters, her best professional instincts told her there was no "Spotlight" story here. Let *Life* do its little human-interest bit. Dallas McCabe and the "Spotlight" cameras had bigger game to hunt.

Thus resolved, she tossed away her cigarette and turned to go back inside. Daniel came through the door, dressed in poncho and boots, just as she was reaching for it. He did not tell her where he was going and she did not ask. She watched him go down the steps and cross toward the woods with a little shrug of disinterest. The rain was beginning to lighten, and there was every possibility that she might actually get out of this place today. She would talk to him about it when he got back. Dallas was certain Masters would be just as glad to be rid of her as she would be to put him behind her.

Her clothes were dry and had been neatly stacked on a chair beside the stove. On the mantelpiece above, the big bowl of what Dallas could only assume to be bread dough had been covered and set aside to rise. "A man of many talents," Dallas murmured, and began to gather up her things.

Of course, she hated the thought of going back to Simon in defeat and resented the fact that he had won. She would have liked nothing better than to return triumphant, with a scathing exposé to throw in Simon's face—but what was there to expose? Masters's secret recipe for apple pancakes? Besides, she had things waiting for her back in Detroit, important things, and she couldn't afford to waste any more time on Simon's little practical joke. He had made his point. Let him think he'd won this one. They both still knew, deep down inside, who was really the boss.

She took advantage of Daniel's absence from the house to change from the comfortable, though by now badly wrinkled, shirt he had loaned her last night into her own clothes. Now that return to civilization was imminent, she could afford to be generous and had to admit that, all in all, Daniel Masters wasn't such a bad guy. He had been far more civil to her than she had any right to expect, given the circumstances, and he was an interesting character, in an offbeat sort of way. He was articulate, fairly polite and a hell of a cook. Of course, he was also chauvinistic, defensive, narrow-minded, and had a temper that almost matched Dallas's own, but nobody was perfect.

She pulled on a pair of gray-cotton ladies' athletic briefs, comfortably bikini-cut, and a matching sleeveless undershirt of the same body-hugging cotton. Dallas had two complete wardrobes: one for work and one for play, and although some of Dallas's lingerie could have rivaled anything Frederick's of Hollywood sold, not a single item in her backpack this weekend was made of silk or nylon. She tugged on heavy woolen socks and a pair of jeans, and was searching through the neat stack of clothing for a warm sweater when she heard the door open behind her.

It was an awkward moment, but it should not have been an overly embarrassing one. She was, after all, decently covered. Dallas turned, with the sweater in her hands, and was caught by the look on Daniel's face—not a predatory one, but nakedly aware. He stood still, the muscles of his face tight, his eyes alert and assessing, and Dallas was uncomfortably aware of how the T-shirt hugged her torso and softly outlined her breasts. She was so aware of it that it actually made her heart speed.

Daniel said blandly, "A perfect illustration of just how stupid it was to send a woman on an assignment like this."

Dallas quickly pulled the yellow turtleneck over her head, tugging it well over her hips, and faced him with as much cool indignation as she could possibly muster. "I beg your pardon?"

Daniel removed his poncho and hung it up before replying, flatly, "No privacy. I don't like to feel like an intruder in my own house."

"Well, you won't have to worry about that any longer." Dallas turned and began to stuff her clothes into her backpack. "I've given it my best professional shot, but I've decided there really isn't any story up here, Mr. Masters. The rain has about stopped, and there's still plenty of time for me to get back down before dark, especially—" now she turned and looked at him hopefully "—if you or someone else has a horse I could borrow."

He nodded, still watching her very peculiarly. "Horses are no good up here," he said, "but I have a mule. You're welcome to it."

Dallas's spirits soared. There was a God. Daniel Masters was the most generous, kindhearted man who had ever been born. This time tomorrow she would be back in Detroit, with a senator on one phone and the chief of police on the other, and the whole world would sit up and take notice because Dallas McCabe was back in town. *Thank you, thank you, thank you. For this I might even give up smoking.*

"I'll take very good care of it," she promised, radiating good will and eternal gratitude with every motion. "I'll feed it a whole bale of hay when I get to town, and I'll pay What's-His-Name—Cal—to bring it right back up to you tomorrow morning." She beamed at him.

Daniel still had that strange look in his eye, as though he had a secret he was not entirely sure he liked. "You don't have to bother," he said. "I'll take you down myself. But—" the curve of his lips was half amused, half rueful, greatly reluctant "—I'm afraid you're not going anywhere today, Miss McCabe. Maybe not for a very long time."

# Chapter Six

Dallas stared at him. A dozen improbable scenarios raced through her head that ranged from altitude-induced hallucinations to Simon lurking behind a wall somewhere ready to spring out and chortle "Gotcha!" A joke—it had to be. Better yet, a nightmare. Daniel Masters couldn't have said what she thought he had said.

But Dallas kept her cool. She responded, quite reasonably, "I beg your pardon?"

Masters did not look as though he were joking. He looked, in fact, rather grim. "Do you remember those floods I told you about?" Dallas nodded mutely. "We're having one. I was just down to check on one of the feeding stations, and I couldn't even get close. The bridge is already washed out."

Dallas's mind raced frantically. "But—but I didn't even come across the bridge. I can get back the same way I came. That doesn't mean I'm stranded!" She looked at him anxiously. "Does it?"

Not a trace of sympathy showed in Daniel's face or tone. "It does," he stated flatly. "That three-foot-deep shallow you crossed yesterday is now an eight-foot-deep rapid with currents so strong they would wash away a mule before he even knew what was happening. And if it's this bad here, it's worse farther down. You crossed more than one stream getting here, didn't you?"

"Well, yes." Trickles, little damp places in the ground—Dallas could not believe any of them could have turned into the kind of raging waterways he described. But what did she know of mountain geography?

*All right,* she told herself. *Be calm.* A little rain wasn't the end of the world. It would clear up, the creek would go down and she would be on her way. Another night here wouldn't kill her. Resignedly, she said, "So how long do you think it will last?"

Daniel crossed the room and picked up a towel, running it briefly over his glistening hair. "It depends on how high the creek gets. I should be able to put down a new bridge in a week or two."

"A week!" Panic, sheer and ungovernable, began to rise. "That's impossible! I can't stay here a week. You don't understand; I've got things to do, people depending on me, stories to get! I can't—"

Daniel looked at her calmly. "They'll have to wait, won't they?"

"Wait!" Dallas parroted the word as though it were not in her vocabulary. And then, more furiously, "Wait? Are you out of your mind? Listen, mister, I know up here on the mountaintop things are pretty laid back and easy, and a day here or there can't make much difference, but in the real world, important things are happening, and I can't just sit up here and wait! I've got a Senate investigation pending. I've got a bunch of firebombing thugs running around loose in Detroit, thinking they can intimidate the press into doing whatever they want, and the entire police department waiting for me to make the first move! Even as we speak, money is probably being passed under the table that could affect the future of the entire automobile industry, and everything I've worked on for the past six months is going up in smoke! I can't just sit here and wait!''

"It must be a terrible burden," replied Daniel mildly, "to have the fate of the entire free world resting in your hands."

"Damn you!" Dallas exploded with an entirely unpreventable though rather childish stamp of her foot. "You don't understand—"

"No, you don't understand." Daniel turned sharply and Dallas noticed for the first time the barely controlled anger that lurked beneath the surface of his implacable features. His tone was even, but his words were clipped. "If you think this latest bit of news exactly makes my day, you're very much mistaken. I didn't invite you here, you know, and I damn sure didn't arrange this storm just to inconvenience you. Do you know what a flash flood could do to this area? Generations of wildlife could be wiped out in one day, topsoil torn away that it would take centuries to replace, and some of the flora would be gone forever. *Forever*, have you got that? You'll have to pardon me, but in light of all that, your senators and your mobsters just don't seem to weigh too heavily on my mind. Now, if you think you can stop the rain and push back the waters with your bare hands, please go right ahead, and we'll have you off this mountain quicker than you can think about it, because nothing would make me happier. But until then, we're stuck with each other, and there's not a blessed thing you can do about it."

Dallas opened her mouth for a rebuttal but found, to her absolute frustration, that there was none. The mere sight of Dallas McCabe and her microphone could make the most powerful men in the country blanch; one half hour of airtime could change the destiny of corporate amalgamations, influence public policy, shape decisions that would affect an entire nation; for one hour every week, Dallas McCabe held fifty percent of America in the palm of her hand, but when rain fell and creeks swelled, her entire life ground to a halt, and all Dallas could do was stand by and watch.

Dallas crossed her arms over her chest and turned to the window, staring impotently at the dripping, gurgling rain. *Damn,* she thought. *Damn, Damn.*

She heard Daniel moving around the cabin with long, angry strides, putting away dishes and rearranging counter space, pushing the chairs under the table with unnecessary force. Belatedly, Dallas realized that this crisis was not strictly a personal one. She turned, concern crossing her face, and asked, "What about you? I mean—the cabin. Is it safe? Do you stand to lose much?"

He paused, and released a breath. One large hand came up to push back his hair from his forehead, and he seemed, with that motion, forcefully to expel tension. "No," he said. "The water never reaches this high. We'll be okay."

Then Dallas remembered something else. "You said feeding stations. What about the animals who go there?"

He looked at her as though surprised she would concern herself, and then his lips curved into a slow, reassuring smile. "Deer," he said. "This part of the mountain gets pretty lean this time of year, so I try to help out a little. I'll just move the stations farther in; they'll be okay."

Dallas nodded, but didn't know what else to say. She turned back to the window. *A week,* she thought. *Maybe longer.* She would go out of her mind.

The silence went on for a long time, broken only by the plopping sound of rain in the mud and the occasional muted crackle of a log in the stove. Daniel, too, was looking out the window, and Dallas wondered if his thoughts could possibly be as bleak as hers. All he had to worry about was a few wet animals and an unwelcome houseguest. Her whole career could be teetering on the edge, and there was nothing, absolutely nothing, she could do. The frustration was so great that she had to grit her teeth to keep from screaming with it. If she ever got back to civilization, Simon would pay for this.

"Well." Daniel spoke so abruptly, and with such energy, that Dallas jumped. She turned to look at him questioningly. "We have a few things to get straight, I guess, if we're going to be living together."

Having mulled the matter over, he seemed now to have it completely in hand. "First," he said, with the decisive air of a man used to organization and impatient to have the details out of the way, "if you're going to stay here, you're going to pull your own weight. You can start by making your bed." He nodded curtly toward the unmade bed. "I don't mind playing host for one night, but I don't have a lot of time for entertaining guests, and up here everyone does his part.''

Dallas gave him an annoyed look. She *would* have made the bed. She had simply forgotten. She did not want anyone to think she was a bad houseguest—not that this could be considered a house, or that she was exactly a guest. "Don't worry," she told him somewhat coolly, "I have manners. I don't expect you to pick up after me, and I have no intention of getting in your way."

He nodded. "Good. Because there's more than enough to do around here to keep you from getting bored."

"Gee, I can't tell you how worried I was about that," murmured Dallas sarcastically. He was beginning to get on her nerves again.

The tiny muscles around his eyes tightened fractionally, but there was absolutely no other expression on his face as he hooked his thumbs casually into his belt loops and gave her a long look. "Well, then. Here's the thing, Miss McCabe. I don't have to let you stay here, you know. It wouldn't be against the law for me to turn you out right now and let you wander around until you found another friendly-looking house, or let you camp by the creek until the water goes down. And that," he finished mildly, "to be perfectly frank, is what I'm more than a little inclined to do. I would really say it's more or less up to you."

Dallas released a half-sigh and directed her gaze briefly to the window again to disguise the needle point of shame and self-reproach she felt. Damn it, it wasn't his fault, and she had been acting alternatively like a spoiled child and an autocrat since the moment she'd met him. She was usually much more in control than this. She usually didn't alienate the subjects of her interviews until the cameras were rolling.

"Look," she said simply, turning to him, "I'm sorry." She meant it this time. There was nothing to do now but make the best of it, and there was no sense in either of them being more miserable than necessary. Besides, there was still the very definite possibility that he would kick her out, and no one could blame him. "I'm usually not so bad-tempered. It's just that—" she lifted her shoulders a little in helpless concession "—I really didn't want to come here, and I guess seeing my car blown up right in front of my face upset me more than I realized—" That was hard to admit, but it was, she had to finally confess, probably true. "And, well…" She smiled a little, half-apologetically. "You tend to rub me the wrong way. But I promise, no more temper tantrums. I won't cause you any trouble. And I appreciate your taking me in. Really."

A small smile quirked at the corners of his lips as he considered this rather left-handed apology, and he agreed, "You rub me the wrong way, too." And his gaze, half amused, half curious, narrowed on her peculiarly. "Your car was blown up?"

She nodded. "Somebody didn't like last week's show."

He continued to look at her, that peculiar half-smile in his eyes, for another moment, and Dallas thought he wasn't half bad-looking when he smiled—when he did anything, as a matter of fact, except glower. Her eyes strayed, without meaning to, to that intriguing patch of firm, exposed chest, and she found herself wondering what Daniel Masters would look like in a T-shirt and tennis shorts, with a haircut and a shave.

What he said next was not what she expected, but then, she never knew what to expect from him. "We've got to have some rules about privacy." He looked at her meaningfully. "This cabin was not built to sleep two."

He glanced around the single room, analyzing the problem of logistics, and then decided, "I can rig up some sort of screen for dressing and bathing, I suppose, although if the weather clears up, you'll probably want to use the shower out back. You can make a pallet in front of the fireplace to sleep on; it's not exactly Posturepedic—" his eyes sparked briefly and unexpectedly at her "—as I found out last night, but it's bearable."

*Fine,* Dallas thought. *His house, his rules, his bed. Be polite.* But she felt some small assertion of her rights was in order, and she said, looking him straight in the eye, "I sleep in my underwear."

Daniel Masters did not blink. "I sleep," he replied, "in nothing at all."

*Great,* Dallas thought, and tried deliberately to push aside the vision of that huge, muscular body completely unclothed. *And that's the way it is, Thursday, September twentieth.*

She inquired only, and with interest, "You have a shower?"

"Um-hm. Solar-heated." He was still looking at her with that funny little glint in his eye, as though expecting her at any moment to launch into a temper tantrum. Dallas had no intention of obliging him. "Also enclosed."

Dallas nodded, and hoped the weather would clear soon. A shower right now—solar-heated or not—would have done a great deal to lift her spirits. *A week,* she thought. *A week up here in the wilderness, with nothing but rain and animals. I'll go mad. I'll return to Detroit counting my fingers and mumbling incoherehtly. I'll...*

But that was a destructive and ultimately pointless train of thought, and she firmly squelched it. With a determined though rather grim smile, she started to move past him on her way to make up the bed.

Daniel said, with a mixture of amusement, wonder, and even a hint of challenge in his voice, "It doesn't bother you at all, does it?"

Dallas looked up at him, surprised. Goodness, but he was tall, and so close now that if she turned, just the slightest bit, her breast would brush against his arm. His scent was a fascinating and definitive mixture of things uncommon to Dallas: strong soap and masculinity blended with just a hint of something feral and untamed, and overlying it all was that spicy scent of cloves she had noticed on his breath last night. Being this close to him, being touched by the scent of him, seemed to make the fine hairs on Dallas's arms prickle, but she wasn't sure whether the reaction was an instinctual animal awareness or an equally primal touch of fear. She demanded, somewhat belligerently, "What?"

*Pretty eyes,* Dallas thought irrelevantly. Warm and brown and deeply intelligent and, just now, holding just the slightest bit of subdued mischief. "Being stranded up here alone with a wild mountain man who's possibly sex-starved and even more possibly just the slightest bit crazy."

Dallas swallowed. She wasn't accustomed to being in any situation she couldn't handle, and, so programmed, it was only natural that she would not recognize such a situation when she stumbled into it. Could she handle Daniel Masters, she wondered now. Would she be foolish even to try?

Instantly defensive, she snapped, "Of course it bothers me. But not for the reasons you think." That was stupid. She had never met a man she couldn't handle. "It would bother anyone in his right mind to be caught in the middle of a flood a hundred miles from civilization." With great effort, she pulled herself away from the almost palpable power of his presence and continued on her way to the bed. But after two steps she had to turn back, curiosity overcoming her. "Well," she demanded, although somewhat hesitantly, "are you?"

"Sex-starved? Or crazy?"

Dallas's brows knit into an uncomfortable scowl, and she felt for some ridiculous reason as though she might blush. "Both. Either."

Now his eyes glinted outrageously, but his expression was perfectly bland. "I'm not crazy," he assured her.

Dallas turned quickly and began to jerk the covers over the tousled bed. *Cute, Masters,* she thought darkly, *real cute. On top of everything else, the man thinks he's got a sense of humor.*

He moved across the room to retrieve his poncho, immediately back to business. "I'm going to dig a trench to try to divert the overflow. It'll probably take all day."

Dallas straightened up, her eyes widening with instinctive objection. The one thing more unbearable than being stranded up here with him was being left up here alone. "But—what about me? What am I supposed to do?"

He hesitated, thinking about it. "I don't suppose you know how to knead bread."

She gave a short, humorless bark of laughter.

He nodded, unsurprised. "Well, there's butter ready to be churned. That doesn't take any particular talent. Come on, I'll show you."

He took her over to the fireplace, where a large pottery churn held what looked like congealed milk. Dallas wrinkled her nose but listened carefully as he showed her how to move the clabber up and down until the butter separated from the milk, instructed her on gathering and molding the butter and preserving the buttermilk, and assured her he would be back in a couple of hours to finish the bread. When he was gone, Dallas looked without a great deal of enthusiasm at the task set before her, but decided in the end that it was better than sitting around counting her fingers. Besides, the rhythmic sound of the butter churn kept her from thinking too much about how empty the cabin was.

The job that should have taken twenty minutes took an hour and a half; her shoulders ached and her hands were chapped, and in the end, she had to gather the butter out of the milk with her fingers instead of with the deft movements of the paddle Daniel had shown her. But this had become more than an occupation to keep her mind off her troubles; it was now a downright challenge, and Dallas applied every ounce of grim energy she had left to removing the curds of butter from the churn, slapping them into a bowl, then kneading a precise pinch of salt into the gooey mass and forming it into a ball. After all that work, the butter she had gleaned was barely as big as a good-sized walnut, and Dallas stared at it in dismay.

"I'd starve," she announced to Daniel when he returned a little before noon. "No, first I'd go crazy, then I'd starve, if this was the only way I had to get my food."

Daniel grinned at the pitiful trophy she had to show for all her efforts with the butter churn. "Looks like we're going to have some rich buttermilk," was his only comment as he went to wash the mud from his hands in the washbasin on the bedside table.

That was meager compensation for blistered hands and knotted shoulders, and Dallas told him so as he opened the front door and tossed out the muddy water from the basin. "Tomorrow," he told her, still with that teasing look in his eyes, "I'll let you milk the cow."

Dallas made a wry face but did not retort. After the hard time she had given him over his choice of lifestyle, she supposed she deserved every comeuppance she got. *I am going to hate it here,* she thought. *I am really going to hate it here.*

With his customary efficiency, Daniel kneaded the bread into loaves while reheating last night's bean stew for lunch. He told her that the creek was still rising, but the rain was slacking off, and it was too early to tell how much damage might be done. The trench he was digging was designed to take some of the pressure off a beaver dam downstream, which, if it burst, could turn several acres of natural mountain flora into swampland overnight. He thought it was working.

Dallas would have liked him to stay longer, if for no other reason than for the sound of another human voice. But Daniel ate quickly, with very little conversation, obviously anxious to get back to work. When Dallas volunteered to do the dishes, he merely nodded and said, "There's plenty of water in the rain barrel; just heat it in that big pan on the shelf over there." He stood, and added, "As a matter of fact, there's enough for a bath, if you want. The washtub is in the pantry." With no more discussion, he took a hammer, nails and a roll of twine from a low shelf, and within moments, had arranged two sheets over the twine support to form a curtained cubicle before the stove. "There. Privacy."

He replaced the nails and hammer, pulled his poncho over his head and advised, "Enjoy." He opened the door, and a large, wet black bird flew in, gazed at Dallas comtemptuously, and settled on the rafters to preen her feathers. Daniel left Dallas with nothing to do but take a bath, and no one for company except Lenore.

Borrowing on the efficiency she had observed in Daniel, Dallas heated water for her bath while doing the dishes. She found the huge washtub in the pantry as he had indicated, and she swept the room with a broom that looked as though it were made of dried shrubs, while more water heated. Five buckets of water filled the tub to a depth of about three inches, and if Dallas had not wanted to wash her hair so badly she would have given up on the project. By the time she had heated enough water to fill the tub halfway, every inch of the cluttered cabin had been swept, dusted and polished; vegetables had been washed, chopped and set on the back burner for dinner—and this from a woman who hired a housekeeper three times a week and considered popping leftover pizza in the microwave oven a major culinary accomplishment; four loaves of bread had been placed in the hearth oven as per Daniel's instructions, and she was telling Lenore the story of her life.

The water was tepid, for by the time Dallas added the last heated bucket of water, the rest of the tub's contents had cooled, and only by drawing her knees up to her chest could Dallas sit down in the tub, but she had worked so hard for the bath that nothing was going to keep her from enjoying it. The soap was dark and rough and smelled funny, but it left her hair squeaky-clean and, as she philosophically informed Lenore, ''Beggars can't be chosers.''

*And so now I'm talking to a bird,* she thought with a kind of wry dismay as she wriggled her body down into the tub for a final rinse of her hair. *And worse yet, talking to a bird in clichés.* Minute by minute she was gaining more respect for her pioneer ancestors and losing confidence in the state of Daniel Masters's sanity. *Three days,* she thought. *Three days maximum of this and I'll go running naked into the forest, screaming and pulling out my hair.*

She dried herself before the stove quickly, shivering, and dressed in the same clothes she had worn that morning. Laundry, she surmised, would be no simple accomplishment, and if she was going to be here for a week she would have to get full wear out of the three changes of clothes she had brought with her.

The absence of a cream rinse left her hair dry and spiky in places, and when Dallas picked up the mirror on the washstand to try to comb it into place, all she could do was grimace and put the mirror down again. Gerard in the makeup department would fall into a dead faint if he could see her now, but unmanageable hair was the least of Dallas's problems. At least she was clean, for all the difference that made.

Dallas was just puzzling over the problem of emptying the enormous tub of bathwater when Daniel came in, covered from head to toe with mud. He had, of course, removed his boots, but his socks were soaked, and Dallas looked in dismay at the muddy tracks his footprints made over the freshly swept floor. "The rain has stopped," he announced cheerfully, stripping off his poncho. A twinkle came into his eyes as he glanced around the cabin. "The place looks good. I take it you got bored."

"Does that mean I might be able to get across the creek after all?" Dallas asked eagerly. "If the rain—"

He shook his head. Even his beard was muddy. "The ground was saturated before this rain; it will take a while for the creek to go down, even if it doesn't rain another drop." He looked slightly grim as he glanced toward the window. "Even if the rain doesn't move farther up into the mountains and cause more flooding here. We'll just have to keep a watch on it for the next few days."

It had been a frail hope, but it still hurt to have it crushed. Dallas tried not to look too despondent as she said, "I put the bread in the oven. I don't see how it's ever going to cook, though. There's no fire."

"Radiant heat," Daniel explained to her, and stripped his mud-streaked shirt over his head. Dallas was determined to give no more than a cursory glance to the broad chest that was revealed. What had happened to his tremendous concern over privacy? "Great—you put some vegetables on, too. We'll have supper in no time. I'm starved."

Dallas was dimly amazed by his energy and his cheerfulness. All she had done all day was clean the cabin and she was exhausted. Daniel had spent the daylight hours digging a trench in the cold and the rain, he was faced with the possibility of a flood that could turn his mountain paradise into cheap swampland, and he had a surly, unwelcome houseguest to contend with. Dallas knew he must be tired, cold and worried, but he took it all in stride. Just another day in the life of a pioneer. Briefly, she envied his ability to deal with stress and wondered if it had something to do with the mountain air.

"You saved the bathwater," he noticed, pleased. "Just what I need. Where's the soap?"

Dallas watched as he stood on first one foot and then the other to remove his filthy socks. "You are not," she questioned carefully, "going to use the same water I just used?"

He strode over to the tub, unbuttoning his jeans. "Waste not, want not."

Dallas gave him a long and measured look. "That is truly disgusting, Masters."

He flashed a grin just before he pulled the curtain. "You never shared a bath? Same principle."

"Togetherness once removed," Dallas quipped, and he chuckled.

There was something distantly uncomfortable about standing there with nothing more than a thin muslin sheet between herself and a bathing Daniel Masters, and suddenly Dallas didn't know what to do with herself. The cabin was too small for her to pretend to be busily occupied in another part of the room, but it felt awkward to be standing there just inches from him while he undressed. It was even more awkward to listen to the sounds of demin unzipping and to watch as a pair of jeans crumpled into the space between floor and curtain.

"It's dark in here," commented Daniel. "Why don't you light the candles?"

Dallas watched, somewhat fascinated, as he kicked aside the jeans and nothing but bare feet and naked ankles, accompanied by a generous portion of strong, dark-haired calf, filled the space between floor and curtain. She swallowed. "Sure," she muttered, under her breath. "Got a match?" She wondered how he was going to fit his huge body into the tub.

In only a moment a box of matches came sailing over the curtain and she caught them just before they hit the floor—and just in time to see one naked leg, and then the other, lift itself into the tub. "The water's still warm," Daniel commented. "Where's the soap?"

"Um...on the hearth." *Okay, floor show's over,* Dallas reprimanded herself and turned busily to light the candles as enthusiastic splashing sounds began. She thought she might be able to tolerate the boredom of staying here after all.

# Chapter Seven

The curtained-off cubicle included that portion of the room that had shelves of towels and clothes, and in only moments Daniel had washed, dried himself and changed into fresh jeans and shirt. In the time it took for the bread to finish baking, he had emptied the washtub, added pork seasoning to the simmering vegetables, and set the table with a huge, strong-smelling cheese wrapped in cloth, and a variety of preserved fruits and chutneys. Dallas watched as he whipped up a thin piecrust, filled it with dried peaches, cut it into tarts, and quickly fried them in a large black skillet filled with simmering butter. Dallas wanted to help, but he was such a model of efficiency that it seemed pointless. They sat down to dinner less than a hour after he had first entered the house.

Though nothing as substantial as meat was served, the meal was wholly satisfying, and Dallas was again surprised by how wonderful everything tasted. Daniel consumed almost an entire loaf of bread, half the round of homemade cheese, and most of the vegetables before the first word was spoken, and Dallas had to wolf down her meal to salvage two of the six peach pies for herself. She was beginning to understand, with ill-disguised amusement, how Daniel kept up his physique, and calories were the furthest thing from her mind as she overindulged on crusty brown bread and butter—a spoonful of which, at least, Dallas had the satisfaction of knowing was made with her own hands.

When she could not eat another bite, she left the remnants of the feast to Daniel and leaned back in her chair, wanting a cigarette but lacking the energy to go outside to smoke it. Dark had fallen fully outside, and the candlelight was warm, reminding her again of the pleasant aspects of being safe and secure inside a sturdy cabin while nature, wild and untamed, roamed outside. She looked at Daniel curiously. "Tell the truth," she invited, for now that the pressing matter of sustenance had been resolved, her mind was at leisure to tackle other concerns. "Don't you ever think you're going to go out of your mind? What do you do with yourself when you don't have a flood to fight or a TV reporter to kick around?"

Daniel chuckled and held out a crust of bread between his thumb and forefinger. On signal, Lenore glided down from the rafters, plucked the bread away, and swooped back up to her roosting place without so much as a wing flutter to announce her presence. "Ninety percent of my time is spent just doing what it takes to live," he answered. "Cooking, washing, planting, cultivating, feeding the stock, preserving food, making clothes, soap, candles...just living. What leisure I have left is divided between writing, exploring the mountain, visiting the wildlife and the neighbors. Are you going to drink your buttermilk?"

Dallas gladly pushed the untouched mug toward him. "But," she persisted, "don't you ever get lonely?"

He looked at her as though the word were unfamiliar to him, as though, indeed, he had never given the matter a moment's consideration. "No," he replied simply.

Daniel finished off the buttermilk in two gulps and stood, gathering up the dishes. If it had been her house, Dallas would have let the dishes pile up until necessity dictated that she either wash them or buy more—which was one reason she had a housekeeper—but in the Masters household, cleanliness was apparently next to godliness. Reluctantly, Dallas got up to help, drying while he washed.

"So," Dallas ventured after a time, running a cotton dish towel over the plate he had handed her, "tell me about yourself. You don't have much of a public biography, you know."

"That's because there's not much to tell." He passed her another plate.

Dallas pursued, as nonchalantly as possible. "Well, what inspired you to go into engineering? Any cute little boyhood anecdotes you'd like to share along those lines?" Dallas thought he smiled, just a little, and very quickly.

"Not a one. I had the average American childhood in the average middle-class neighborhood; mediocre grades in grammar school, a little better in high school. I played football but was never much of a star, won second place at a science fair one time for my model of the atom. I spent most of my time camping and hiking with my dad. Mom died when I was five. Dad spent his whole life on an assembly line, and the only thing he wanted was that I should go to college." Daniel shrugged, not looking at her. "So I went. Engineering was where the money was, and I decided to be an engineer. End of story.''

Hardly, Dallas thought, musing about it. Behind the words somewhere was a lonely boy who had spent his life trying to please his only living parent—a devoted father whose only wish was that his son should have a better life than he did. ''I wonder,'' Dallas said softly, ''what your father would think about you now?''

Daniel looked at her. His eyes were steady, his voice firm. ''He would be proud,'' he replied with conviction. He turned back to the dishes, and his eyes strayed for a moment to the window and the twilight outside. His voice gentled a little as he added, ''Dad loved these mountains. He lived for the times he could get away from the time clock and come up here. He used to say this was the only place in the world a man could be free. I think,'' he added simply, ''Dad is the only person I've ever known who could understand why I'm doing this.''

''He's dead?'' Dallas asked, as tactfully as possible.

Daniel nodded. ''The year before I moved up here.''

Dallas wondered how much his father's death had had to do with Daniel's decision, but she thought she knew the answer. Perhaps seeing his father die, tied to a job he didn't like, had prompted Daniel to make sure the same thing didn't happen to him.

But Dallas had to voice her opinion. ''Seems pretty pointless to me,'' she observed noncommittally. ''You came up here to escape the rat race, but you only got into another kind of race. Still the same old computer mentality. Organize this, finish that, hurry up with the other thing, every minute of the day neatly filed away and labeled. The only thing that's different is the name of the pressure.'' She looked at him slyly. ''It doesn't seem to me as though you're any better off up here than you would be back at M.I.T.''

Daniel was totally unimpressed. "So who said I was trying to escape from anything? As for the computer mentality—" the smile that curved one corner of his lips was rather condenscending as he plunged his hands once again into the steaming water "—one of the first things I learned when I came up here was that you can't change what you are. All you can do is make better use of it."

"So what was it, anyway?" Dallas insisted, beginning to feel the nagging rise of the old frustration again. "What great compulsion made you leave an important, satisying career to dedicate your life to baking bread and talking to birds? I mean, you weren't an accountant, Daniel, or a three-fifty-an-hour burger chef—you were doing important work, changing people's lives. You were talented, highly skilled, very much in demand—"

"Contributing in a meaningful way to society," interrupted Daniel dryly.

Dallas bristled. "Something wrong with that?"

He looked at her, his expression guarded, his tone perfectly bland. "Is this in the nature of an interview?"

Dallas released a well-controlled sigh. "No. This is in the nature of boredom. I'm just curious, that's all."

Daniel washed the last plate in silence. The candlelight gleamed off the burnished fall of his hair and shadowed the thoughtful lines of his face. The dark hairs on his wrist were wet and molded to the strong lines of muscle and bone of his arms, and Dallas was fascinated for a moment by the movements of his hands, absorbed in so simple a task as washing dishes.

Then Daniel said, rather disinterestedly, "I'm not trying to make a statement with my life or my lifestyle. I'm just living, and I'm doing it this way because it suits me. And if you're really all that curious—" he handed the last plate to her, his eyes revealing nothing "—read my book."

He lifted the basin of dishwater and went to empty it outside, and there was nothing left for Dallas to do but put away the dishes.

Daniel returned to put away the dish basin and wipe off the counters, and Dallas left him to it. It was obvious that he was not going to go out of his way to make conversation with her, and she really needed a cigarette.

It was chilly outside, starless and foggy. Dallas found a dry perch on top of the covered wood bin and drew her knees up to her chest, wrapping her arms around them for warmth while she smoked. The atmosphere was spooky—dark, isolated, almost surreal—and it took her a moment to realize why.

There was no noise. No distant traffic sounds, no door slamming far away, no muffled voices. No sirens, no rumble of a truck from the freeway. Those low-level, almost unheard background noises—the hum of generators, the buzz of streetlights, the high-decibel throb of all the machinery that kept the world turning—they were all gone. Not even an airplane passed over. The culture shock affected Dallas on a inexplicable primal level that was like a shiver running right through her soul. The streets of Detroit were filled with danger, treachery and cunning, but those were known threats, familiar and manageable. This place was wild, untamed and completely unknown. Dallas could not handle what she did not understand,

and everything about this place made her feel helpless. She did not like that feeling. Not at all.

A soft square of yellow light opened as Daniel came
out, then closed again. He said quietly, looking at the
night, "It makes you feel small, doesn't it?"

Yes. That was the feeling. Small. Dallas inhaled
sharply on her cigarette and responsed. "I still don't
see the point." The sound of her own voice made her
feel better. More in control. "You said it yourself—
you're just living. Not accomplishing anything, not
working for anything, not *doing* anything, really. Just
passing time. I don't see how anyone can live like
that."

He laughed softly, not looking at her. His shadowed form in the night seemed huge. "Shall I play
philosopher for you? It seems to me that one of the
biggest problems with modern society is goal achieve-
ment. What *I* do, what *I* accomplish, what *I* want.
We're so involved with what we can do, what we can
make and what we achieve that the last thing we ever
think about is who we really are."

*Damn,* Dallas thought. *Why don't I have my tape
recorder? Or my notebook, at least?* This was the stuff
interviews were made of. Trying not to sound too interested, she said, "And do you know that? Who you
are?"

He answered in a moment, "It's like an American
traveling abroad, you know? We think we own the
world. 'You can't do that to me, I'm an American' has
got to be the most popular phrase in the Berlitz books.
But the same kind of superiority complex afflicts the
whole human race, I think. The first winter I was up
here, the roof leaked, there was six inches of snow, a
fox carried off my chickens and I damn near starved;

the deer ate my winter garden, in the spring the floods came and wiped out my fresh crop, and I felt like shaking my fist at the sky and yelling, 'You can't do this to me, I'm human!''' A rueful smile of remembrance crept into his voice, and, almost unwillingly, Dallas was drawn into his story; she almost understood. ''But you stand alone on this mountaintop on a night like this, or you walk through the forest in the still, heavy heat of summer, and you know who you are and what your place is. The fish were here before us, the ants, even the cockroaches—they were all here long before we were and will be here long after we're gone. We may busy ourselves with exalted things we like to call accomplishments—building and tearing down and moving and dreaming—but in the end, all we're doing is living, just like the fish and the cockroaches and the ants. The only difference is, when we go, we leave scars to mark the place we were. All I'm trying to do by living the way I do is to leave as few scars as possible.''

Dallas wanted to object, to protest with all her education, experience and intellect that such a life was futile, wasteful, self-defeating. But somehow she knew whatever words she spoke would sound hollow. The silence and the vastness of the night seemed to echo the truth in his words and for the first time in her life Dallas couldn't think of a single thing to say.

Daniel looked over at her, as though expecting the retort that should have come, and he was pleased when it did not. The atmopshere between them seemed warmer then, friendlier than it had been since Dallas had come bursting into his life a scant twenty-four hours ago, and Dallas found that she liked that feeling. For no reason at all, she smiled at him in the dark, and she thought Daniel smiled back.

Daniel took something from his pocket, like a stick of candy, and leaned back against the wall of the cabin, chewing on it. The familiar scent of cinnamon and cloves drifted over to her. Dallas finished her cigarette and tossed it out into the mud, where it landed with a sizzling sound. She half expected Daniel to reprimand her for littering and was surprised when he only said, casually, "Now it's your turn. Tell me the story of your life."

Dallas laughed a little, somewhat uncomfortably. She was used to being on the receiving end of an interview. But for lack of any more scintillating topic of conversation, she shrugged and replied, "Pretty predictable, actually. I grew up in a little neighborhood outside Detroit that was starting to go seedy before I was even in my teens. My folks were divorced; my mom was a night maid. I spent a lot of time on the streets, raising hell. But I was good in school." She smiled a little, remembering those carefree days of her youth. "Good enough to get a college scholarship, at least. I don't know, I just liked learning things. Insatiable curiosity, I guess, the makings of a reporter even then. My teachers always used to say 'that's a very good question, Dallas,' and I'd get so mad because they never gave me any good answers." She flashed Daniel a grin through the darkness. "One day I got sent to the principal's office for mouthing off at a teacher who complimented me on my 'good questions.' I told her to write a five-hundred-word report on the subject and have it on my desk by tomorrow. Cracked the class up." She winced a little at the memory. "The principal was not amused." Dallas leaned back against the wall, her face softening as she revisited those years. "Then, at night a bunch of us would pile into somebody's old Chevy and go cruise the Dairy Queen, listening to the Beatles and David Bowie and looking for trouble—finding it more often than not, too." She smiled. "I had a good time growing up," she decided. "Really good. Then I went off to college and had a pretty good time there, too—a whole new set of challenges. I majored in journalism but ended up at a TV station, bitten by the broadcast bug. The rest is history."

He was silent for a moment, and Dallas thought her life's story had been sufficiently boring to cause Daniel to turn to other topics of conversation now. Hopefully, to himself. But he surprised her by asking, "Do you live alone in Detroit?"

A week ago, if someone had asked Dallas to describe the place she lived, she would not have been able to. She spent so little time at her apartment, and she had never been very concerned with the details of domesticity; an apartment was just an apartment. But now it came back to her, with something that felt like a sharp twinge of yearning. She thought of the plush wall-to-wall gray carpet, the deep-cushioned sofa and chairs where she sometimes napped while waiting for a telephone call or an important meeting, the shelves lined with research books and journalism awards, the cable TV and VCR, the efficient little kitchen with every timesaving device known to man, the refrigerator filled with TV dinners and frozen waffles, the queen-sized bed and the bathroom with a real toilet and a porcelain tub with hot water that came right out of the taps.... It was all she could do to restrain a soulful sigh as she replied, "Yes." But there was no point in torturing herself over something that might as well have been on another planet, so she glanced back at him and inquired, "What are you eating?"

He held up a slim stick of what looked like candy, and replied, "I'm not really sure. It's some kind of root that the people around here use for seasoning; you boil it in ginger and it turns hard and sweet, like rock candy. I'm addicted to it, I'm afraid. Want some?"

Dallas started to demur, but he broke off a piece and came over to her. Dallas was so surprised when he sat down beside her and held the piece of candy before her lips that she opened her mouth automatically; he popped it inside. "Um," she murmured as the sweet-spicy taste spread over her tongue. "Good."

She could feel the hard muscle of his thigh against hers, and he was so close that his warmth reached her with a feeling of power and enormous male presence. Dallas tried to relax, but it wasn't as easy as it should have been.

Daniel leaned back against the wall and stretched one long leg out to rest over the porch railing. "You're not married, then."

She hesitated. "No."

He glanced at her. "That has the sound of a long story."

Dallas swallowed the gooey candy, thought about it and shrugged. "Not really." She shook out another cigarette and lighted it. "I was, once." And she turned the question on him. "What about you? Is there a woman in your past?"

He laughed softly, a deep, rolling, warming sound that made Dallas think how easy it would be to like him. "You mean as in the woman who broke my heart and sent me into exile? I'm afraid not. I was always too busy to let anyone get close enough to break my heart.'' He glanced at her slyly. "A lot like you, I suppose. Another disease of modern society.''

Dallas was immediately defensive. "I don't feel diseased.''

His eyes, bright and alert, were still on her. That made Dallas very uncomfortable. "What happened to your marriage?''

Dallas inhaled deeply on the cigarette, determined not to let him goad her. "We wanted different things. He wanted a full-time wife—children, car pools, PTA, the whole works. I wanted a career.''

"And?'' prompted Daniel perceptively.

"And I didn't like the idea of someone else controlling my life; he couldn't deal with taking second place to my career. It was a mistake from the beginning. People like me should never marry.''

"The overachiever syndrome,'' he mused. "It'll kill a relationship every time.''

Dallas wanted to inquire pertly what he, the original hermit, could possibly know about relationships, but instead, asked curiously, "Overachiever? What has that got to do with anything?''

"Overachievers,'' he responded thoughtfully, "wrap themselves up in what they *can* do so they don't have to deal with what they *can't* do—like make someone else love them. They're never satisfied with anything, most especially with themselves, and certainly not with another person. They keep looking for bigger and better challenges because they simply can't face the ultimate challenge—giving up part of themselves to someone else.'' He glanced at her, half challenging, half teasing. "Only an overachiever would walk fourteen miles up a mountain to do an interview with a crusty old hermit for a story she thought was stupid, just because she didn't want to go back and have to admit to someone that she couldn't do it.''

Well, there was no arguing with that logic. She said carefully, ''You sound as though you speak from experience. Is that what you are—an overachiever?''

The dim square of curtained yellow light coming from the window behind them was just enough to show Dallas the outline of his face, and his eyes, deep and rich and night-bright. He was looking at her in the absorbed, searching way a man looks at a woman he is thinking of kissing, and even though he did nothing more than look at her, Dallas's pulse began to speed as she thought what it would be like, what she would do, if he did try to kiss her.

Only a slight flicker of his eyes told her that his gaze had moved downward to her lips and then up again. *He's wondering,* thought Dallas, *what I would be like in bed. He's wondering why we're sitting here talking about philosophy and psychology when he hasn't seen a woman for heaven-knows-how-long, and we're all alone here with nothing to do, and it would be so easy.* Dallas knew she should put an end to that speculative look in his eye right away; she should assert her rights as a journalist and a woman and get a few matters straight right now. She should probably even resent his train of thought, and the assumption that just because she was female and here, she was available. But, in truth, Dallas was wondering, too.

Still looking at her, he said softly, ''I suppose I was. Until I learned that surrendering control can be even more important....'' His hand came up, large and warm, and very lightly smoothed a strand of hair away from her face. "And just as fulfilling as maintaining it."

His face was very close, his breath warm and scented on her cheek. His hand, so large and so strong, was strangely gentle in its touch, lightly cupping her scalp, his fingers just brushing against her face. But power radiated from him with a kinetic force waiting to be unleashed, and Dallas wondered what it would be like to surrender control to this man. Anticipation shortened her breath, hoarsened her voice a little, and her eyes seemed to be captured by his, even as she replied. "I thought you said that the first thing you learned up here was that you can't change what you are."

The blatant sensuality upon his face slowly relaxed into a smile, then a half-rueful chuckle. His hand drifted down to her shoulder, rested there briefly and companionably, and then left her altogether. "You're good, Dallas McCabe," he admitted, and there was a twinge of admiration in his voice that almost made up for the disappointment Dallas felt. "Right on top of everything. The next time I want to give an interview, you'll be the first person I call."

"Well." Dallas released the breath she had not even been aware she was holding and managed a philosophic smile as she tossed her half-smoked cigarette over the railing. The moment, for whatever it might have been, was gone and she assured herself that it was just as well, even as she was wondering how she had let it slip by.

Dallas got to her feet, suddenly needing to put some distance between herself and Daniel, and smoothed her hands on her jeans as she invited, "Shall we go inside and watch a little television?"

He was still chuckling silently as she stood. "Thanks, but it's almost eight o'clock and well past my bedtime. I found my old sleeping bag for you; it should make the floor a little more comfortable."

Comfortable was not the word Dallas would have used, but she was not certain whether her restlessness was due, in fact, to the hard floor, or to the uncertainty of the incompleted scene that had taken place on the porch. The floor was padded with the sleeping bag and two quilts; she was warm by the stove, and Daniel had even loaned her a feather pillow, but even though her body was tired, she twisted and turned and could not seem to keep her eyes closed. She wondered why he had not, after all, kissed her. She wondered what would have happened if he had. She wondered why she hadn't kissed him.

She heard Daniel turn, after a time, in the big soft bed, his voice came from the darkness, rather sleepy and muffled. "You doing okay?"

"Sure." She fluffed up the pillow with her fist. "I hear sleeping on the floor is good for back trouble."

"Do you have back trouble?"

Dallas pulled the covers up over her shoulders and tried to get comfortable on the pillow. "Not before tonight." It was probably best, she decided. His beard would be scratchy and she had never liked big men.

There was a long silence, and Dallas thought he had probably fallen asleep. Easy for him. When she got back home, she resolved, she was going to spend a week in bed. First, she was going to take a long hot bubble bath, and then she was going to go to bed—to her own bed, with a real mattress and innerspring coils.

His voice came again, unexpectedly, drowsily. "We'll take turns with the bed, okay? You can have it tomorrow night."

Dallas's surprise registered in the silence. Take turns. Not share. Strange. One would have thought, given such a perfect opportunity, he at least might have tried. "Yeah," she agreed softly, and tried to make out his form in the dark. "Okay. Thanks."

He turned again, with a rustle of straw mattress and quilts and a sleepy sigh. "Good night, Dallas McCabe."

It was probably for the best, Dallas decided, and closed her eyes. "Good night,...I guess."

# Chapter Eight

Four days had passed. Dallas had not, in fact, started pulling her hair out and counting her fingers, and sometimes that worried her. It worried her even more that often, for long periods of time, she could not even remember what life was like before she came here. The world seemed to begin and end with the borders of one forest on one mountaintop; it always had been and always would be. *That* was unsettling.

Nothing remained of the rain's presence except earth that was damp an inch below the surface and the roaring gush of a once-quiet creek a hundred yards away from the cabin. Every morning Dallas went with Daniel to measure the waterline by means of a submerged tree, but so far, very little discernible progress was being made toward returning the waterway to its natural boundaries. *Forever,* Dallas always thought glumly after these trips. *I'm going to be here forever.*

On the second day, Dallas had remarked dully, only half-teasing, "I wonder who's president now?"

Daniel looked at her blankly. "Who was president before you left?"

Then it was Dallas's turn to stare. Two elections had taken place since this man had last seen a newspaper.

Countless advances in medicine, science and technology had been made. He did not know what a yuppie was, had never eaten a Chipwich. He had never heard of "Hill Street Blues" or the space shuttle *Discovery*. The realization was so overwhelmingly depressing that Dallas had to go lie down.

Daniel kept himself so well-occupied during the day that it was almost as though he forgot Dallas's presence, which was irritating. While she longed for the sound of a human voice, the mere presence of another intelligent—or even semi-intelligent—being in her life, Daniel Masters was so well-accustomed to its absence that he hardly noticed. He really *did* like being alone and was easily capable of going an entire day without seeing or speaking to Dallas once.

Dallas had met the cow who needed milking, the chickens who provided fresh eggs daily, and the burly mule who would one day be her ticket back to civilization, but she was not interested in furthering her acquaintance with any of them. The cow had a tendency to kick; the chickens, with their squawking and pecking, terrified her; and the mule was stupid. So Daniel took care of the animals with no offer of assistance from Dallas; he also took care of the meals and the house and the myriad details of which simple existence was comprised. Every day Dallas felt more helpless. Basic tasks like preserving vegetables eluded her, as did the weaving of oak baskets and, yes, even the mending of her own torn shirt. The frustration was immense. She watched Daniel spend one entire morning stirring a huge, bubbling caldron of lye and grease into soap, and an afternoon melting tallow for candles, and beneath the dumb amazement that anyone would invest so much effort for an item that could be purchased for less than a dollar at the local grocery, there gradually began to emerge a sense of awe and even respect. Dallas knew she had been here too long when she started admiring, even envying, Daniel Masters's adjustment to this life-style.

Dallas also knew she had been here too long when she held in her mind all day the image of Daniel, his bare chest gleaming and muscles rippling, splitting logs with an ax. Or when her skin began to tingle when she heard his step on the front porch and when she lay awake at night listening to the sound of his deep breathing only a few feet away.

Sometimes, to keep her mind off her misery and her boredom, and as a desperate measure to keep in touch with reality, Dallas would list in her mind all the things she missed. Chocolate-chip cookies. Pizza. "Tonight." Nylon carpet. Fabric softener. Shampoo. Men in polo shirts. Men without polo shirts.

The worst part was, of course, that for all of her misery and privation, nothing—absolutely nothing—would come of this. A week, possibly more, of her life would be wasted, and she would return to Detroit with nothing for her trouble more useful than a knowledge of soap making and a picture in her head of a bearded man with deep-brown eyes and a laugh that could make her heart beat faster when she thought of it. Already, because the workaholic in her would not die, she was beginning to see day-to-day life with Daniel Masters in cutaway shots and voice-overs, and at least twice an hour when she was with him Dallas had to close her mouth on a question that was to be asked in her interviewer-voice. Unfortunately, this was not a magazine interview, and the background research that was being forced on Dallas so graphically was worth nothing without the cameras. Without Daniel's willing cooperation there could be no story, and cooperation along those lines was, so far, the one thing he refused to give.

Not, Dallas continued to assure herself, that there was any story here, anyway. She was just bored, that was all, and he was the only subject of any interest to be had. Just because she was beginning to find him somewhat fascinating was no indication at all that the viewers of her prime-time network show would have the same reaction. But Dallas didn't seem to be able to deny the fact that her fascination with him was growing deeper and more absorbing with every day.

IT WAS EARLY MORNING. The sky was clear, the air cool, the creek rushed vigorously in the background, and the birds chirped. The trees had deepened their orange-yellow colors in the days Dallas had been there, and had even added shades of maroon and violet, and Dallas had to admit the view was quite spectacular. Rolling hills in peaks and valleys of blue-green forest splashed with random color surrounded the cabin on every side, thrusting into the brightening sky, catching the sun in the spark or glitter of a mountain pool or lake, vibrant and alive as far as the eye could see. It would have made a fantastic postcard.

She was standing on the front porch, smoking. The effort it took to go outside every time she wanted a cigarette had decreased her consumption somewhat, but, still, the carton was diminishing at an alarming rate. Dallas's worst nightmare was that one day she would reach into her backpack and find the cigarette carton empty and the creek still flooded. Sometimes she broke into a cold sweat thinking about it, and she made a conscious effort to smoke less and save more.

The door opened, and Dallas turned around to greet Daniel, who was no doubt off on one of his daily treks through the woods. Heaven only knew what he did on these trips—something to do with plants and animals, Dallas thought—though sometimes he brought home baskets of berries or strange-looking flora that he served for dinner and that Dallas was wise enough not to inquire about too closely. Usually she waved good-bye to him, sweetly urged him to have a good day and reminded him not to forget his briefcase, to which he replied with either a grin or a grunt, depending on how closely he was paying attention. He always carried his rifle and usually a basket or a sack; today he carried the rifle and two of the large burlap sacks. Before Dallas could even open her mouth, he had snatched the cigarette out of her hand and tossed it aside, grabbed her wrist and was pulling her along with him as he strode down the steps and across the yard.

"What—what in the world are you *doing*?"

"Putting something else in your lungs beside poison." He tugged imperiously on her wrist and lengthened his stride until she had to run to keep up, then he increased the pace until they were both running and he grinned over his shoulder, "Come on, lady— *breathe*!"

That was much easier said than done and Dallas was gasping and pleading for mercy after only a few minutes of running uphill and over broken ground, ducking branches and tripping over clumps of wild grass. When she stumbled and almost fell Daniel caught her around the waist and, laughing, allowed her to lean against his chest for support, patting her back in mock solicitation as she struggled for breath.

Dallas's throat and chest were aching and she had a stitch in her side, her muscles were rubbery and she was so thoroughly exhausted that she couldn't even appreciate what would have, at another moment, been a singularly pleasant experience—being held in Daniel's arm, with her face pressed against his broad chest and his strong thighs blending into hers. She was spending so much effort just getting her breath that she couldn't even yell at him, as she would have like to have done, or kicked him in the shins, which probably would have been more effective.

His eyes were dancing as he took her shoulders and held her a little away from him, looking down at her severely. He wasn't even winded. "Do you need a lecture on all the junk you've been breathing for the past twenty-odd years of your life? The hydrocarbons and sulfur dioxides, nitrogen oxides, bituminous vapors, peroxyacyl nitrates—and that's not even to mention the cigarettes."

"You—you crazy person!" Dallas gasped hoarsely, her fist bunched against his shirt as she struggled for breath. "Don't you know...I'm ...high risk for heart attack? I'm from...Detroit, for Pete's sake! You could have...killed me!"

"Six months up here, and you'd be in better shape than you were when you were sixteen." He put an arm companionably around her shoulders and began to lead the way again. Dallas, too weak to protest, stumbled along. "Your life span would be increased by twenty percent."

"Who'd want a longer life span," grumbled Dallas, "under these conditions?"

He laughed. "I feel the same way about Detroit."

He kept his arm around her as they walked, and it was a nice, though strange, sensation. Since that first night on the porch, not even the remotest hint of intimacy had passed between them—not a glance, not a touch, certainly not a word. Sometimes it almost seemed to Dallas that Daniel was going out of his way to avoid being near her, but she tried not to spend too much time puzzling over it. She wondered what had made him decide that he wanted companionship today.

"Where are we going?" she asked when she had regained control of her breathing enough to speak an entire sentence without pausing.

"To finish gathering the apples I had to leave the day the rainstorm started. I only hope there are enough of them left to make it worth our while."

Dallas lifted her shoulders in an agreeable shrug. "It's better than sitting around the house all day watching soap operas, I guess." In fact, the prospect of spending a whole day with him sent her spirits soaring to a level they had not experienced since she had crawled out of the creek and landed at his feet, and when he flashed her that wonderful grin of his, her heart started beating fast again.

They walked through a sparse stretch of forest, down a hill, and then picked up the path of the stream again. Dallas had not been away from the cabin since she arrived; certainly she had no desire to visit again that awful stretch of wooded moutainside she had learned to abhor on her journey up here. But today, walking with Daniel, it seemed different. It smelled good, sweet and fresh and earthy, and when Daniel pointed out to her the various herbs and shrubs that

# A FIRST CLASS OPPORTUNITY FOR YO

- ◆ **Grand Prize** – Rolls-Royce ™
  (or $100,000)
- ◆ **Second Prize** – A trip for two to Paris
  via The Concorde
- ◆ **Third Prize** – A Luxurious Mink Coat

**The Romance can last forever**… when you take advantage of this no cost special introductory offer

## 4 "HARLEQUIN AMERICAN ROMANCES®" – FREE!
Take four of the world's greatest love stories – FREE from Harlequin Reader Service®! Each of these novels is your free passport to bright new worlds of love, passion and foreign adventure!

But wait…there's _even more_ to this great _free offer_…

## HARLEQUIN TOTE BAG – FREE!
Carry away your favourite romances in your elegant canvas Tote Bag. With a snap top and double handles, your Tote Bag is valued at $6.99 – _but it's yours free with this offer!_

## SPECIAL EXTRAS – FREE!
You'll get our free newsletter, packed with news on your favourite writers, upcoming books, and more. Four times a year, you'll receive our members' magazine, Harlequin Romance Digest®!

## MONEY-SAVING HOME DELIVERY!
Join Harlequin Reader Service® and enjoy the convenience of previewing four new books every month, delivered right to your home. _Great savings_ plus _total convenience_ add up to a sweetheart of a deal for you.

## BONUS MYSTERY GIFT!
P.S. For a limited time only you will be eligible to receive a _mystery gift free_!

# TO EXPERIENCE A WORLD OF ROMANCE.

## How to Enter Sweepstakes & How to get 4 FREE BOOKS, A FREE TOTE BAG and A BONUS MYSTERY GIFT.

1. Check ONLY ONE OPTION BELOW.
2. Detach Official Entry Form and affix proper postage.
3. Mail Sweepstakes Entry Form before the deadline date in the rules.

H·A·R·L·E·Q·U·I·N
FIRST·CLASS
*Sweepstakes*

## OFFICIAL ENTRY FORM

### Check one:

☐ Yes. Enter me in the Harlequin First Class Sweepstakes and send me 4 FREE HARLEQUIN AMERICAN ROMANCE® novels plus a FREE Tote Bag and a BONUS Mystery Gift. Then send me 4 brand new HARLEQUIN AMERICAN ROMANCE® novels every month as they come off the presses. Bill me at the low price of $2.25 each (a savings of $0.25 off the retail price). There are no shipping, handling or other hidden charges. I understand that the 4 Free Books, Tote Bag and Mystery Gift are mine to keep with <u>no obligation to buy</u>.

☐ No. I don't want to receive the Four Free HARLEQUIN AMERICAN ROMANCE® novels, a Free Tote Bag and a Bonus Gift. However, I <u>do</u> wish to enter the sweepstakes. Please notify me if I win.

See back of book for official rules and regulations.      154–CIA-NA3X
Detach, affix postage and mail Official Entry Form today!

FIRST NAME_____ LAST NAME_____
(Please Print)
ADDRESS_____ APT._____

CITY_____

PROV./STATE_____ POSTAL CODE/ZIP_____
"Subscription Offer limited to one per household and not valid to current Harlequin American Romance® subscribers. Prices subject to change."

# ENTER THE H·A·R·L·E·Q·U·I·N
# FIRST·CLASS *Sweepstakes*

Detach, Affix Postage and Mail Today!

**Harlequin First Class Sweepstakes**
P.O. Box 52010
Phoenix, AZ 85072-9987

Put stamp here.
The Post Office
will not
deliver mail
without postage.

gave off the scents, she was fascinated. He showed her deer tracks in the soft earth, and once a chipmunk scampered across their path and made Dallas laugh out loud. He paused to point out in the trees across the stream a series of wooden boxes he had built as nests to lure a certain type of duck back to the habitat it had abandoned a generation ago. So far, he told her with an unmistakable note of pride in his voice, two families of ducks had returned, and next year he expected more.

"Why did they leave?" Dallas wanted to know.

He dropped his arm from around her shoulders as they emerged from the woods onto a narrow path of worn-down grass that led downhill. Dallas was sorry for that. "Who knows? The coal mining that used to be done up here upset the balance of nature in ways we'll probably never know. The mountain is just beginning to recover, and it will probably never be what it once was."

Dallas looked at him curiously, trying to understand. "Do you really think that you can help?"

He smiled at her gently, shaking his head. "No. I can only try to live in harmony with what's left."

And that, among all the strange things Dallas was beginning to understand about Daniel, was the strangest. He was a believer, but not a crusader. He might be a naturalist, but he hardly ever gave in to the impulse to launch into lectures about it. His philosophy, his way of living, seemed to be ingrained so deeply that he never thought about it, could never consider changing it; it was simply an inextricable part of him. He really didn't want to change the world. He just wanted to be left alone. And that concept, to

Dallas, was so totally alien that she supposed Daniel Masters would forever remain an enigma to her.

Dallas froze in her tracks as a high, broken screech, like a wounded animal of enormous proportions or a woman in pain, pierced the stillness of the autumn day and echoed across the hills. It sounded as though it was coming from a point directly behind her left shoulder, and a chill went up her spine as she whispered hoarsely, staring, "What's that?" Immediately her mind flashed back to the terrifying moment when she was alone on the trail, herself against a fierce raccoon, and to the warning, *Panthers, grizzlies...*

Daniel grinned, glancing back at her. "Wild turkey." He extended his hand to her. "They're not flesh eaters."

Dallas released her breath and took his offered hand gratefully. "This place is spooky," she mumbled, by way of apology or excuse for her nervousness. But his fingers, so large and strong around hers, did a great deal to mitigate whatever uneasiness she might have been feeling. And that was strange, too. Dallas had never had that feeling before, of being safe simply because a man was near. She had always been able to take care of herself.

"Not as spooky as, say, a Manhattan subway at 3:00 A.M.," he responded cheerfully. "Or rush hour on any freeway in any major city of the world."

She glanced at him shrewdly. The sun, glinting off his long, dark hair and highlighting his profile, made him seem a part of the landscape, as indestructible as the earth, as enduring as the sky overhead. And very, very attractive. "So," she commented, "it's only two-footed animals you're afraid of."

If she expected to get a rise out of him with that, she was to be disappointed. He only said, soberly, "Shouldn't I be? The two-footed animals are the only ones who have the power to destroy all this." With a single broad sweep of his hand he encompassed mountain, trees, sky and earth.

There was something Dallas could relate to: commitment, compassion, caring. It struck her with surprise that Daniel, in his way and in this place, was doing no more than what she did every day of her life. He was protecting the underdog, conducting his own lone battle against apathy and disintegration. The difference was that, in Daniel's case, the battle was a silent one, and the underdog was the ravaged earth.

"I guess we're more alike than I thought," she murmured thoughtfully.

It was a peculiar thing that she did not have to explain what she meant. He looked at her, and his deep-brown eyes were gentle and full of understanding, and in that brief yet endless moment in which knowledge was shared in his eyes, Dallas felt as though the entire world had just opened up at her feet. He looked at her as though he saw everything and knew everything that had ever been and ever would be true about her, and the sensation took Dallas's breath away.

He said softly, "Yes. We're a lot alike, you and I. In more ways, I think, than I even want to know right now."

And then he turned, gesturing with the rifle toward the area ahead. The moment was gone, but Dallas's heart was still beating, slowly and loudly, from the power of it. "Here we are," he said, and they started down the hill.

The stand of apple trees was hardly large enough or organized enough to be truly called a grove. There were less than a dozen trees of mixed variety scattered randomly in the clearing, their trunks knotty and their gnarled branches bent and groaning with the weight of their fruit. But Daniel had kept them cultivated and cleared their bases of weeds and grass, and the picture they made, standing against the cobalt sky with colorful fruit scattered upon the ground, was striking—the Garden of Eden in the midst of a primal forest.

Dallas needed no encouragement to run the last few yards down the hill toward the clearing. A sudden surge of adrenaline filled her that had something to do with the warmth of Daniel's hand around hers and the poignant moment that had just passed between them, and she wanted to laugh, to run with the wind in her hair and the sun in her face, and with all the world as her playground.

She grasped the trunk of the largest tree to stop herself, swinging around until she was leaning against it, flushed and bright-eyed, laughing and gasping, as Daniel drew up. "Got you that time!" she declared, and his eyes sparked with the pleasure he saw in hers.

"That is what is known in these regions, ma'am," he drawled, "as cheating. You have the prettiest eyes I've ever seen."

Laughter died in the surprise of that statement, but Daniel had already turned away, casually laying his gun upon the ground and inspecting the apples he saw lying there. "Looks like the birds have already beaten us to it."

Dallas shrugged and slid down until she was sitting on the ground, resting her back against the tree trunk, her arms folded around her upraised knees. "Just as well. I'm too tired from all that exercise to pick apples. Don't we get a lunch break?"

Daniel's eyes danced as he tossed aside one partially decimated apple. "Not unless we pick it off the ground."

Dallas made a face. "I should have known. And I was worried about gaining weight." She looked around contentedly while Daniel continued to examine and discard apples, letting the sun and the aftermath of exercise and the still autumn air work their insidious tranquilizing effect. "I haven't had a vacation in four years," she commented after a time.

"Too busy making the world safe for democracy, hm?"

Dallas chuckled a little, too languorous to take the bait. "I guess."

"We're going to have to climb the trees if we expect to get any good apples," Daniel said, and then he surprised her by coming to sit on the ground near her. Not too near—not near enough to touch—but close enough for Dallas to feel his presence and smell that subtle scent of his that was a mixture of spice and earth and woods and was more effective than the highest-priced cologne on the market, as powerful as an aphrodisiac.

He lounged back with his weight on one elbow, one knee partially upraised, his strong body shadowing Dallas. The sun was in his eyes, and he squinted a little, producing a spray of tiny, weathered lines along his tanned cheekbones. His hair fell in a luxurious sweep over his ears and collar, and Dallas wanted to touch it. The beard wasn't so bad, she remarked to herself absently. It only drew attention to the full, gentle shape of his lips.

For a while they sat there in companionable silence, absorbing the sounds and the scents of the world around them, and then Daniel said, "I used to spend every summer up here when I was a kid. My dad and I would camp all over these mountains."

This was the first time Daniel had ever spoken voluntarily about himself, and Dallas's interest was immediately sparked. "So that's how you learned all that survival stuff that it takes to live up here."

He smiled a little and glanced at her briefly. "Some," he admitted. "My dad thought those camping trips were an important lesson in self-reliance, and they were, in a way. But I went away to college, then got wrapped up in the corporate world, and it didn't take long to forget all I had learned up here."

He was silent for a while, and Dallas did not press him. His eyes were focused lazily on a distant hillside, and the way the light was reflected in them reminded Dallas of a cut-glass crystal. She found pleasure in just looking at his face.

"Then," he continued, "when I started teaching, I remembered this place, and I came back. Every summer, all summer, just me and my backpack. That's when I really started learning what the mountain was all about and what it meant to the people who lived here...and what living was all about, I suppose." He picked up a stone and turned it over in his hand, examining it. "I learned how to make what I needed from the land provided, how to cultivate and protect it and appreciate it and be a part of it." He did not look up from his study of the small, gray-green stone he held in his hand. "Then one day I found out that the microchip I had spent five years of my life helping to develop was being used in the guidance-control system of the MIG, and it didn't take long to put my priorities into place. I bought this land and started building my cabin.'' He opened his hand to her and looked up. ''An arrowhead. Do you want it?''

Dallas took the small, pointed rock from him slowly, strangely moved and a little confused by all she had learned about him in the past few minutes. When one balanced nuclear war against the peace and natural beauty of this place, it was difficult to argue with his choice, yet Dallas wanted to argue with it. She wanted to assert that disassociating oneself from society never solved society's problems, that hermitage was pointless and futile, that the MIGs would have been developed and tested with or without his help—but somehow all those arguments seemed shallow. Daniel wasn't a fanatic; he wasn't preaching his principles or fighting for a cause. He was simply doing what was right for him, because he could not have lived any other way.

Dallas said quietly, her eyes upon the stone in her hand, ''Daniel, what will happen if you lose your court case and the government takes back your land?''

''They think there's a uranium deposit here. They'll open up a mine, strip the forests, foul the waterways, drive away the wildlife, and use the uranium to build their bombs. Technology will have won again.''

Dallas's throat tightened with this; the fighting spirit in her flared to life and she thought, *No, damn it, they can't do that. Not to this gentle man, this quiet place.* She said quickly, ''Let me do the interview, Daniel. 'Spotlight' has power, more than you can imagine.'' Her hand tightened around the stone with intensity and instinctive determination. "We can help. By the time I'm finished, everyone in America will be on your side, and even if by some chance you did lose your case, no corporation in its right mind would take on the mining contract. We'd hound them into the ground. The case would probably never be brought to court, once our show aired." Already, an avaricious gleam of excitement was coming into her eyes at the prospect.

"Why, we'd investigate every rumor of graft, we'd air every scrap of dirty laundry, we'd go right into the judge's chambers if we had to, and not even the U.S. Government wants that kind of trouble. There are other uranium deposits; they'd be quick enough to find them and leave you alone."

Daniel looked at her, his deep eyes a mixture of amusement, wonder and grudging respect. "The lady tiger at work, hm? Do you get this excited about all causes, or is it only the lost ones that turn you on?"

She leaned forward a little, her posture revealing restrained impatience. "Daniel, I'm serious. I—"

But he reached forward then and lifted the hand that had closed around the arrowhead. Gently, he opened the fingers. "Do you know how old this is?" he inquired, picking it up.

Dallas shook her head, her breath strangely suspended with the light grasp of his fingers on the pulse of her wrist, the thoughtful, tender look that had come over his face. "The last time the Indians hunted here was two hundred years ago. This arrowhead could be older than that. When you think about time in chunks that big, it helps to put things in perspective, doesn't it?"

Dallas shook her head, not understanding at all. "You can't just refuse to fight. You have to—"

"I'll fight," he returned mildly, "with the truth. That's all I can do." He returned the arrowhead to her. It held the warmth of the sun and of his palm. "Here, keep this. I've heard it brings luck."

Dallas stared at him helplessly. Obviously, he had made up his mind. And how could she convince a man to defend himself? How could she help him when he refused to cooperate? She looked down at the smooth stone in her hand, at a loss. "Maybe you'd better keep this," she said at last, unable to keep the note of sourness out of her voice. "It looks as though you're going to need it."

He laughed softly and closed her hand around the stone. The warmth of his fingers lingered over hers for a moment. "Oh, no, you're the fighter, not me. And it's only the warriors who need talismans."

With a brief, almost imperceptible squeeze of her fingers, he released her hand and got to his feet. "Come on," he said, "let's get those apples. The day is moving fast and we've got a lot to do before dark."

With a suppressed sigh of exasperation, Dallas got to her feet and tucked the arrowhead into her pocket.

It was hard to hold on to her sense of frustration, or even to think like the professional she was, when the day was so bright and Daniel's laughter was so warm, and the sounds and the scents of nature were everywhere. Never before had Dallas, once hooked on a story, let her resolve waver for even a moment, but with Daniel, in this carefree demiparadise, it was easy to forget who she was and why she was here. Maybe that was why he stayed, Dallas thought. It was easy to forget all the threats and pressures of the outside world when you were wrapped up so completely in the day-to-day living of your own personal Eden.

Daniel had no trouble reaching into the lower branches of the trees for the apples the birds had not yet damaged, but Dallas had to climb into the limbs to reach the fruit. She hadn't climbed a tree since she was twelve and the single scraggly birch in her fast-distintegrating neighborhood had given up the ghost; she had forgotten how much fun it could be.

"You do that very well," Daniel called up to her, his eyes sparkling with sunlight and humor as he tilted his head to look at her. "For a city kid."

"Hey, you're talking to the regional tree-climbing champion of 1969. Catch!" She plucked off a huge red apple and tossed it to him; he caught it one-handed, laughter dancing in his eyes.

"You'd better be careful up there. That limb doesn't look too—"

But as he spoke, Dallas heard a cracking noise beneath her feet; she grabbed for an overhead branch but came away with only another apple. She began to totter.

Fortunately, she was standing on the lowest branch. As she pitched forward, squealing more with laughter than alarm, Daniel caught her firmly by the waist. They were both laughing when he swung her securely against him, his arms wrapped around her, the length of her body pressed against the strong form of his, her feet a few inches off the ground.

A dizzy exhilaration swept Dallas as she looked into Daniel's face, so close—his eyes so bright and filled with laughter, the open curve of his lips and the flash of white teeth—and she thought, *How could I have ever thought he was unattractive? He's magnificent.*

His arms were strong around her, supporting her in midair, his body hard and as warm as sunshine against hers. Playfully, Dallas wrapped one arm around his neck and with the other hand brought the apple before his lips. "Lunch?" she invited coquettishly.

Daniel's eyes lightened, then deepened, as they swept over her—her hair, sun-golden and wind-tousled, her face flushed with laughter and her eyes as clear and as light as tinted cellophane, dancing with pleasure. His eyes moved to the apple she held temptingly before him and he murmured, "Somehow this scene seems familiar to me."

Dallas let the apple drop from her loosened fingers as his face moved close to hers, as his lips claimed hers. Without hesitation, his tongue filled her mouth, heated and sweet, tasting of cloves and fresh air. Her arms went around his neck even as every muscle in her body abruptly turned to rubber; her pulse soared and her skin flamed, and she literally lost her breath. The mastery of him filled her, the instinctive chemical responses of her own body drew her closer to him until she felt as though she were melting into him, and she thought dizzily, *This is good. Oh, this is so good.* Earth and sunshine and Daniel Masters penetrating every pore of her body, kissing her, absorbing her, blending into her, making her want to let it last forever.

The fever built as the initial wonder of discovery and exploration faded into unvarnished need. Daniel's hand moved down her back and spread over her buttocks, learning of her, claiming her. Dallas could feel the ache of her breasts against his chest and the stinging awakening of desire within her loins. Her fingers tightened around the strong, broad cords of his neck, beneath his hair, and her tongue explored his mouth with the same greedy urgency with which his had explored hers. His desire was hard and demanding against the soft flesh of her abdomen, and Dallas wanted to drift backward onto the soft bed of grass beneath, bringing him with her, feeling his body melting with hers, filling hers, making love to her. How long had she wanted him, she wondered through the distant haze of rising ecstasy. Since the first moment she saw him, the first night? No, later than that, more subtly than that—a need that grew with exposure until now it cried out to be filled, could not wait for fulfillment.

Dallas was not aware that his grasp had loosened until she felt her feet touch the ground, nor that the hungry, unmasked demand of his kiss was gradually coming under restraint until, in fact, his mouth had left hers. His lips closed hers with one final, very brief kiss. Daniel supported her very lightly with his hands upon her waist; Dallas looked up at him, flushed and weak and confused. Her breath was shallow; her pulses still roared; every inch of her skin ached for him, and she even involuntarily swayed toward him. Daniel stepped back.

His color was high and his breathing was still a little uneven. But beneath the undampened fire of residual hunger in his eyes was something else— something sober, firm and completely enigmatic to Dallas. He looked at her for a moment, and her head whirled with confusion and loss, then he bent to pick up the discarded sacks of apples. "We'd better start back," he said simply. "We've still got a lot of work to do this afternoon."

# Chapter Nine

*Wait a minute,* Dallas thought dumbly as she followed the path Daniel was breaking through the woods. *Did I miss something here? Didn't this man just kiss me like a man kisses a woman when he means business, and didn't I have yes written all over my face, and didn't he want me as much as I wanted him? What happened?*

As far as she could tell by Daniel's stance, absolutely nothing had happened. He had picked up the sacks laden with apples and flung them over his shoulder, retrieved his gun, and was leading the way back home before Dallas even had a chance to catch a steady breath, before she was even sure her watery knees would support her. He hadn't said a word; he had not given her a chance to say a word. It was just over, as though it had never been.

Never had desire come upon Dallas so quickly, so intensely, and so overwhelmingly as it had when Daniel Masters had taken her into his arms—and never had fulfillment been wrested from her so abruptly. She searched her memory, trying to figure out what had happened, what she had done to offend him or make him angry or simply turn him off, but try as she might, she could not come up with a single thing. They had been enjoying each other this afternoon; he had opened up to her for the first time on his own. She had felt close to him. Then what had happened?

Dallas, accustomed to meeting every problem head-on, could not be silent any longer. She quickened her pace a little to keep up with his, catching the branches over wooded undergrowth that he brushed aside. She was hot and sweaty and a little short of breath by the time she finally formed the question, "Daniel, did I imagine what just happened between us under the apple tree?"

His broad back kept moving in front of her, yet she forged ahead to keep up. He responded easily, "No, you didn't imagine it."

*Okay,* she thought. *Good sign. He's talking to me.* She suggested, half teasing, "You're not interested in sex?"

His step faltered a bit, but he did not turn around. She thought she heard the release of a pent-up breath with his soft reply. "Oh, yes. I'm interested."

*But not with me,* Dallas realized slowly, trying to subdue the hurt of rejection. *That much is pretty clear.* And then a sense of outrage surged to the surface and she thought heatedly, *Why the hell not?*

She stopped, ready to demand an explanation and get this thing out in the open before her sexual self-confidence was completely destroyed. "Daniel—" But just then he released a bramble she was not quick enough to catch and it snagged her sweater and she swore softly.

Daniel turned. "Sorry," he began, and then stopped.

"It's okay," Dallas mumbled, working the material loose from the thorns. The moment was gone. She should have known better than to try to conduct an intimate conversation in the midle of an uphill hike, anyway.

Daniel said very quietly, "Dallas, don't move."

"Oh, for goodness' sake," she said, exasperated, embarrassed, and at the end of her patience as she released the last thorn. "There, it's—"

"Be *still*!"

Dallas stared at him, openmouthed at his rudeness, but when she saw the look on his face, everything within her froze. He was not looking at her at all, but his eyes were fixed on the ground—on her boot. Dallas saw the small movement of his finger as he silently released the safety catch on the rifle, and then she felt something soft and heavy move onto the toe of her boot.

Dallas never knew how she kept from screaming, fainting, jumping back or jumping forward. Perhaps, in the end, it was only the paralysis of terror that saved her. Her heart started to pound, and she thought each beat would be its last; her throat dried up, and she couldn't feel her fingers or toes. The whole world shook and pulsed in tones of brown and green, and Dallas watched the biggest snake she had ever seen slither slowly, ever so slowly, across her feet.

*Oh, God,* she thought. Oh, dear God.... Her mind was so numb, she couldn't even finish the prayer. She could only watch as, inch by inch, second by second, that hideous crawling weight moved over her boots, and a hundred flashing half-finished terrors assailed her. Diamond-shaped paterns—poisonous? Huge—anaconda? Daniel—would he shoot? Would he miss the snake and shoot her? Oh, dear God. She saw the rattles on its tail, and she thought she was going to pass out.

The snake slithered into the bushes. Daniel replaced the safety on his rifle. They looked at each other.

*No,* Dallas commanded herself firmly, *you are not going to throw up.* This was the woman who had faced down mobsters and street thugs and angry teenage boys with switchblades; she would not be reduced to hysteria by one creepy little snake.

It was the biggest snake she had ever seen in her life. It was the *only* snake she had ever seen in her life. Dallas thought she was probably going to be sick after all.

Daniel smiled at her, hesitantly, bracingly. "That's one good reason," he said, gesturing toward the rifle, "for carrying a gun."

Dallas swallowed hard; she tried for nonchalance. Her voice was a little hoarse. "Was that...a rattlesnake?"

"Um-hm. These mountains are thick with them."

*Great,* Dallas thought in a sinking spell of weakness. *Oh, great.*

"Why—" she cleared her throat "—why didn't you shoot it?"

He made a small sound that could have been laughter and shook his head. "Because it's an exercise in futility. The snakes are here; we just have to live with them. Also—" the curve of his smile was definitely meant to be encouraging as he cocked his head toward her "—because I didn't want to miss and hit your foot. You okay?"

"Oh, sure." Dallas tossed her head nonchalantly and tucked her hands into her jeans pockets to hide their trembling. "You should see the size of the snakes we have in Detroit. They make that one look like a minnow."

He laughed and pushed aside another branch, once again leading the way. Dallas moved quickly to walk beside him. She said uneasily, after a time, still trying to convince her pounding heart that the crisis was over, "What's the other reason?"

He glanced down at her curiously. "What?"

"You said that was one good reason for carrying a gun. What are the others?"

"Oh." He looked unconcerned. "We get wild-dog packs sometimes. Or a wounded panther or bear, or a mean boar, or a mother defending her young. Man is still the alien here, you know. It doesn't hurt to be prepared."

Dallas felt that sinking feeling beginning again. She did not ask whether he had ever had to use his gun. She didn't want to know. *Come on, Dallas, brace up. You're a big, strong girl, in command, in control. You're not afraid of anything. You can take on the world with one hand tied behind your back, everybody knows that. What are you getting so weak-kneed over?*

Because out here everything she had ever known about being in control and in authority evaporated like mist in the desert, and she didn't feel strong at all.

Daniel's arm came around her shoulders firmly; his brief squeeze was bracing and his smile warm and understanding. "Hey," he said softly, "you did good, Tiger. Your camera crew would have been proud of you."

Dallas swallowed the dryness in her throat and smiled weakly. *Right,* she thought. *I'm doing just fine. There's nothing Dallas McCabe can't handle.*

But it felt awfully good to have the strength of Daniel's arm to lean on for the rest of the walk back home.

DALLAS SAT ON THE FRONT PORCH in the dark, smoking. Behind her a candlelit window glowed softly, and inside the cabin Daniel was writing. She could hear the muffled click of the typewriter keys and it was a comforting sound. Civilized.

They had spent the afternoon peeling and slicing apples. Some of the apples had been spread over wooden racks to dry in the sun and in the heat of the fire at night; others had been cooked with cinnamon and brown sugar into applesauce; others boiled and placed in sterile jars for consumption later in the winter. It had been a long, hot, exhausting job, but Dallas was not tired. She was still on edge, restless, energized from the many conficting demands and confusions of the day.

*What are you doing here,* she asked herself, staring out into the moonlit shadows and valleys that spread before her. *What are you going way up here on the top of the world with a man who kisses you one minute and ignores you the next, where killer rattlesnakes roam the woods, and wild dogs and boar and God-knows-what-else lurk around every corner, and there's not a Seven-Eleven or a McDonald's in sight?* She might as well be on another planet. Everything about this place, this man, baffled and unsettled her. Nothing was familiar; nothing behaved the way it should. Dallas was accustomed to walking into a situation, assessing it, taking charge of it. She came, she saw, she conquered. It was a simple as that. But from the moment she started up that mountain trail, she had been awkward, off-guard, ill-equipped, helpless. And the advent of Daniel Masters into her life had done nothing to make matters easier.

Lenore, only a darker shadow among the silhouettes of the porch rail, clucked softly and ruffled her feathers. Dallas squinted to make out the beady black eyes that were focused on her. "Go figure it, bird," she muttered. "Four years of college, three years of making coffee and writing copy, seven years on-the-job training with hard news…and I end up making applesauce with Ralph Waldo Emerson. It's a crazy world."

Lenore, in obvious agreement, squawked loudly and fluttered to a nearby branch, where she could survey with appropriate disdain the crazy world and all the fools who inhabited it.

The clicking of the typewriter keys from inside the house ceased; in a moment there was the scraping of a chair, and footsteps approaching the door. Daniel came outside, and Dallas didn't look around, even though every nerve in her skin prickled with awareness of him.

"You look very contemplative," he commented after a moment.

Dallas took a final draw on her cigarette and tossed it aside. "I was just thinking," she answered with a sigh, "that I'd sell my soul for a Big Mac." She glanced at him. "Writer's block?"

He came over and sat beside her on the wood bin, propping one foot on the rail. Once again Dallas was overwhelmed with his presence. "No. I just needed a breath of fresh air. Aren't you cold?"

A moment ago Dallas had indeed been aware of the night's autumn chill. Now she felt very warm. She shook her head. "It feels kind of nice."

Silence fell, and it was not the kind of silence that could be ignored easily. The air between them seemed to spark with things unsaid, and Dallas found herself straining with every sense for some signal from him. Was he thinking about this afternoon under the apple tree? Was he wishing he hadn't turned away? Was he wondering, even the slightest bit, what Dallas had made of his behavior? Did he care how she was feeling now?

Abruptly, but as easily as though he were only continuing a conversation that had been temporarily sidetracked, he turned to her. "So," he invited, "tell me about Dallas McCabe, lady tiger of the world of electronic journalism."

Dallas leaned back against the wall, trying to relax. "What you see is pretty much what you get. Just a woman trying to make a living."

"With a passion," he put in.

Dallas shrugged a little and repressed a rueful grin. "Yeah, I guess you could say that. I enjoy my work."

"You *are* your work."

He said it as though it were meant to be a condemnation, but Dallas was not offended. "Anything wrong with that?"

"Not at all." His response was easy and casual, and he, too, leaned his head back against the wall. Dallas liked that feeling of closeness, of being at ease together. "You remind me a lot of myself—or myself as I used to be. I think I told you that. It's the excitement of the challenge, isn't it? The power thrill, the taste of conquest."

"I'm not sure I like the way that sounds," Dallas murmured, growing suspicious.

"It's not a bad thing," Daniel assured her. His eyes, in the moonlight, were like pieces of velvet—very deep, very soft, very sincere. "It's what makes greatness."

"Or survival," Dallas pointed out. "You can't tell me you moved up here to live the way you do just for the fun of it. There was a challenge here. There had to be."

He nodded, his silky hair making a soft rustling sound against the wall. "You're right. But there's a difference in fighting for what you believe in and fighting just for the sake of fighting."

Dallas knew he was referring to their disagreement of the afternoon, when he had refused her insistence of help with his legal case. Her instinct was to protest, to tell him that her concern was not just for the sake of an exciting fight, but honesty made her hesitate. How much of her sudden enthusiasm for doing this interview was motivated out of concern for him and what happened to this place he loved—and how much of it was the result of boredom? Damn it, it *would* be a good story—she could see that now. She had gotten to know Daniel, to understand some of his values and to appreciate, if only in a small way, the life he led here. She could make other people understand, too, and contrast the simple values he held with the superpowers that were threatening to destroy them. Her adrenaline surged at the thought of going up against the big guys, of fighting the god of technology for the sake of freedom of the individual. Simon had been right; this case was tailor-made for her. And if she played up the Defense Department angle...

Guiltily, she caught her mind racing—onward and outward, ever focused in the big story, riding the crest of enthusiasm, carrying the banner of justice, tasting the kill. Was Daniel right? Was all her life nothing more than a fight for the sake of fighting?

"It doesn't matter why I do it," she said in a moment, somewhat defensively. "The point is, I get things done. Okay, there's satisfaction in that." She shrugged. "Maybe it's ego, maybe it's excitement, maybe it's the thrill of winning. I can't apologize for what I am. I've broken a lot of headlines in my day, crashed a lot of barriers, crossed boundaries, smashed stereotypes...and I like it," she admitted without a trace of shame. "I like knowing there's nothing I can't do, nothing I can't conquer, no frontier too dangerous or too distant for me to explore."

"Except one," he said softly.

Dallas looked at him curiously.

"You're still single, aren't you?" Daniel pointed out gently. "And let me guess—no long-term affairs, no live-in lovers, no emotional commitments, in fact, of any kind. No, don't get your hackles up—that's not an accusation." His smile was rather tender, far too observant. "Or if it is, it's one that's been thrown at me often enough to make me an expert. And it's sad but true: the easiest thing in the world is something the strong can't seem to do—love someone."

Dallas didn't know what to say. There was nothing she could say. She felt opened, touched, exposed in a very vulnerable way, because as much as she would have liked to deny it, everything Daniel had said was true. She knew it, though she tried not to think about it. It bothered her, though she tried not to notice. Her biggest weakness was the one thing she could not control; her only fear was commitment to another person. Love, and all it implied, was still an unexplored frontier to Dallas, and she knew as well as she knew herself that it would, most likely, always remain so.

She turned her head against the wall to look at him, and his face was very close. A small, almost-wry, almost-tender smile curved her lips, and she said thoughtfully, "You're a very strange man, Daniel Masters. Maybe I should read your books."

He returned her smile, and there was a gleam of indulgent affection in it that made Dallas feel warm all over. "Couldn't hurt," he admitted modestly. "Fourteen ninety-five a copy, but I give friends a discount."

"Am I your friend?" she asked softly. A thrill ran through her at the way he looked at her, and her instinct then was to touch him, to kiss him, to lay her head against him and to hold him. When had she begun to like him so much? When had it become so important to her that he like her as well?

Daniel's eyes were as brilliant as the moon, and they seemed to be absorbing her, caressing her, wondering at her. "That," he replied, rather huskily, "is up to you, isn't it?"

Then Dallas did touch him. She reached up and laid her hand against his face, her fingers lightly touching the corner of his lips. His beard was soft, like raw silk, an intriguing texture that made her fingertips tingle. And he looked at her, simply looked at her, with a gentleness and a need so strong it seemed to charge the very air between them and draw her by inches closer to him until her lips touched his, and she kissed him.

His hands drifted around her, embracing her, then holding her tight, pressing her to him. His mouth opened beneath hers and they drank of each other. Distant night sounds and sweet mountain fragrances swelled and faded, advanced and retreated and blended at last into the taste of him, the sensation of him, the power of him, that seemed to fill Dallas's bloodstream until all she knew was her need for him. Every sense surged to life and carried her outside herself, and she wanted him with a passion she had never known before.

One hand curved around his neck; the other floated over the breadth of his shoulders and muscled back, across his denimed hip and down the length of his thigh. She could feel the catch of his breath with her touch, and when his strong fingers tightened on her waist, she trembled. She wanted to feel his hands upon her breasts, his lips upon her bare skin; she wanted to feel their bodies naked against each other and entwined with each other, and she wanted it more than she had ever wanted anything in her life.

"Let's make love, Daniel," she whispered. "Now." Then her mouth was lost in his again; a renewed surge of passion, a quickening of breath and a flood of heat encompassed them both and built within and between them, sweeping them away.

His hand slipped beneath her sweater, and then her T-shirt, electrifying the bare skin of her back for an all-too-brief moment before his fingers were atop the material again, kneading and caressing, and pressing her closer. Dallas's fingers tightened on his knee and then moved slowly up the inside of his thigh. She wanted to insinute herself closer to him, to know more of him, to be a part of him.

She felt his muscles tauten as her hand moved; he made a low sound deep within his throat as her fingers brushed over him, the hardness and the power that was male. Her will left her in a single rush of dizziness and desire, and she thought, *I do want you, Daniel. Oh, how I want you.*

And then, in a rush of breath, his mouth left hers; his fingers closed firmly around her wrist. He moved her hand away.

For what seemed like an eternity, Dallas sat there, bereft of him, listening to the uneven sound of his breathing and trying to tell her heart to stop beating; she was dazed, disoriented and incredulous. Her skin was on fire; her breath was shallow and jumpy; her head whirled with residual passion, and there was an ache deep inside her that remained unfulfilled. Would remain unfulfilled, she realized in a slow chill of disbelieving shock. He had turned her down. He didn't want her.

Daniel was leaning back against the wall, taking slow, deep breaths, staring out at the hills. He did not touch her. He wouldn't even look at her. Dallas couldn't believe it, but it was true. The lady tiger had been quite unmistakably rejected.

A rush of embarrassment and hurt all but swept away the clinging ache of arousal, and a new kind of heat crept over Dallas. She wanted to bury her face in her knees and never have to look at him again. She wanted to crawl away into the smallest hole she could find and pull the ground in on top of her. She wanted to wither up and disappear. *Twice in one day, Dallas. Good God, can't you take a hint?*

Daniel's profile was shadowed and unmoving. The silence went on forever, heavy and thick with the sounds of two mismatched hearts beating. Somewhere a night frog chirruped briefly, and then even he was still. Dallas thought she would scream if she had to listen to the sound of her own breathing one more second.

"Well," Dallas said. She smoothed her damp palms on the knees of her jeans and stood, walking away from him. "That was fairly humiliating."

"Dallas—"

She turned, an unpreventable flash of anger mixing with the hurt and the shame to form hasty, spiteful words. "What is it with you, Masters?" she demanded. "Don't you like women? Is that why you live up here with nothing but birds and plants for company?"

She felt him stiffening, sensed the hardening of his eyes through the darkness. He said quietly, "That was beneath you, Dallas. Shall we behave like adults, or do you want to sit here and toss insults back and forth like a couple of overheated adolescents on their first date?"

Already Dallas regretted her lapse into temper, and the childish words only added to her embarrassment. She said stiffly, half turning from him, "No, thank you. I think I've had enough insults for one day." And that didn't sound any more mature than what she had said before. She flushed under the cover of darkness and thought about biting her tongue.

Daniel said lowly, "Do you think I'm enjoying this? Do you think this is really making me happy?"

*I don't know what to think!* Dallas wanted to scream at him, but she didn't. She tightened both hands in her pockets and took a short breath. "Look, I'm sorry, okay?" she said, not looking at him. "Obviously, I misread—"

"You're a sexy woman, Dallas," Daniel interrupted tersely, almost harshly. "And, obviously, you didn't misread anything. You've been driving me crazy since the first night you spent here, and I want you like hell. Is that what you wanted to hear?"

Dallas stared at him. Without thinking, she blurted, "Then why—?" and closed her mouth with a snap, cursing herself silently. *You're a real glutton for punishment, aren't you Dallas? You couldn't just leave well enough alone.*

She could feel Daniel's eyes, low-flamed and sober, fixed upon her in the darkness. This would have been the appropriate moment to turn and make a dignified exit, but where would she go? Off into the woods? Back into the one-room cabin, where he must eventually follow? No, there was no escape from this mortification. She hated this place. Nothing like this ever would have happened in Detroit.

"I won't be another one of your conquests, Dallas," Daniel said simply.

She had thought her amazement could not be surpassed, but she had not expected that. She stared at him, and it seemed the words were tangled in her throat for the longest time before they burst out incredulously. "Is *that* it? Some kind of convoluted male-ego thing? Wake up, mister. This is the 1980s'; women are allowed to be aggressive! Some men— grown up, well-adjusted men—even like the idea that feelings can be shared equally! Do you think I go around seducing men for a living? That I carve notches on my belt to keep score?"

Her voice was growing shrill, and it echoed obscenely in the calmness of the night and in Daniel's pacifist endurance of the onslaught. Dallas stood there, her eyes flaming and her cheeks burning, and she felt like an utter fool. *This is stupid, Dallas. You're yelling at the man because he doesn't want to make love to you. Dear God, it's finally happened. This place has driven you right out of your mind.*

At long last, Daniel released a soft sigh. He stood and walked to the other side of the small porch. His movements were graceful and controlled, but tension emanated from every inch of him. The air was heavy with it.

Daniel leaned against a supporting rail, half facing her, gazing out over the shadowed landscape. At last he said quietly, "You can't meet every situation in life like a storm trooper mowing down obstacles, Dallas. You've got to learn that there are just some things you can't control. You can only sit back and let life move in its natural course, in its own time."

Control? What was he talking about—control? Everything about him, about this place, made Dallas feel helpless, at odds, utterly confused. She had never felt less in control in her life. And what a time for him to start wandering off on some philosophical tangent that made absolutely no sense to her.

Dallas ran her hand slowly through her hair as a calming motion, releasing a long, soft breath of restrained emotion. At least he was talking to her. And she could not walk away from him tonight without knowing why, without at least trying to understand. "Daniel," she said quietly, letting go of the last of her indignation and shock, and seeking now no more than the simple truth, "I'm sorry if I moved too fast or pushed too hard, but I thought..." Intently, she searched his figure in the dark, seeking some sign of softening, of reciprocal emotion, even of forgiveness. She took another breath. "I know, when I first came here, we didn't get along so well. You had every right to resent me and, well, I wasn't too crazy about you, either, I guess. But lately, we've gotten to know each other, and maybe understand each other a little better. I like you, Daniel, Lord knows why." She tried to smile, but it faltered. "And I thought..."

He looked at her. "I like you, too, Dallas," he said softly. "A lot. More than I should, or ever intended to. And if you think it's easy having you here, watching you move, hearing the sound of your voice, seeing the way the sun plays on your hair and turns your eyes to silver...listening to you undress at night and knowing you're lying there only a few feet away... Sometimes making love to you is all I can think about, and keeping myself away from you takes all the willpower I ever had."

Dallas's heart started to beat again. He *did* want her. He *did* think of her; he did see her as a person and as a woman. "Then," she faltered, "I don't understand. We're both adults; we like each other and we want each other."

"Because it's not that simple." Now his voice was short, shot with the underlying tension that was Dallas's first indication of how much it had cost him to push her away. "Because real life is more complicated than the kind of instant gratification you're used to. Because liking and wanting each other isn't enough. Our life-styles and our values are poles apart; you don't know me and I don't know you, and neither of us really cares much about what's important to the other. Because, except for a freak of nature, you and I would have never met and would have been perfectly happy that way—and because as soon as the creek goes down, our paths will part again, and we'll never even miss each other.''

Once again, Dallas was plunged into confusion, and she stared at him for a moment, speechless. Far in the back of her mind a dim knowledge echoed, *But I will miss you, Daniel. I really will,* even as she said, somewhat nervously, ''Wait a minute. We're not talking long-term commitment here. I'm not trying to change your life.''

Daniel looked at her sharply. ''Aren't you? Isn't that what you've been trying to do from the first minute you stormed in here, determined to make a cause célèbre out of me? You want to turn this mountain into a battleground; you want to make my home a television studio. You want me to do my shopping at the supermarket and get a Jeep instead of a mule. You want me to take my laundry to the Laundromat and install an electric dishwasher, and while we're at it, why not put a satellite dish in the backyard?'' Dallas flinched, but he continued, ''Now you want to make me into the kind of casual-sex partner you're used to in Detroit—a good time was had by all, and no one remembers names in the morning.'' His voice softened a fraction as he insisted, ''That's not *me*, Dallas, and it's not appropsrirate for this time, this place. Don't you think I could have it all if that's what I wanted—easy life, easy money, easy sex? But real life is too important to waste like that. Up here nothing is cheap, nothing is easy, nothing is meaningless, and things last *forever*. Can you understand any of that?''

The worst part was that Dallas thought she did understand, if only fractionally, but the hurt and the defensiveness were too thick to allow her to admit it. He had just implied that her life was shallow, her affections meaningless, and if there was a grain of truth in those implications, Dallas was not ready to face it. She sought, instead, the simple solution. "Maybe I was right the first time," she said somewhat stiffly. "You are running away. You live up here all alone because you can't deal with real people and real emotions."

"No," he said gently, and his eyes, in the moonlight, were filled with compassion. "Real emotions are the only thing I'm interested in. It's the game playing, the lack of commitment, the refusal to become involved with real life that I can't deal with. And I think you know that, don't you?"

Dallas swallowed hard, and she could not withstand his gaze, even in the darkness. What was he asking of her? No commitment was possible between them. Nothing permanent could come of this. He knew it, and she knew it...and that was why, she supposed, he was asking nothing of her.

He came over to her and took her face, very gently, in his hands. The scent of spices and Daniel fell over her. And then he kissed her, very lightly, upon the forehead. "Dallas," he said huskily, "you are a beautiful, exciting woman. Sometimes you make me wish I could change, but I can't. If it were right between us, we'd both know. But there's no point in fighting what is."

She dropped her eyes, and then she had to look at him again. "Sometimes," she said, "I think it wouldn't hurt you to fight a little for what you want." But then she smiled a little wryly and shrugged. "And

I guess it wouldn't hurt me to learn to stop trying to whip the world into shape with one hand tied behind my back. But I guess we can't help being who we are." Her eyes searched his in the shadows—open, sincere, briefly vulnerable. "I am sorry, Daniel," she said softly. "For everything."

He smiled, and when he moved his hands away, his fingers lingered briefly to caress her hair. "Still friends?"

Dallas swallowed again and managed a weak smile. "Sure," she returned flippantly. "If that's the best we can do."

But he did not smile. "It is," he assured her soberly, and turned to go inside.

It was Dallas's night for the bed, but for the first time, she did not look forward to a comfortable night's sleep in the luxury of the straw mattress. As a matter of fact, the bed was cold, far too large, and very lonely, and she hardly slept at all.

## Chapter Ten

Daniel brought out old Buck, the mule, and announced to Dallas the next day that he was going to visit a neighbor around the mountain. Dallas was welcome to come along if she pleased. The prospect of actually meeting another human being sounded almost too good to be true, and she agreed readily. That was probably all that was wrong with her anyway—culture shock. She had been stranded too long with no one but Daniel to look at, no one but Daniel to talk to; insane fantasies and bizarre behavior were not completely unexpected under those circumstances.

And that, Dallas had finally rationalized, was all that was developing between them. Two starving men, trapped on a desert island, would eventually begin to look at each other and see pork chops. Dallas McCabe, isolated for an unnatural period of time away from all that was familiar, had begun to look at Daniel Masters and see heaven. He was right. Under other circumstances, they never would have noticed each other at all. Proximity, someone had once said, was an infallible aphrodisiac, but the logical mind could surely overcome its insidious effects.

But knowing all that did not keep Dallas's pulse from speeding when she watched Daniel step into the wooden box that enclosed the outdoor shower and toss his jeans over the side, or stop the small, melting sensation that spread through her stomach when he smiled at her, or keep her skin from tingling when he grasped her waist to seat her on the balky old mule for the journey across the mountain. Not, Dallas assured herself firmly, that she would ever again make the mistake of trying to bring whatever erotic fantasies she harbored about him to life, but, strangely enough, the events of the night before had only made Daniel more intriguing. He was indeed a remarkable man.

And that was frustrating. She should have been angry, bitter, uncomfortable, still wrestling with her bruised ego and her humiliation. But Daniel allowed no chance for awkwardness to develop between them. He arose as cheerful as ever, made breakfast while Dallas showered, talked to her about the plans for the day as easily and as naturally as he ever did. And Dallas slowly began to realize that, far from despising him, she actually felt closer to Daniel than ever. It seemed that the more she learned of him—both good and bad—the more she liked him, and the more involved with him she became. And Dallas was not at all sure she was happy with that turn of events.

The neighbor they were going to visit was a woman by the name of Miss Emily, and her place was about five miles away. For the first time, it occurred to Dallas that perhaps Daniel had more than one reason for keeping himself away from her, and to her very great surprise, she felt a small stab of jealousy. She couldn't help inquiring, as casually as possible, "A woman? Does she live up here all alone?"

The mule carried Dallas and two baskets of pre-served foodstuffs and other goodies, which were tied together and flung over the animal's back like saddle-bags. Daniel led the way on foot, tugging on a rope tied around the mule's neck. The mule's bony back and shuffling pace were not comfortable, and the baskets kept bumping against Dallas's legs; she was beginning to think that Daniel had gotten the better end of the deal. But every time she started to volun-teer to walk, she remembered the snake and dug her fingers more securely into the mule's bristly neck.

Daniel replied, not looking around. "Hm-hm."

Dallas remembered Daniel's derisive remarks when she had first arrived, about the mountain being no place for a woman alone. She wondered what kind of paragon this lady was, and her less-than-worthy emo-tions were pricked again as she let her imagination roam. There was Dallas McCabe—squeamish, clumsy, bad-tempered and loud-mouthed, with her big-city talk and her big-city ways, representing everything Daniel had turned his back on and come up here to forget. And there was Emily—strong, country-fresh, peaceful, self-sufficient, as good as the earth and as enduring as the mountain. Some choice. What an id-iot she was.

Dallas kept her eyes upon the breadth of Daniel's flannel-covered back, the easy swing of his shoulders, his silky-haired head, and she had to twist the knife a little. "She must be some lady. How long has she lived up here?"

"All her life," Daniel replied easily, guiding the mule around a fallen tree that half obscured the trail. "It was her family who sold me the land. She's been by herself for about ten years now, I guess. Her husband died, and her boys grew up and went down the mountain to find wives, never came back. They keep trying to get her to come live with them, but she won't leave her home." Daniel shook his head a little in fond amazement. "She's quite a woman. You're going to enjoy meeting her." He cast a twinkling glance over his shoulder. "This is one person who'll be glad to sit for hours and answer all your reporter's questions."

Dallas released an entirely imperceptible breath of relief mingled with embarrassment. A widow with grown children. Silly Dallas. She *did* have it bad.

The day was surprisingly warm and summerlike. A few puffy clouds were scattered high in the sky that Daniel had assured her, without her even asking, did not forecast rain. That was good, Dallas told herself. The longer they went without rain the faster the creek would go down and the sooner she could go home, never to see Daniel Masters's strong back or raven-colored hair again, never to hear the sound of his rolling laughter or teasing tone.

The air was sweet with the scent of herbs and autumn flowers, the birds were busy in the trees, the landscape was a brilliant palette of every color in the spectrum, and the ground a crunchy carpet of gold and red and brown and green. For a while Dallas tried to distinguish the scents Daniel had taught her, but she couldn't remember any of them, and her attention kept straying back to Daniel—the way he walked, the soft tune he hummed under his breath, the shape of his hand, large and strong and competent, as it tugged the guide rope on the mule. He was a man in complete harmony with his universe—content, at ease, in control—as different from Dallas and all she knew as night was from day, but she couldn't stop wanting him.

That was not a comfortable train of thought, and, in fact, was distinctly unsettling. She would not fall into that trap again. Daniel had made himself very clear, and he was right. It was only sex, after all. Nothing special. And the minute she got off this mountain, she would forget all about Daniel Masters and his strong arms and broad shoulders and gentle eyes. She would probably even laugh at herself for all these foolish fantasies.

Deliberately, she began to think of something else. *Häagen-Dazs ice cream, butter-rum. Pretzels and beer. Polyester. Taxicabs. Pigeons. Instant banking, supermarkets, neon. Billy Joel, bagels, elevators, pepperoni, movie marquees, calendars, telephone-answering machines, telephones...*

It didn't help. Not at all.

MISS EMILY'S PLACE was a ramshackle split-board cabin with a leaning stone chimney and one window. The ragged patch of yard surrounding it had been scraped bare by the chickens and geese, who squawked and scattered as Daniel and Dallas and the mule came up; and a split-rail fence with several rails missing enclosed four filthy, noisily squeaking hogs. A couple of sheep nibbled at some bushes on the far side of the cabin, and a goat was tied to a stake near the porch steps. Dallas's first impression was one of absolute squalor.

But the inside of the house was quite different. The front door was standing open, and Daniel tethered the mule on a low-hanging branch of a cedar tree before taking the baskets down and escorting a somewhat hesitant Dallas up the unsteady front steps. Morning sunlight streamed through the single window and showed Dallas a small room that was scrubbed within an inch of its life, colorful hooked rugs on the bleached floor, yellowed lithographs on the wall, a pottery container of brilliant wildflowers on the table. From the wood-burning stove came the smells of chicken frying, bread baking and vegetables stewing. Everything about the room welcomed one.

Beside the stove stood a tiny, ancient woman in a long print dress and a crocheted navy shawl. Her thin white hair was pulled back tightly over her pink skull and wound into a neat knot. Daniel placed the baskets on the table, strode over to her, lifted her off her feet and kissed her soundly on the cheek. The small woman responded with a squeal of delight and a severe tap on his head with a wooden spoon, and Daniel set her on her feet, declaring, "How did you know I was coming? Is that strawberry cobbler you're making?"

"It is," responded Miss Emily pertly, using the spoon again to slap his hand as Daniel reached around her for the bowl of preserved strawberries. "My nose has been itchin' off all morning; I knew company was just around the bend." She turned her bright, dark eyes on Dallas. "And who's this pretty young thing?"

Dallas still stood rather awkwardly at the door, and Daniel turned, extending a hand to her as though to urge her inside. "This is Dallas McCabe," he answered. "A friend of mine from the city. Dallas, this is Miss Emily Booth."

Dallas smiled. "How do you do?"

Miss Emily took her own sweet time about looking Dallas over, those quick, alert eyes missing not a single detail. Finally she responded, "City girl, eh?" And she nodded once, decisively. "She'll do, I reckon." She demanded of Daniel, "She your woman?"

There was a moment of awkward silence, which Dallas made no effort to break. What could she have said, anyway? *No, I'm just a person who came all the way from Detroit to ruin Daniel's life.* She tried not to imagine how she would have felt, what it would have been like, if Daniel had looked at her at that moment and said, "Yes."

With his silence, Miss Emily apparently reached her own conclusions, and she told him severely, "You'd better marry that girl quick. It's no good, a man living alone. And you remember that quilt."

To Dallas's very great delight, a faint stain of color tinged Daniel's cheekbones, and he looked distinctly uncomfortable even as he laughed. "I remember," he said.

Dallas inquired curiously, "What about the quilt?"

"I gave it to him," returned Miss Emily promptly. "It's a marrying quilt, and no unmarried man sleeps under a marrying quilt and stays unmarried for long. It ain't natural."

Dallas's amused glance met Daniel's for a moment, and the laughter in his eyes faded. Before she could determine what emotion came to replace it, however, he turned to give Miss Emily another quick squeeze and said, "You've got some rails missing out of your fence. I'd better take care of it."

"Now you," Miss Emily nodded briskly to Dallas as Daniel left and she turned back to the stove, "you come over here and let me show you how Daniel likes his cobbler. I'm not going to live forever, you know, and it's for blessed sure the poor man needs somebody to take care of him.''

Dallas tried to look properly demure, but her lips were twitching as she did as she was bidden.

Had Dallas been more of an observer of life, she should have no doubt learned by now that miracles happen when one is least expecting them, that answers often come without one's seeking them, that secrets unfold in the most unlikely places. Dallas had come with Daniel today for nothing more than something different to do, but she left Miss Emily's cabin with the one thing she had sought from the first day she had come to the mountain: understanding.

Miss Emily was an authority on everything from childbirth to planting by the signs, and she was not reticent about imparting her knowledge. At first, Dallas was amused by the old woman's ramblings, sprinkled as they were with superstition and folk culture, but gradually she found herself being drawn into the stories Emily told; soon she was hopelessly fascinated.

"The menfolk," Emily told Dallas with a chuckle, while illustrating the intricacies of making buttermilk cornbread, "like to think they're the strong ones, takin' care of us and all, and it don't hurt none to flatter them, I reckon." She nodded toward the window, where Daniel could be seen, shirtless and sweating, splitting another load of firewood for Miss Emily's stove. "Lord knows I appreciate the help. But let me tell you something, missy, my grandmother built this cabin, log by log and stone by stone, while her man was off hunting game one fall. After he'd been gone a month, didn't seem likely he'd be coming back, so she set to it herself. Cut the trees, split the logs, and all the while growing big with child. Sturdy as a rock, too, this place is. Course, Papa put on the cedar shingles and added a room when he got back from the war, but up till then 'tweren't nothing but an old log cabin, snug as it could be, just the way she built it.''

Dallas found that story quite impressive, to say the least. "What about her husband? Did he ever come back?"

"Yes siree, he come strolling in with the first snowfall, and there Gran was, sitting by the fire, nursing her firstborn." She gave a derisive little snort and bent to slide the heavy black skillet filled with cornbread into the oven. "These young gals today, they think they're something, going off to work in the factories and bringing home their paychecks and leaving somebody else to mind their young'uns. They should've lived when times was hard. Back then, there weren't no question about what you wanted to do; it was just what you *had* to do. Lord knows, we made it this far doing what had to be done, don't see what all the commotion is about, just because we got the vote."

Emily told Dallas how to keep weevils out of the flour and how to make bread rise on a rainy day; she told her about the Christmas her husband had brought her the wood-burning cookstove on a mule-drawn wagon, all the way from Greenville. "Sold two of our best hogs for it," she remembered. "I 'bout took a rolling pin to his head when I heard that, but, Lordy, was I proud to see that brand-new stove hooked up to my kitchen. Before that, we cooked on the hearth fire, you know, which weren't no fun. World of difference with this here. I still don't know how your Daniel manages on that contraption he has, but it's better than a hearth fire, I guess.''

Dallas liked that, the way Miss Emily said ''your Daniel.'' And she wondered what the old woman would say if she ever saw a microwave oven.

But nothing that came from a microwave oven could possibly have tasted as good as the food that Miss Emily put on her table. The vegetables came from her own garden, and the assortment of platters that filled the table reminded Dallas of a smorgasbord. There were six kinds of vegetables, some preserved, some fresh; two meats, two breads, a large cut-glass relish dish filled with radishes, beets, sliced bell peppers and onions, and a spicy condiment made of tomatoes, hot pepper and dill that was delicious. ''Now you know where I learned to cook,'' Daniel told her with a twinkle, and Dallas had to admit that, as good as he was, he had a lot to learn before he surpassed his teacher.

Miss Emily told Dallas the story of how her mother had won the relish dish at a county fair. A storm had blown up on their way back to the mountain, and the wagon had gone over a cliff. Mother and children had jumped out in time, but Emily's father had been thrown down the mountain and broken his neck. The storm was so severe that they couldn't even reach him until the next morning, and a cloud came over Emily's eyes as she told how they had hidden in a cave all night, her mother crying and clutching the relish dish and rocking back and forth—and then how they had gone out the next morning and buried her father. The relish dish, which was probably even now worth less than ten dollars, was Miss Emily's proudest possession.

Daniel's eyes met Dallas's across the table at the conclusion of the story, and the moment between them was deep and quiet and completely unstrained. And the way Daniel looked at her...there was something different in his eyes. He was looking at Dallas as though he had never seen her before, and as though he was wrestling with a cautious wonder over what he saw. And gradually Dallas understood his confusion.

She had spent the entire morning with Miss Emily, talking to her and listening to her, and not once had she remembered she was a reporter. She had been living each story as it was told, wrapped up in the memories and the meaning of it; when she interjected a question, it was motivated by her own need to know more and understand more and feel more of what she was learning, not because her reporter's mind was writing copy. Not once had Dallas chided herself for not having the foresight to bring a tape recorder; not once had she reached for a nonexistent pen to scribble notes. And it wasn't until this very moment, and with a small shock, that Dallas realized what a magnificient addition to the hypothetical Daniel Masters show this interview would make.

But then she tried to picture Miss Emily, who had never seen a television set, in front of lights and cameras, spinning her simple tales, expounding her nononsense philosophy for millions of jaded viewers, and she couldn't. The two images—life as it had existed untarnished on this mountain for centuries, and the bright-eyed monsters of modern technology—were mutually exclusive. That was when Dallas understood, at last, what Daniel had been trying to tell her from the beginning. Their two worlds weren't just different; they were a contradiction in terms. This was

not to say that either one was more important or more
intrinsically valuable than the other; it was simply that
at no point did they intersect, and to allow the intru-
sion of one into the other would mean the destruction
of them both.

Daniel looked at Dallas, and it was as though he
shared this slow and reluctant dawning of understanding with her. Dallas wondered if it had come to
him in just such a moment of revelation, when he had
seen his two worlds standing side by side and he had
known he had to make a choice. What courage it must
have taken for him to do so, and something inside
Dallas swelled with awe and wonder at the scope of the
man she was only now beginning to know.

Daniel smiled at her, and it was a gesture as warm
and gentle as a loving handclasp, filled with recognition and welcome. It was the rarest of all moments of
human communication, in which a look, a smile,
could penetrate the very core of the soul and leave its
gentle mark of wonder there forever. It was an understanding so brief that it could never be defined or re-
captured, but so pure that it would never be forgotten.
Even as something deep within Dallas opened in
wonder and began to flower, she felt the shadow of
sadness, because knowing him, understanding him,
did not make him hers.

Daniel went back outside to finish his work while
Dallas and Emily did the dishes. "He's a fine boy,"
Emily remarked, fixing a meaningful look on Dallas.
"Never seen a person work harder or learn faster.
You'd think he was born in these hills. Powerful lot of
help to me, he is. He's got the neighborly spirit, and
that's just as important as a strong back, let me tell
you. Never lets a person go in need as long as he's got

it to share, and that's the way it's supposed to be. Nice little place he built for himself, too. It'll stand many a winter. Couldn't be prouder of him if he was my own.''

Feeling fairly certain that Emily's train of thought was leading to a long dissertation upon Daniel's virtues as trustworthy, kind, a good provider and a staunch family man, Dallas said casually, ''I understand you sold Daniel his land.''

Emily nodded, scraping leftovers into a bucket for the hogs. ''Didn't have much use for it myself, too much work with no menfolk around. All I need is my little patch of ground and m'garden.'' She gave a little snort as she turned to place a handful of plates in the tub of steaming water. ''And can you believe it? Now them government fellows is saying 'tweren't my land to sell. Says I, why this land has been owned by the Booths far back as Indian days, every parcel of it registered all proper-like in the courthouse; the first Booth ever to set foot on this mountain bought it at an Indian auction from the very same government that is trying to say they never sold it at all!'' She gave a short cackle of laughter, shaking her head. ''That's what happens when you get too big for your britches, and it's as true for governments as it is for people. They just got too blessed big, can't keep up with their own business. But your Daniel, he gave 'em what for, you can bank on that. There's no way in this sweet world that he's going to let anybody take away what's rightfully his.''

But was he? Dallas tried to remember everything the research department had dug up on this case. Neither side, if she recalled correctly, had overwhelming evidence against the other, and if it had been an ordinary civil case, it might have been tied up in court for years. But when the United States Government was involved...What if Daniel did lose? How could she let him lose?

What could she do about it?

THE SUN WAS LOW in the hills as they made their way across the mountain toward home. The baskets were once again strapped across Buck's back, filled this time with gifts from Miss Emily's kitchen, but Dallas walked beside Daniel. She told him she need the exercise to work off the calories from dinner, but the real reason was, of course, that she simply wanted to walk beside him.

His blue-flannel shirt was untucked from his jeans, buttoned only to midchest, sleeves folded up to his elbows. Dallas restrained herself from reaching out and wrapping her fingers around one of those strong forearms, tucking it beneath hers and keeping him close as they walked. She also refused to let her eyes shift too often to the expanse of chest bared by the unbuttoned shirt. What a strong throat he had. How she would have loved to lay her hand flat against his chest and explore the textured planes and contours there, or just to rest her head against his shoulder and feel his arm around her waist as they walked. The coming night had already cooled the air, and it would have been nice to walk close to him, touching, sharing warmth.

But she had no intention of making a move to initiate such closeness. The day had been special in a way it was yet hard for Dallas to describe, even to herself; it was as though Daniel, by admitting her for a few hours into his world, had given her a precious gift, one richer and far more meaningful than a few moments of passion could have been. Everything seemed different now, seen in a new light, even Dallas's own desires. She was not about to spoil the tenuous closeness that was beginning to develop between them by some rash and selfish move toward further intimacy. She was not even certain that was what she wanted anymore.

After a time Dallas said, "Thanks for letting me come today, Daniel. She is—" Dallas shook her head a little with the inadequacy of her own expression "—fascinating."

Daniel smiled as he glanced at her. "I thought you'd like her. I guess, in a lot of ways, Miss Emily is a symbol of everything I value about life up here, about life in general."

*I know,* Dallas thought. And how could she dispute such values as honesty, simplicity, individual rights, devotion to the quality of life? Weren't those the very things that she had spent her crusading career fighting to protect? But, dear Lord, how much simpler things had been when Dallas hadn't understood him so well, or cared so much about what happened to Daniel.

To distract herself from the confusing course her thoughts were beginning to take, Dallas forced a smile, glancing up at him. "Did you really chase a reporter away with your shotgun?"

His eyes twinkled with startled amusement. "Who told you that?"

"Cal." It seemed a million years ago that she had stood in the dusty general store and listened to three old men debate the ferocity of their local hermit-celebrity, almost as though it had happened to another person. "Someone else said it was a four-by-four, though."

The sparkle in his eyes only deepened and seemed to be laced with a secret smugness. "Now, you know me better than that," he asserted. "I never resort to violence when there's a peaceful solution. Besides," he mused, "that particular reporter was probably the most abrasive young jackass I've ever met. He deserved to be scared a little."

Dallas laughed. "More abrasive than I was?"

"It's a close call," he admitted, "but you had an unfair advantage." The dancing amusement in his eyes softened in indulgent affection as he looked at her. "You were good-looking."

The moment between them held and began to deepen into warmth, the teasing in his eyes gradually turning into a gentle, absorbing study that took Dallas's breath away. She knew that what he said next would be very important, that the words would be soft and the tone tender, and that when he had spoken, something inside her would have changed...and Dallas wasn't sure she wanted to hear what he might say.

It was Dallas who broke the eye contact. "Thank heaven for small favors," she murmured lightly, and picked up the pace of their walk again. She tried not to wonder what he might have said if she had given him the chance. She wondered what he would do if she slipped her arm around his waist, casually, companionably. Just for the sake of being near him.

Aware of a very definite need to keep the conversation going, Dallas inquired after a moment, "Daniel, what *do* you do with all your money?"

Immediately she realized how much like a nosey-reporter question that sounded, and she remembered his distinctly unfriendly reaction the last time she had asked about his finances. She couldn't help casting a quick, anxious glance his way, and was relieved when he chuckled softly. "Honey, there's not that much of it to do anything with. Most of my royalties are endowed to various wildlife and conservation funds; what's left over goes to taxes and lawyers." His glance was easy and amused. "So if you're thinking of asking for a loan..."

"Actually," Dallas responded without thinking, "I was wondering if you needed one."

He stopped, and looked at her, puzzlement clear in his eyes. Dallas felt a flush creep all the way down to her toes, and she could have bitten her clumsy tongue. Hadn't she learned by now not to interfere in his business? Hadn't he accused her only last night of trying to change him? Would she never learn to leave well enough alone? "What I mean is—" she began, and then stopped, looking at him helplessly. "Daniel," she said simply, "it's going to take a lot to fight the government in court. A lot of power, a lot of money. Sometimes the truth just isn't enough."

He smiled at her, and the tenderness in his eyes went straight through her heart. "I'm fine, Dallas," he said. "Thanks."

"Daniel," she insisted, though she hated to. Her eyes were dark with pain and her voice was very sober. "You could lose. What then?"

A slight shadow came over his features as he acknowledged the concern that could not have been too far from his thoughts these past months. But then he smiled again and settled his arm around her shoulders in a brief, reassuring squeeze. "That's what appeal courts are for,'' he told her. ''And I've got the rest of my life.''

Dallas was suddenly struck by it, walking through the woods in the shelter of his arm, with the colors of the sunset streaming through the trees and setting the horizon on fire. What an extraordinary man he was. The last of the pioneers, strong and true and sure, the embodiment of all the independence of spirit and the simplicity of virtue that made mankind noble. Dallas had known many men; she knew their weaknesses, their vices, their petty ambitions. She had seen corruption and she had seen greatness, and she thought that that was all there was to know. But in Daniel Masters was everything that was important to her, everything she valued in the human race, all in one package: dedication, commitment, independence, compassion, strength against all odds, and devotion to simple values. Dallas could have spent the rest of her life looking for exactly those qualities without ever finding them, yet they were all here, in this man.

She looked up at him. The sunlight washed his face with red and gold, crinkling his eyes, sparkling on his beard. His expression was composed and content, the shelter of his body strong and warm against hers. Dallas looked at him, and she knew her life had changed.

But with the slow, sweeping wonder that filled her like a burst of sunshine, there was a shadow of despair. She had spent all of her life searching without knowing what she was looking for, waiting without knowing she was waiting. Why did it have to be Daniel? Why did it have to be here?

## Chapter Eleven

Days passed, and as inevitably as time, the swollen creek began to recede. Each morning when Dallas went to measure the waterline on the submerged tree, it had fallen by several inches, and though she forced a cheerful grin and a thumbs-up sign to Daniel, inside, her spirits fell at a much more alarming rate. She couldn't understand it. She should be happy. Home was in sight, freedom close enough to taste. Already Daniel had felled the trees that would be required to build the new bridge; all that remained now was to split the wood into planks, and in only a matter of days the bridge could be laid across the water, and Dallas would be on her way home. Back to the sounds of traffic and ringing telephones, business suits and briefcases, indigestion and Excedrin headaches. She couldn't wait. She was excited. And every morning she prayed the waterline would be higher.

Dallas read Daniel's first two books. Every night while he sat at the table writing, Dallas lay upon the floor before the stove, reading. The fact that a great deal of the time she was distracted by the way the candlelight softened the planes of the author's face, or the way his large, workman's hand played over the typewriter keys with such efficacy in no way diminished Dallas's enjoyment of his work. And sometimes she would look up to find that he was watching her with an abstract, gentle attention in his eyes that made her wonder whether she looked that way when she was watching him. And even though the glow that spread through her at such moments was so intense that it made her giddy, Dallas could not help chiding herself. *Way to go, Dallas. You started out with a crush on Johnny Appleseed, and now you're acting like Dorothy Lamour in an old movie. Grow up, will you?*

Daniel did not ask what she thought of his books, and there was no need for her to tell him. The truth was obvious, and it was a truth Dallas already knew. Daniel's heart and soul were in his writing, mingled as inextricably with the mountain and its way of life as sunshine was with light. With every page she turned, Dallas learned more of him, and with everything she learned, she felt herself being pushed closer to the border of something very dangerous, something from which there would be no turning back.

Dallas spent a lot of time studying the research her staff had done on Daniel's case. Those were the times when she most acutely felt the frustration of isolation, when she yearned for a telephone or a library or a small computer terminal. One telephone call and she could have some of the best legmen at ''Spotlight''— therefore, the best in the country—working overtime to ferret out scraps of little-known information, doing in-depth studies, digging up every possible bit of relevant material. A three-minute long-distance call could answer a dozen questions; an hour with her Rolodex could put the best legal minds in the country at

Dallas's fingertips. But for now, she had to make do with what she had, and that was precious little.

According to the report, the dispute over land ownership dated back to the Depression era, when most of this part of the Appalachians had been declared a national forest. Before that time, the accuracy of surveys was in question, so that, even though Daniel had land plats to prove his ownership, and Emily had records to prove her right to sell, the government held that its survey was the accurate one. Obviously, the only reason the matter had come to dispute at this late date was because of the plans to open a mine, and just as obviously, as soon as the government won its case, it would be a simple matter to have this section of the mountain removed from national forest protection and contracted for mining. Oh, what a story Dallas could make of this. If only she could get back to Detroit, start nosing around in federal offices, get a few uncomfortable officials before the cameras, uncover a little dirty laundry... *Oh, Daniel, it would be so simple. It would be spectacular. It would be you and I, working together, fighting the system and winning.*

But she said nothing further to Daniel about the court case. He had good lawyers, she assured herself, and certainly she was no smarter than they were. Reading and rereading her own research department's scanty report was doing nothing but giving her a headache, and she could find no answers. She was not going to pressure Daniel about doing the interview, and that was the only way in which she could have been any concrete help to him. It was only a pity that the one thing she could do to show Daniel how much she cared was the one thing he did not want.

DANIEL WAS DOWN BY THE CREEK, working on the bridge. It would be a very simple structure, he assured her, just as the one before it had been, for there was little point in wasting an engineering degree on something that was washed away twice a year. Little was required except split logs and rope with which to tie them together, and Daniel thought he might be able to put the bridge in place within a couple of days. Dallas smiled bravely but did not volunteer to help.

Dallas was spending the afternoon doing laundry and supervising the stew Daniel had put on the stove for dinner. The big washtub was set outside, next to a kettle over an open fire that kept Dallas supplied with hot water. She poured boiling water over soft lye soap and stirred it until the soap was dissolved, then added the dirty clothes and cleaned them by scrubbing them against a thick sheet of corrugated metal. The harsh soap and hot water were turning her hands the shade and texture of fresh lobster; her shoulders ached and her back felt as though it would crack in two; she was hot and sweaty despite the cool temperature of the day. Beating the clothes against rocks, she observed bitterly, blowing a strand of damp hair out of her face, would have been easier—and a lot more effective.

"What is he in such a hurry to get that bridge built for, anyway?" she muttered to Lenore who, the last time Dallas had looked, was perched upon the rail that surrounded the chicken house, preening her feathers. "I've waited this long; it's not as though I have a bus to catch or anything."

But she knew perfectly well what his hurry was. The sooner Dallas was out of the way, the sooner Daniel could get on with his life, and it wasn't as though she were a welcome guest here. Chance had brought them together, and an accident had kept them together this long; there was no rhyme or reason to their time together and no reason to prolong it. It was an interlude, that was all, a handful of days out of their lives that served no ultimate purpose and would leave nothing changed when it was over.

Dallas paused in her vicious up-and-down scrubbing, a look of bleakness coming briefly and unexpectedly over her face. The only problem with that philosophy, of course, was that something had changed in the time Dallas had been here, something inside her. It wasn't going to be so easy to say goodbye to Daniel Masters.

She wanted to go home. She *did* want that. Tires screeching, horns blaring, sirens wailing, skyscrapers, production meetings, cameras rolling, people moving... Her heart began to speed in anticipation simply with the thought of it. That was where she belonged, smack in the middle of life and all its energy, doing things and getting things done, charging full steam ahead, leaping over obstacles, challenging the impossible. That was *Dallas*, and those were the things she couldn't live without. But Daniel...

She wondered whether Daniel might ever come to Detroit, and for a brief time the daydream cheered her. *Sure, why not?* Surely he left the mountain sometimes, surely even he took a vacation, so to speak. They could go to the theater, and she would take him to the finest restaurants. They could stand and watch the city lights playing on the river. They could spend one whole day at a movie marathon and have Polish hot dogs and dark beer. Maybe he would come to see her in Detroit. Just a friendly visit.

Dallas transfered the soapy laundry to the tub of rinse water in one heavy armload, grimacing and jumping back a little as the hot water splashed out of the tub when she dumped the wet clothes in it. She paused to push her hair out of her face with a damp, puckered hand and made an unpleasant face as she looked down at her water-splotched jeans and ratty sweater. "Gerard would die if he could see me now," she muttered. Her nails were cracked and peeling, her hair straight and stringy, her cuticles a mess, and her clothes would have to be thrown out after she left the mountain. She would have to make a special stop at a beauty parlor before she even flew to Detroit. Although heaven only knew what even the best beauty specialist could do about her nose, which kept getting sunburned and peeling and getting sunburned again, until its texture was now like old leather.

*Yes,* she thought longingly. *A beauty parlor. Some new clothes. A hot bubble bath, a cool glass of wine made from real grapes, a trashy paperback novel to read in the tub. Designer sheets. Central heating.* And maybe Daniel would come visit her in Detroit. It wasn't entirely out of the question.

But it wasn't very likely, either.

Quickly, before that train of thought could depress her, Dallas bent over the washtub and began to wring out the soggy laundry with her hands, piece by piece. "I'll tell you one thing I'm not going to miss," she muttered to Lenore, standing at last with her arms weighed down by still-dripping laundry. "This."

Deliberately, almost grimly, she listed in her mind all the things she was looking forward to as she hung the clothes on the line: washing machines; all-night grocery stores; tequila; morning DJ's and the sounds of Bruce Springsteen; the smell of smog on a crisp fall day, corn chips and piquante sauce, fist fights at Darien's, the screeching brakes of delivery trucks at 6:00 A.M., cats knocking over garbage cans at midnight; plastic plants; plastic anything. Home...

WHEN ALL THE LAUNDRY WAS HANGING in the sun to dry, the wash water emptied and the open fire extinguished, Dallas stretched her weary shoulders and rounded the cabin. She would check on dinner, and then see how Daniel was doing. But first, she was going to relax. Daniel had put a crock of fresh milk in the spring that morning, and she thought she might just get a mug, go down to the spring and pour a cup, then sit out in the sun and read awhile. That was one thing she would miss. Nothing in the world tasted better than fresh milk.

The front door was open, and Dallas did not remember leaving it unlatched. Not that it mattered much, excpet that there were still a number of flying insects this time of year, and Dallas did not like fighting them off at mealtime. She came into the darkened cabin, calling, "Daniel? Why did you leave the door open? I—"

Dallas had closed the door behind her and was halfway into the room before she realized that the shadow crouched in the corner of the cabin was not Daniel. For a moment it was only curiosity that stopped her footsteps, and she formed a half-challenging question, "What—?" just as her eyes adjusted to the dimness and the creature began to move.

It was a bear. Never in Dallas's life had she imagined an animal as big as this one was, and as she stood there, rooted to the spot, it raised up on its hind legs, the bulk of it filling the space between table and wall, its head seeming to come within inches of touching the ceiling. It opened its mouth, pink jaws parting to reveal sharp teeth, and it emitted a roaring yowl loud enough to shake the very foundations of the building.

The blood froze in Dallas's veins. She could feel her face go white. Her heart stopped beating for a split second and then lurched into a painful, throbbing series of explosions in her chest. Perspiration flooded from her pores and her throat went dry. She tried to scream, but all that came out was a hoarse croak, and even that was drowned out in the bear's next ear-shattering growl. She thought, *Holy Mary, Mother of*— and then the bear took a lurching step toward her.

She had been terrified on the trail when she faced down a dusty raccoon. She had thought she would die of fright from the encounter with a snake. But this...this was quite different. This was a bear. It was everything she had ever been afraid of about this place in one neat package. It was a killer, it was enormous, and she was trapped inside the room with it.

The bear kept coming, knocking over jars and baskets and pieces of pottery with its bulky body, sending pots and pans scuttling to the floor with a clatter. It roared again, and Dallas tried to scream.

*Wait*. What was it she had been told about wild animals? Harmless. Hadn't those men in the store said they were harmless? *The only time you have to be afraid is when they don't run from you.*

This bear wasn't running.

*Oh, dear Lord...dear God, help.*

The huge animal dropped to all fours. Its flabby body shook with the impact and so did the floor. *Oh,*

*God, oh...* Dallas's panicky eyes looked around the room: the fire poker; Daniel's shotgun above the mantel. The bear was between the stove and Dallas, blocking her access to the weapons. He was still now, but likely to launch an attack at any moment. Hadn't she heard somewhere that bears could move faster for their size than any other animal known? Where had she heard that, she wondered distractedly. "Wild Kingdom"? *National Geographic* magazine? Oh, what difference did it make; she was going to die.

The bear shifted its weight, making low, growling sounds in its throat, seeming to size up the situation. Dallas was so close that she could smell its wild scent. If it started toward her again, it would have her in its jaws before she could take a breath.

Slowly, on feet that felt like lead, she began to inch around the table. She never took her eyes off the bear, and it never took its eyes off her. Her breath sounded like the hissing of a steam engine in her ears, ragged and labored. Her heart was going to burst with its very next beat. Inch by inch, second by second, she put distance between herself and the carnivore. She would never make it. The bear was going to attack. She saw a muscle twitch beneath its rough, dark hide and she stopped still, certain she would never move again. But the bear held its position.

At last she felt the firm surface of the door behind her. She groped for the latch and couldn't find it. Her head started to roar. Then she found the latch and sobbed out loud when it wouldn't open immediately. The bear started to move.

Dallas stumbled out into the sunlight, gasping and shaking, slamming the door closed behind her. She fumbled for the latch and finally locked it firmly in place, and then she leaned against the door, her chest heaving, her head whirling. From inside the cabin came a mighty roar and Dallas jumped away, almost falling backward down the steps. She started to run in halting, half-stumbling steps, greatly impaired by her own shortness of breath; she tripped over an exposed root and did fall, but was immediately on her feet again, backing away, watching the cabin with a fixed, terrified gaze for signs of the bear's egress.

She saw Daniel strolling casually toward her, but she was shaking so hard and breathing so hard that she could not even make herself call out to him. Daniel lifted his hand to her in friendly greeting, but nothing came from her throat except hoarse, gasping, incoherent sobs for breath. Daniel began, "Well, I'm almost finished—" and then he was close enough to notice the expression on Dallas's face.

In three running steps he closed the distance between them, grabbing her by the shoulders, his face taut with alarm. "Dallas, what's wrong?" he demanded. "What happened?"

Every muscle in Dallas's body had turned to jelly. She could hardly get a coherent word out. Every breath was a dragged-in sob. "I-in—in there!" She pointed weakly with a shaking arm. "B-bear! In-inside! It—"

But no further explanations were necessary as another roar and a crashing sound from inside the cabin told the rest of the story.

Daniel glanced toward the cabin, then his eyes came back to her, wide with alarm. His hands tightened on her shoulders. "A bear? You locked him inside?"

Dallas nodded, choking on a breath, and he released her abruptly, his face darkening as he turned toward the cabin. He yelled at her, "What the hell did you do that for?" And he started to run toward the cabin.

More crashing sounds and furious growls emanated from behind the closed door, and for a moment Dallas's shock mitigated her fear. She ran after him. "Daniel, don't! He'll kill you! He—"

"Bears don't attack!" he shouted back at her and flung open the door of the cabin.

Dallas stopped at the bottom of the steps, her heart in her throat, as Daniel paused on the threshold, looking inside. Dallas could not see what he saw, but whatever it was it caused him to let out a particularly vicious and highly descriptive curse. The response was an equally disgruntled growl that caused Dallas to bring her trembling hands to her ears. And then, as she watched, Daniel moved deliberately, albeit cautiously, inside.

Dallas's lips began to move in an automatic, mindless recitation of a prayer, and from inside the cabin came the sounds of footsteps, another crash or two, Daniel's low voice. Dallas closed her eyes.

When she opened them again, Daniel was backing carefully down the steps, a loaf of bread held at arm's length before him. The huge black bear was lumbering on all fours after him, his nose trained on the scent of the bread. With a gasp, Dallas pressed herself against the side of the cabin as man and bear came down the steps, moved across the yard and disappeared behind the cabin.

Relief left Dallas even weaker than terror had when she saw Daniel coming back around the cabin. He stopped before her and she managed. "Is he—is he gone? Is it safe?"

Daniel stood before her, his hands on his hips, his face grim, his eyes blazing down at her. "What in the world," he demanded lowly, "possessed you to do such a crazy thing?"

Dallas stared at him. She couldn't believe it. He was angry. He was angry at *her*. She had just escaped death by a hairbreadth and he was angry! "What are you talking about?" Incredulity strengthened her voice and made it high-pitched. "There was a-a *wild animal* in there, ready to attack."

"He was *hungry*!"

"For me!"

"Like hell!" He was shouting now, his eyes snapping, his hands clenching into fists. "Are you a complete idiot! Don't you know *anything*? Bears are not aggressive animals unless threatened! He wouldn't have hurt you."

"Are *you* crazy?" she shouted back, the combined pressure of panic, life-and-death struggle, and, now, utter amazement over this unwarranted attack, combining to push her almost over the edge. "Everyone knows that grizzlies are killers."

"There are no grizzlies in this part of the country!" It was a roar almost as fierce as the bear's had been, and the force of it took Dallas's breath away. Instinctively she shrank back, staring at him, as she could see the effort it took for Daniel to bring his temper back under control. "It was a plain old American black bear," he said. His tone was level, his words clipped and distinct, but an angry color still stained his throat, and his eyes were smoldering. "It even so happens he's a *friendly* bear. He comes here because I feed him, every fall, right before hibernation, and he's already so fat and lazy he couldn't have attacked if he had wanted to. For God's sake, couldn't you even see *that*?''

*No, no,* Dallas thought, *I am not hearing this. This is not happening to me. I just survived the most harrowing experience of my life, and he's yelling at me because I offended a bear.* She looked at him, still breathing hard, her fists clenching in instinctive self-defense, and she cried, "All I saw was a bear! How was I supposed to know he was a friend of yours? I thought he was going to kill me! What was I supposed to do?"

"Use a little common sense, for the love of Pete!" He turned with an impatient hiss and an abrupt gesture back toward the cabin. "You could have run away. But why the hell did you have to lock the door?"

"So he wouldn't run after me!"

Daniel looked at her with such utter contempt and churning anger that Dallas felt herself wither, and then he turned and strode up the steps into the cabin. Dallas stood there, her head reeling, her breath still coming in gulps, and tried to convince herself that she had imagined the entire past half hour of her life. She had walked into the cabin. She had seen a bear. It had growled at her. She had run away, and locking the door behind her was the smartest thing she had ever done in her life. Then why was Daniel angry with her? What the hell was she *supposed* to have done?

Daniel should have been comforting her, holding her, telling her how happy he was she was unharmed, complimenting her quick thinking, telling her everything was all right. Didn't he know how frightened she had been? Didn't she get any points for valor? Didn't he care at all?

Dallas's chin came up a fraction; her eyes narrowed. Her hands tightened at her sides as though in preparation for battle, and she stalked up the steps after Daniel, determined to demand an explanation and an apology, and to defend herself if she must.

Daniel stood just inside the threshold, for in truth he could get no farther. Dallas looked around at what was left of his cabin, and she understood the reason for his anger; her own anger evaporated into a hollow, sinking sensation in the pit of her stomach.

Every chair, as well as the table, was overturned. The contents of the shelves now littered the floor—towels, linens, clothes mixed in gooey array with broken jars of preserved foodstuffs, smashed crockery and tableware. The butter churn was broken and thick yellow-speckled milk spread slowly over the hearth and dripped onto the floor. Three jars of honey had been smashed upon the counter, and the basket of eggs Daniel had gathered this morning was shredded, its contents splattered in yellow and white gobs over counters, walls and floor. A twenty-pound bag of flour had been ripped open and evidently carried across the room, trailing flour until it was abandoned for the more enticing lure of a large jar of molasses. Molasses and flour now formed a messy glue in the middle of the floor, in which several of Daniel's shirts and miscellaneous articles of clothing were tangled.

And it wasn't just the mess. Flour, cornmeal, coffee, jars of preserved vegetables, dried fruits, butter, cheese, dozens of jars of food Daniel had put aside for the winter were scattered everywhere. The rocking chair had been turned over and its woven seat ripped out. A table leg was broken. Two shelves had fallen down. Candles were cracked. A pane of window glass

Daniel had been saving in case of emergency was smashed. That such utter devastation could have taken place in so short a time was mute testament to the wiles of nature when brought against the limitations of man.

"Look at this," Daniel said softy.

His voice held a note of weary incredulity mixed with disgust, and Dallas ventured a hesitant glance at him. "I guess it wasn't such a good idea to lock him in here after all," she offered.

Daniel didn't bother to reply. He took a step inside, kicking at a torn and tangled knit afghan. The silence, like the tension, was thick. "A summer's work," he said slowly, looking around the room. "Gone. Fifteen minutes, and it's gone."

Dallas didn't know what to say. *Damn it, how could he blame her?* She hadn't known any better. What was she supposed to have done?

Finally, with a heavy sigh, Daniel bent to pick up the afghan. He straightened up, squared his shoulders, and looked around once again. "Well," he said, "we've got a lot of cleaning up to do."

Dallas couldn't stand it any longer. The tension, the guilt and the unspoken blame built to the boiling point within her and she burst out impatiently, "Look, I'll pay for the damange, okay? I don't know what makes you think it was my fault but—"

He turned on her, his eyes smoldering, his lips tight. "That easy, huh?" The words were practically spat out. There was such anger and such contempt in his eyes that Dallas felt it strike her like a physical blow. She had never expected to see those emotions on Daniel Masters's face. She had never expected to have them directed at her. "Write a check, pass the buck, and everything's all right. Well, let me tell you something, lady, it's *not* that easy here, and your quick fixes won't work. You can go back to your disposable society and sweep your own mistakes under the rug, but I've just lost half a year's supplies, and nothing you can do will bring that back, do you understand?''

Dallas's color flamed, and, unexpectedly, her eyes began to sting—not with anger, but with hurt. He looked at her with fury and disgust in his eyes and he spoke words that were nothing but true, and everything that had been tentatively building between them over the past few days came crashing down around her feet. They looked at each other, and whatever shallow pretense they might have held about knowing each other, understanding each other, sharing with each other was stripped away, leaving nothing but the raw and painful truth. He was right. Dallas didn't belong here. She had no part of this way of life, or this set of values, had no understanding or need for it. Maybe her world was cheap and shallow, where an accident meant no more than a minor inconvenience and higher insurance rates, and a mistake could be covered with a credit card, and a loss could be replaced with a checkbook and a phone call—but it was *her* world, the only one she knew, and there was no point in trying to change it now.

Dallas looked at him, and she felt her small and tenuous hold on something she had not even known she valued begin to slip away. But she couldn't stand there any longer, facing down the accusation in his eyes or westling with her own helplessness. She didn't know how much longer she could hide her hurt, or her sorrow. And she didn't know what else to say.

She turned and walked outside, closing the door behind her.

## Chapter Twelve

Dallas sat on the large tree stump that Daniel used to split logs, telling herself not to be an idiot, but she was unable to prevent the past hour's combination of fear, outrage, incredulity and hurt from welling up into hot, sloppy tears that spilled down her cheeks no matter how hard she tried to force them back. Angrily she scrubbed her cheeks, took deep breaths, tried to focus on the horizon. But again and again the fiery colors of an autumn afternoon blurred and melted together, and the emptiness in the pit of her stomach was the painful evidence of sobs unreleased.

How foolish she was to think she had begun to feel a harmony with this place. Only this afternoon, hadn't she been thinking how much she would miss it, wishing she could postpone leaving; for a while she had almost begun to think of herself as a part of this place and of Daniel. But you can't change what you are. Daniel had told her that the first day she was here. And what she was had nothing to do with Daniel and the life he loved. She simply would never understand it, and she wanted to go home, where she belonged.

Dallas searched in her jeans pocket for a handkerchief or a tissue, knowing she would find no such thing. What she came up with was the arrowhead Daniel had given her on that long-ago day under the apple tree. The day when she had first thought she was coming to an understanding of him. Slowly she turned the ancient stone over in her hand, sniffing back tears. "Good luck," she muttered thickly and blinked rapidly to keep her eyes from blurring. "Sure." She had brought Daniel nothing but bad luck since she had come here, and no Indian artifact was going to change that.

*Oh, Daniel,* she thought heavily, looking down at the stone, *I wish there could have been a chance for us. I wish I were different. I wish I could appreciate the things you do and love the things you do, and in my own way, I do care. But I could never live like this. If I lived to be a hundred, I would never understand all you understand, or have the passion for this life-style that you do, and I could never share it. It's sad. Right now I feel as though it's breaking my heart, but it's just one of those things I have to accept. That's life, and there's no use pretending it could ever be different.*

She heard the footsteps; with her peripheral vision she saw Daniel approaching. She made a meager effort to compose herself, but there was no time to hide the signs of her tears before Daniel sat beside her on the wide stump.

He put his arm around her shoulders and drew her close. "Dallas," he said gently, and brushed her hair with a kiss. "I'm sorry. I shouldn't have shouted at you."

Surprise and wonder caught Dallas's breath and completely dried her tears as he took her chin lightly between thumb and forefinger and lifted her face. His eyes were very sober, his face gentle and intent.

"Honey, you were right. You did the only thing you could have, and I guess I went a little crazy." He tried to force his lips into a semblance of a rueful smile, but it faded almost immediately. "It was just that when I saw you, and you told me—I was so frightened for you, Dallas." His voice had hoarsened a little with that, and his fingers tightened on her shoulder. His eyes searched her face intently, almost anxiously, as though he were wondering whether she would believe him, or as though he were trying to assure himself that she was, indeed, unharmed. "When I realized what had happened and I thought how differently it might have gone—it could have been an unfamiliar bear or an injured one, or you could have threatened him or angered him—when I thought of what could have happened, well, I lost it." Again he tried to smile. "Forgive me."

Dallas didn't know what to say. Warmth seeped through her, and wonder. Cautiously she reached for the moment but didn't know how to take it. His arm was around her, making her feel warm and secure, his chest protecting her, his eyes looking at her with such depth and concern. The pain and the uncertainty and the fear of the past hour were washed away and lost in the tenderness of his eyes, and Dallas did not know what to do.

She said, a little uncertainly, "The cabin...all your things..."

He smiled, and she felt the tautness of his muscles relax fractionally. "I know I should say it doesn't matter, but you know it does. We've got a hell of a mess on our hands. But—" and now his gaze deepened again and the planes of his face grew intense as he looked at her "—it doesn't matter as much as you do. And that's the truth."

He kissed her. His lips covered hers as softly and as naturally as sunshine awakened a sleeping earth; it was a gentle kiss, filled with tenderness and care. Dallas unfolded beneath it, each petal of dormant emotion brought slowly to life. The sweetness of it brought tears to her eyes that evaporated like dew in the afternoon into sheer, quiet joy. The passion that sparked so easily between them was for this time no more than a background fire; they basked in its glow but did not let it consume them. They tasted each other, they melted into each other, they explored each other. And when their lips parted, there was no urgency, no disappointment, no frustration, because a part of each of them, perhaps the most important part, still clung together.

Dallas leaned her head upon his shoulder, one hand resting on his thigh. Daniel's arm encircled her waist lightly; his other hand covered hers. They rested that way, quietly, for a long time.

How strange it was that, after all the turmoil that she had undergone in the past hour—no, ever since she had come here—could be wiped away so sweetly and so completely by a single kiss. Dallas kept waiting for the uneasiness to come, the dissatisfaction, the urgency, the wanting more, but it never did. It was enough just to sit in the golden-red glow of the forest and the sun and be close to Daniel. Contentment. What a strange feeling. Perhaps it could only be fully appreciated after moments of extreme stress—or perhaps it was simply something Dallas had never known before. However it came to be, Dallas wished it could last forever.

*Daniel,* she thought, *maybe there could be a chance for us. If we would let it be. If we would only let go and let it be.*

But the concept of letting go was a strange one to Dallas, and she could not examine it for long. Instead, she found herself saying softly, "Daniel, don't you ever miss civilization? Don't you ever think of coming back, even for a little while?"

And what she was really trying to say was, *Won't you come back with me? Won't you try it, just for a little while?* Because it would be so hard to leave him.

Daniel smiled, slowly, rather distantly. He turned her hand over beneath his and found it still clutched the arrowhead. He took up the stone and began to toy with it absently. "Sure," he admitted. "I think about it sometimes. And I miss it. The Red Sox games, the 'Movie of the Week,' popcorn," he said, and his eyes held a glint of teasing. "The kind they serve at movie theaters, with all that salt and artificial butter. I miss popcorn a lot. And wearing a suit." His eyes took on a half-amused, reminiscent shade, the kind of look a man might have while looking at a picture of himself in a high-school annaul—half disbelieving, half fond. "When I think how I used to hate wearing a tie...but now I miss it. And other things, like restaurants with heavy silver and linen tablecloths, and the corner bar where everybody knows the regulars. And, God, sometimes it drives me crazy, wondering what's playing on Broadway now."

"*A Chorus Line,*" Dallas said, a little breathlessly. An insane kind of hope had begun to flower with every word he spoke. She could offer him all of that and more. She could give him the things he missed; they could share them together. "It's still playing. The longest-running musical in Broadway history."

His eyes sparked briefly with amazement and pleasure. "No kidding? Would you believe it—that's the last show I saw. And the last movie was..." His brow furrowed, trying to remember. Finally he relented with a laugh. The movement of his shoulders when he laughed was a subtle intoxicant to Dallas, and his fingers squeezed her waist in quick affection. "I've forgotten. It mustn't have been very memorable."

"Well, there've been some memorable ones lately," Dallas assured him, and her eyes searched his with fervent, excited hope. "Daniel—"

But even before she could finish the sentence, she saw the soft refusal in his eyes. "I think about it sometimes," he said gently, "but that's all—just thinking." He looked down at the arrowhead he held between his fingers, and then up again. His expression was troubled and reluctant as it traveled across the horizon, and Dallas knew what he was thinking, what he was trying to find a way to say to her. She acknowledged it with a dull sinking of hope and was glad she had not put her request into words. He would never come to her in Detroit. He didn't belong there, any more than she belonged here.

Then, slowly, his expression cleared, became transformed with a quiet infusion of pleasure, and he said softly, "Look."

Dallas turned her gaze to follow his, and she saw, outlined against the brilliant reds and yellows of the forest, the stately silhouette of a large black bird, gliding regally between earth and sky. With hardly a flutter of a wing, it rode the air currents, swooping close to the ground and then soaring upward again, silently, effortlessly, in mastery of all it surveyed. It was a moment that should have been captured on film—nature at its simplest and its finest, breathtaking in its beauty, humbling in its nobility. Dallas could do nothing but watch with suspended breath as the bird ascended over trees into the sky, until it at last became lost in the sun.

"A hawk," Daniel said. And then he looked at her. A low, burning passion had come into his eyes, and he spoke quietly, intently, but with very little expression at all, as though he stated the obvious and expected no particular acknowledgement for it. "Golden eagles nest here. And the bald eagle is beginning to come back. Can you believe that? Less than two thousand of them left in the country, and I've seen two of them with my own eyes. That's an experience, Dallas, like nothing I can explain. It's as though..." He hesitated, searching briefly for the words. "It's as though I'm tied here by bonds as old as time and as strong as nature itself. Not a choice I had to make, but a choice that was made for me."

His expression sobered as he looked again at the arrowhead in his hand. "I know," he said slowly, choosing his words carefully, "that not everyone can understand, and not everyone can see the value in the way I live, but I don't want everyone to understand. It's enough that I do. To me, there is no other choice, nothing more important, nothing more satisfying, than simply living day by day and learning about nature and life and the way things were meant to be. This is it, Dallas," he said, and his eyes traveled slowly over the landscape: the woods that were putting on their gay party robes, the sun that glanced off them, the rich brown earth that nourished them, the busy forest creatures that fed from them. Life, endless, busy, un-forgiving, but ever-constant. "The last frontier," he said quietly, "the great planet Earth." He pressed the arrowhead back into her hand. "We make it here, or we don't make it at all. Is there anything more important?" he asked simply.

Dallas looked at him, everything within her aching, not with yearning, but with understanding. How could she fail to know, to understand the essence of what he was saying, and to acknowledge the importance of it? For Dallas there were battles, the conquests and the conquerors, and the outcomes of those little wars could mean the uplifting of the quality of life for hundreds of thousands of people. But, for Daniel, the only battle was in the preservation of life itself, and without the silent struggle he maintained, all others would be pointless.

She looked at him, and the helpless answer was *I know*. For she did know, and there was nothing, absolutely nothing, she could do.

"Dallas, I've been thinking about what you said the other night," Daniel said quietly, after a time. "Maybe the time has come to take off the gloves and fight just as dirty as the other guy is doing." He looked at her, and a determination had come into his eyes. "I want you to do the interview, Dallas," he said. "If that's the only way to save what has to be saved, then do it."

This was her chance. This was what she had been waiting for, hoping for. She could make this into the story of a lifetime, and it *would* work. Once she put the "Spotlight" staff on this case, once she brought in the cameras and set up her shots, no stone would be left unturned, and she would have all America up on its feet cheering for Daniel Masters on Sunday night. The people of the country had a right to know what was being threatened in the name of progress, to be informed about the underhanded tactics used by their own government against the rights of the indidivual. That was Dallas's job; it was what she was good at, and this time she could use her expertise to protect something she cared about in fact, as well as in principle. She could help Daniel. It would work.

Exhilaration filled her, tightened in her muscles and shone in her eyes as she began to make her plans. Simon had said the cameras could be sent in on the fifteenth. She had no idea what day it was now, but she was certain she hadn't been here a month yet. They would have to come in by helicopter, of course, and plan to spend at least two or three days filming. She wanted to get an interview with Emily and plenty of shots of the surrounding landscape. Lord, she had a lot of work to do. She had to get to a telephone. She wondered it she could get Daniel to repeat some of the things he had said about freedom and the last frontier, for voice-overs. Why in the world hadn't she taken notes? It would be one of the best shows she had ever done. She could almost see it now.

She could see the helicopter, with its noise and its fury, landing in this peaceful clearing, scattering chickens and chopping up earth. She could see her camera crew, trailing wires and power packs, cussing like sailors and calling everyone "baby" and tossing chewed-up cigar butts everywhere; Emily, her simple home invaded by high-wattage bulbs and close-up lenses; Daniel, reciting copy into a microphone. *My God, Dallas, what are you doing?*

Her eyes fell in confusion, and Daniel, immediately sensing her change of mood, prompted gently, "Dallas?"

For a time she was silent, turning the rock over and over in her hand. Then she smiled and shrugged a little, and said, "I was just thinking about this story I heard. It seems that a bomber was shot down over a primitive South Seas island during World War Two. The natives had been living their own peaceful way for centuries. They'd never seen an airplane or even heard of one; they were completely untouched by modern civilization. And to this day, they worship that fallen bomber. Their whole culture is centered around it." She glanced at him uncomfortably, feeling foolish. "An accident, a moment out of time, changed an entire civilization forever, just like that."

She looked down at her hands again, not knowing how better to express herself, not even certain what it was she was trying to say. It just didn't jibe. It was stupid, but Dallas couldn't see herself bringing into this quiet place all the technology and contradiction of a modern age that Daniel had worked so hard to avoid. Maybe nothing would be permanently changed if she did...but maybe everything would be.

Whatever the case, Dallas knew for certain there was no way to capture on film the specialness of this place and the importance of it. There was no way to bring into the living rooms of America the essence of one man's existence alone with nature—sometimes in harmony, sometimes in battle, the way life itself was—as he tried to preserve just one corner of the world from modern invasion. Because he had been right, when he originally refused the interview. After the "Spotlight" story, he wouldn't be able to turn away

*Time* and *Newsweek*, and the first thing he knew, he would be doing lecture tours and appearing on "Tonight"; then would come the weekend nature buffs, the hikers and the campers and the tourists. Was it a chance worth taking? Wasn't the entire venture self-defeating?

Looking up at him, she said simply, "I'm not sure that's what we want to do, Daniel."

His eyes softened with understanding of what she didn't know how to say. No, it was more than understanding; it was appreciation and gratitude. His hand moved slowly up her back in a caressing motion until it cupped her neck beneath her hair, and Dallas slowly melted into the warmth in his eyes. "You," he said softly, "are beautiful."

Dallas wanted then to wind her arms around him and press herself close, to offer her lips to him and let the passion that had simmered so subtly between them since the first moment he touched her find its full and final release, but something restrained her. The moment seemed too gentle, too full of truth and wonder, to be pushed. She let herself bask in it, let its tender glow fill her, but even that became too intense after a moment, and she had to look away, forcing a totally false dry smile and a nonchalant lift of her shoulders.

"I feel like a fool," she corrected, "turning down the chance for a story like this." She shrugged again, examining the arrowhead. "I guess," she continued lightly, "I just got a sudden picture of being haunted by all those Indians whose sleeping spirits I'd be disturbing." And then she stopped, growing thoughtful. She turned the arrowhead over in her hand. "Land auctions," she mused. "I remember reading about those. The federal government bought up a bunch of land from various tribes and then auctioned it off to settlers in the late 1700's'.'" She looked up at him. "Shouldn't that all be a matter of public record?"

He nodded. "It should be. But the government's record of this particular auction has been lost or destroyed somewhere along the way. That's why their claim is so strong—the first accurate survey we have is the one that claims I'm trespassing."

"I can't believe there isn't some kind of record of the purchase somewhere," Dallas insisted, brooding.

Daniel smiled. "Nobody keeps anything for two hundred years—apparently, not even the federal govenment."

Dallas snorted. "Nobody except Emily," she replied, remembering the crowded room and its assorted treasures, many well over two hundred years old. "The govenment should have her keeping their records. I'll bet she hasn't thrown away anything since—" Dallas stopped, and the possibilities of what she was saying dawned on them both at the same time in shades of wonder, incredulity and hope. Dallas said, somewhat breathlessly, "Good Lord, you don't suppose she—"

Daniel's face was both jubilant and astounded. "She does," he said lowly, his tone stunned. And then, with rising relief and joy he added, "How could I be so stupid? We've spent all this time looking for the records of the auction, records of the Indian treaty— all we needed was one record of one sale! And Emily has a copy of the original document. She showed it to me when I was about fifteen, and all I remember is being disappointed because there weren't any real Indian names on it. It completely slipped my mind." He laughed out loud in wonder and delight, and the pleasure that snapped in his eyes went through Dallas like electricity, making everything inside her sing. "Dallas McCabe, you are incredible!" he said, and pulled her to him in a quick, joyful embrace.

Dallas laughed in pleasure and surprise as he eased his arms and she looked up at him. Her spirits soared, with a problem so easily solved, but she felt it only fair to point out, "Your lawyers would have thought of it, eventually."

"Maybe," he agreed, his eyes still shining with quiet relief. "But you saved a lot of steps—and a lot of worry on my part." The smile in his eyes briefly deepened to teasing. "And all without the aid of a single camera."

She laughed. "I guess the old arrowhead did bring good luck after all."

His gaze softened and sobered. "For both of us," he said, and pulled her to him again, gently, sweetly, just holding her. "I'm glad you came into my life, Dallas McCabe," he said simply.

Dallas's heart began to beat that slow, full rhythm again, her veins pumping life-giving warmth, her chest filling with sweetness and yearning so intense it felt like the taste of tears. *My God, I'm happy,* she thought, and she turned her face against Daniel's chest, tightening her arms around him. *I could stay like this forever.*

And that was when she knew. She loved him. She did not know how it had happened, or when, or even why, but it was unmistakably true. For the first time in her life, Dallas McCabe was in love.

Daniel moved a little away from her, smiling down at her gently, almost absently. His face was tender, his eyes content, all of him beautiful, strong, enduring. *I love you,* she thought, because she couldn't help it.

But the realization left her dazed, confused, very uncertain, and she had to break the eye contact. She couldn't deal with this. She didn't know *how* to deal with this. Getting to her feet and forcing a nervous smile, she said quickly, "Well, I guess we'd better get started on the cabin."

For a moment Daniel looked a little confused, and Dallas wondered, for a heart-stopping minute, what he had been thinking, what he had been about to say. But he recovered himself quickly, and his smile seemed much more natural than hers.

"I'm ready," he agreed, and stood.

He rested his hand on her shoulder in an easy, friendly manner as they went inside, and Dallas was thinking helplessly, *But I'm not. I'm not ready for this at all.*

## Chapter Thirteen

They worked until well after dark, possibly until close to midnight, before the cabin was even habitable again. There were still a lot of repairs to be done, and much was lost that simply could not be replaced, but they did the best they could. Dallas was physically and emotionally exhausted by the time the last candle was blown out and she snuggled down into her sleeping bag before the fire, and she should have fallen into an immediate and sound sleep. But she couldn't sleep.

The evening of forced activity had kept her too busy to think, but now, in the dark and the quiet, all those disturbing questions and uncertainties and startling realizations kept circling in her mind and wouldn't leave her alone. It was impossible, of course. It was totally ridiculous, out of the question, patently absurd. Dallas couldn't be in love with Daniel Masters. Dallas McCabe couldn't be in love with anyone; she was too busy, too purposeful, too involved with the many other, far grander projects that occupied her life to have anything left over for love. Daniel had said it himself: *You can't change what you are.* And Dallas had known from the time of her first marriage, perhaps even longer than that, that she was not the type of woman who could ever be committed to a loving relationship; she wasn't the kind of woman who fell in love.

Yet she *had* been changing—slowly, subtly. From the very first moment she had been cast into this alien and hostile environment, she had been changing on the inside. She had learned to relax. She had become more malleable, more open-minded, more generous. This afternoon she had sacrificed the story of a lifetime for some idealistic principle she couldn't begin to explain, even to herself. The old Dallas McCabe would never have done that.

The Dallas McCabe who had arrived here less than two weeks ago never would have cried when a man shouted at her, or felt her spirits soar when he smiled, never would have put his needs above hers, never would have found it in her heart to grow to care about an old woman who raised hogs and goats and cherished a carnival relish dish above all other possessions in the world, nor would she have carried an Indian arrowhead in her pocket as a talisman. Dallas did not recognize herself anymore, and it was a frightening feeling.

She turned over quietly on her back, drawing the quilts more securely around her against the chill of the night. Her eyes were wide-open, fixed upon the black of the ceiling. *Oh, Daniel,* she thought dully, *how did this happen to me? What have you done?*

Dallas had always thought that love, when it happened, would be like a lightning bolt—swift, sudden, sure, wreaking havoc with all around it, knocking its victim completely off her feet. But for Dallas it had been a more insidious thing, creeping up on her while she wasn't looking, wrapping itself around her when she least expected it, planting itself deep within her without her ever having known it. It was the realization of what had happened that knocked Dallas off her feet, for it had certainly been going on for some time. And it was definitely wreaking havoc with her life.

She tried to sleep. She closed her eyes and tried to let the sound of Daniel's deep, even breathing work a hypnotic effect. Of course, it did exactly the opposite. When she closed her eyes, all she could feel was his face; all she could feel was the golden, melting sensation inside her stomach that his kiss had brought upon her this afternoon. It was so sweet, so intense, unlike anything she had even known: deeper than sex, better than sex, making her want more, and wanting it to last forever.

It was very cold inside the cabin. Dallas curled herself up inside the quilts and tried not to think of Daniel's warmth, or how it would be to be held in his arms through the night. Firmly, she squeezed her eyes shut and tried to block out those dangerous thoughts. What a scary, lonely thing this was. Dallas was not prepared for this; she didn't want it; she couldn't handle it. And what a strange thing it was that Dallas McCabe, so accustomed to blazing new trails and conquering new frontiers, should find herself at such an utter loss when it came to matters of the heart.

Dallas twisted and turned, trying to get comfortable and to get warm, trying to calm her restless mind or at least think of something else, but it was no use. Daniel filled this room; he filled her mind. Nothing about her would ever be the same because he had touched her life. How could she just go back to Detroit and pretend nothing had happened? How could she pick up her life again without him in it? How could she forget him?

She sat up, giving up on sleep. It was definitely chilly in here, and that was not helping matters at all. She reached her hand out toward the stove, but even it wasn't warm. Shivering and wrapping the quilt around her shoulders, Dallas got up on her knees and lifted the latch on the stove door, swearing softly at the clatter it made. Daniel turned over heavily in bed, and Dallas hesitated, not wanting to wake him, before she eased the creaking door open. There was nothing inside the stove but dead ashes. Apparently, in all the furor of activity during the evening, Daniel had forgotten to bank the fire.

Shivering more elaborately now, Dallas retrieved a book of matches and a piece of the scrap paper Daniel kept by the stove. She struggled to keep the quilt around her shoulders as she struck a match to the paper, waited until it caught, then tossed it inside the stove. The minute she turned to get a piece of kindling to aid the burning process, the paper went out. Dallas struck another match.

She struck five matches, each one burning her temper but nothing else. The paper would catch and burn for an inch or two, but the moment she tried to coax the flame onto the dried stick of kindling, it would die into cinders. "Great, Dallas," she muttered, poking at the paper and getting nothing but sparks that evaporated in midair. "You're going to solve the problems of the world, and you can't even light a damn fire." She didn't know why this should irritate her so, but it did. She struck another match.

Daniel pushed himself up in bed. His voice was sleepy. "Dallas? What's wrong?"

*Just like a man,* she thought in some annoyance.
*He's sound asleep while my whole world is falling
apart.*

"The fire went out," Dallas replied, keeping her
voice a near whisper, even though there was hardly any
reason for it at this point. "I didn't mean to wake
you."

Dallas heard the rustling movements as he got out
of bed, his bare feet on the wooden floor, the scrape
of material as he pulled on his jeans. Deliberately, she
did not look around. She kept her eyes on the last
dying match inside the stove.

Daniel knelt beside her. He smelled of sleep and
warmth and masculinity—subtle, drugging scents that
wrapped themselves around Dallas and made her want
to draw close. She kept her eyes on the stove. "I guess
if civilization had been depending on me to discover
fire, we'd still be wearing bearskins and eating raw
meat. It's beyond me how millions of acres of timber
can be destroyed by forest fire each year when I can't
even get a piece of paper to burn."

There was a smile in Daniel's voice as he took up
another piece of paper, twisted it into a spiral, and
took the book of matches from her. "There's a trick
to this," he assured her, and struck a match to the
spiral. He waited until the paper was burning health-
ily, then propped it against a half-burned log inside the
stove. Over that he built a neat tent of kindling, and
when that was flaming, he added a log and closed the
door.

He sat back, wiped his hands on his jeans, and pro-
nounced, "There. Nothing to it."

"Says you," muttered Dallas, and he chuckled.

The room was lighted only by shadowed moonlight, and Daniel was sitting very close. His hair was rumpled and his eyes drowsy-soft. The grayish light filtered over his bare chest, with its gentle shading of hair, and over his arm muscles and his shoulders. Dallas remembered how enormous he had seemed to her when they first met. He didn't look so overpoweringly huge now; he just looked like Daniel.

He was smiling at her, in the absent, half-contemplative way a man might who isn't certain whether or not he is dreaming. In a moment, as almost a natural extension of the smile, he reached out and smoothed her tousled hair. He let his hand fall to the quilt that still protected her shoulders, but no farther. "It is cold in here."

Dallas nodded, suddenly nervous. She drew the quilt more tightly around her, though what she really wanted to do was to open it and draw him inside with her. "The temperature certainly dropped fast."

His smile deepened a fraction. He never moved his eyes from her, and they seemed bottomless, fathomless, quiet and gentle and he just looked at her as though he could do so forever. "It's that time of year. Maybe we'll get snowed in."

Her heartbeat jumped a little, not because of what he said, but because of the way he said it. As though nothing would make him happier, as though he had read her deepest fantasy and put it into words.

Everything in her heart must have been written in Dallas's eyes in that moment, because in his eyes there seemed to be an answer. It was another one of those instants of contact in which words were spoken that were not spoken, in which truths were revealed like long-kept secrets, and both accepted the communication naturally, easily, as though it were only what they had been waiting for all their lives.

Daniel said quietly, "This afternoon, when I asked you to do the interview, it was only because that was the only thing I could think of to get you to stay longer."

Dallas felt the half-believing joy in that statement and its implications go through her like an intoxicant, shining in her eyes, toying with her breath. She searched his eyes, looking for some sign of regret for the confession, or teasing, and found nothing but the simple truth. "All you had to do was ask me," she whispered.

His other hand came up to stroke her face, very lightly, from temple to cheek on one side, tracing the shape of her chin and throat, and Dallas pressed her face, imperceptibly and unpreventably, into the caress. At last, both his hands rested on her shoulders, near her throat; his thumbs spread over her bare collarbone in the place where the quilt did not quite meet, his fingers coming together at the back of her neck, beneath her hair. His face was so tender, his eyes lighted with a low, dark blaze that seemed as anxious as it was needful. He said huskily, trying to smile, "Have you noticed? The great naturalist has committed a cardinal sin. I've been fighting against nature since the moment I met you." The smile faded as his eyes drifted slowly down the length of her body, and up again until they seemed to rest upon the point where her clenched fists held the quilt closed. And all the while, without seeming to move at all, he was drawing her closer, until now his sigh, heavy and long, fluttered across her cheek and feathered her hair. "Oh, Dallas," he whispered, searching her eyes, "I don't know how this happened. God knows I did my best to keep it from happening. But I think the time has come for both of us to let go of a little control."

He moved his face toward hers, but Dallas was already lifting her lips to him. They met in a kiss that was open and deep and everlasting. The barriers were broken and the shields cast aside at last; they simply let the power of their need speak for them, and it seemed there could be nothing more right, nothing more natural.

Dallas let the quilt slip away as she wrapped her arms around Daniel's neck, his smooth, warm skin beneath her fingers, his muscles tautening against hers. What started out as a mere inevitable coming together soon became greedy, and Daniel's hands traveled to her waist, tracing the outline of the curves beneath the brushed cotton of her undershirt, pressing into her softness, hardening against her back as he held her to him. Heat spread between them and weakened Dallas's muscles making her head roar, stripping her breath, tingling in her skin. Hungrily, Dallas drank of him, her hands moving over his back in a futile effort to draw him closer, her numbed fingertips aching for the feel of his skin, drawing on his strength. Gradually, so that Dallas hardly knew it, he lowered her to the floor until they were lying side by side, his large, slightly unsteady hand moving in a slow, light, greatly restrained caress up and down the length of her torso from breast to hip—gently, almost reverently.

He kissed her chin, and her jaw, and then, very delicately, her throat. The fan of his breath was hot and unsteady as, with an exquisitely light touch, his forefinger came up to circle her peaked nipple. Everything within Dallas quickened and melted with the caress, yearning toward him, aching for him, and when his lips brushed near hers again, she lightly traced the pattern of them with her tongue, again, drawing him closer by fractions of millimeters until his mouth covered hers in another deep, drawing kiss.

His hand closed upon the fullness of her breast and she arched toward him, wrapping one leg around one of his, pressing herself closer, and him closer, as close as they could possibly get. Still, it wasn't enough. It was so right between them. Nothing had ever been more right in Dallas's life.

He moved on top of her, his long, jeaned legs against her bare ones, his torso brushing hers, his weight resting on his elbows on either side of her. His forward falling hair shadowed his face as he looked down at her; his breath mingled with hers. Dallas lifted her hand to touch his soft beard, and her fingers were trembling. His look—so sweet, so tender, so adoring—was as powerful and as binding as a caress. He spread his fingers through her hair, his thumbs resting against her cheekbones, and he whispered, "So much wasted time, Dallas. How helpless you make me feel."

Her unsteady fingers moved across his lips, not because she wished to silence him, but simply because she wanted to touch him. "You make me helpless, too," she whispered, her eyes searching his and opening to him her every need, her every desire, drawing the same from him. "You always have. I never expected this to happen, Daniel. I never expected to...love you."

There. She had said it, and she felt his catch of breath, saw the lightening of his eyes with her words.

He moved his hands beneath her, gathering her close. His face lowered slowly and buried itself in her neck, as he inhaled the fragrance of her, seeming to draw his very life force from her. "Then it's too late for both of us," he said hoarsely, tightening his arms. "Because, God help me, I think I love you, too."

They held each other, and let the power of mutual confession shake them and bind them, until at last the depth of need overcame them, and whatever fear or uncertainty remained was washed away by the demands of urgency. Daniel left her with pulses pounding and limbs trembling, to strip off his jeans, and then he knelt astride her, his warmth a tantalizing shadow above her that made her reach into the darkness for a taste of it. But he caught her hands in a single one of his, he pressed her palms to his lips briefly, then released her hands. In a single fluid motion, he slipped his hands beneath her T-shirt and pulled it over her head; then he dragged down her panties and discarded them as well. When he gathered her into his arms, lowering his full weight onto her for only a moment, every nerve in Dallas's body, from the center outward, was jolted into the sensation of the two of them being together at last, naked and pressed against each other.

Dallas was ready for him. She wanted him with a deep and physical ache that was almost explosive in nature; she wanted him with a more consuming, less easily definable urgency that threatened to break her heart. But Daniel was not to be rushed. He stilled the restless motions of her hands; he soothed her fevered demands with light, brushing kisses, and he lifted himself a little away from her.

Dallas had never thought of Daniel as a skillful lover. She had always imagined their lovemaking as fierce and primal and intensely satisfying, a swift and intense coupling that would shake the foundations of her world. Nature, simple and unadorned, stripped of the vestiges of civlization and reduced to its most basic, most fulfilling elements. But Daniel, as she should have known, was so much more than one-dimensional, and he was determined to draw every nuance of pleasure from the night they shared. With agonizing gentleness, his hands and his lips explored every curve and crevice of her body, worshiping her, delighting in her. He made her weak and then infused her with the quick strength of demand. He made her moan with pleasure and gasp with need, and though she thought there could be nothing deeper than the hunger she felt for him at the outset, he taught her, with patience, the intensifying pleasure that came with knowing him, of belonging to him, as he did to her.

Dallas could see the tremor of his arm muslces as he held himself above her, the intensity that lined the gentle planes of his face, the quiet vulnerability in adoration-softened eyes, and her heart swelled with love for him. The strands of his hair that fell forward across his forehead and his cheekbones were damp with perspiration; his breathing was as uneven and as labored as her own. She curved her hands around his biceps, wanting to touch him, then slipped them beneath his arms to his back, wanting to draw him closer. Her knee pressed against his hip, and her other leg traced the outline of his upward, and she whispered, "Yes, Daniel. Please, let's not wait any longer." He lowered himself into her, a sweet ecstatic filling that stretched the very boundaries of the universe to its limits.

He slipped his arms beneath her and gathered her upward, pressing her against his chest, and they clung to each other, holding each other tightly to the rhythm of their pounding hearts and suspended breaths. They wanted it to last forever, this union, this melting of one into the other as he settled deeper into her, and even deeper. But they could not prevent the instinctive demands of their bodies, and even their souls, for more. Then it was fierce, then it was primal, and then the world did shatter and leave them both dazed, transported, weak in each other's arms and knowing that nothing would ever be the same again, for either of them.

They lay wrapped together in a tangle of quilts on the floor, muscles still quivering, breaths gradually calming, basking in the warmth of the stove and the glow of a thousand exploding universes. Dallas's head was tucked into the curve of his shoulder, her knees drawn up between his, his arm wrapped around her waist. His hand lightly stroked her hair; her head was curled against his chest, absorbing the sound of his heartbeat.

*I never knew,* Dallas thought distantly, wonderingly. *I never knew it could be like this. I never knew love and sex could go together, that it could feel this wonderful afterward.* For still he filled her, every part of her heart and soul, with something so deep it was almost metaphysical, something that left her feeling washed with sunshine from the inside out—something so magnificent, and so strong, that it would bind them together forever.

Daniel crooked his forefinger under her chin, lifting her face a little. He smiled down at her, the moonlight showing the small crinkles at the edges of his eyes as he did so. "I sure do wish you hadn't played so hard to get," he teased. "This could have happened much sooner."

Dallas laughed, but the laugh became choked in a sudden urge of powerful emotion as she was consumed by the urge to try to put into words what could not be described. She tightened her arms fiercely around him and she buried her face in his chest, saying, "Daniel..."

But he stopped her with a brief tightening of his arms and a light kiss upon her hair. "Sh," he whispered. "I know, Dallas. I really do."

And that was the miracle of it. He did know.

At length they moved to Daniel's bed. They didn't sleep, they didn't make love, and for a time they didn't talk. They simply basked in the wonder of being together at last, of holding each other and needing, for the moment, nothing more. The bed was soft, the layers of quilts warm and heavy, and like other of nature's creatures, they burrowed into their den, secure against the coming winter. Strong legs entwined with slim ones, the soft parts of one body molded into the hardness of another, fingers were linked, heartbeats slowed, breaths synchronized. There had never been anything more beautiful, Dallas thought drowsily, than lying here with him in this protected nest on top of the world. And it seemed, at that moment, as though she had never wanted anything else in her life except this.

Daniel said at last, looking at her, "It's crazy. You know that, don't you?"

Dallas nodded. She knew, but in the euphoria of the moment, she didn't care. And, from the look in his eyes, neither did Daniel.

He smiled a little, and sighed, and lay back against the pillow, his fingers making absent twining motions in her hair. "God, how strange life is," he said softly. "If I could put together all the things in one package that I needed and wanted from a woman—the courage, the determination, the unflappable spirit, the compassion, the generosity, the nobility, the quirky humor—even the damned stubborn temper..." The curve of his lips deepened briefly, and then faded altogether. His voice hoarsened. "It would all be you. But we could have gone our whole lives without ever meeting each other, and now..."

He didn't finish, and Dallas didn't want him to. Now she didn't know how she was going to live without him. Now she didn't even want to try. She tightened her arms around him and pressed her face into his chest, clinging to him as though that very action could prevent the inevitable.

Neither of them knew what they were going to do now, but, for the night, it was enough to simply love each other.

A HANDFUL OF DAYS REMAINED to them; crisp, bright mornings and passion filled nights. They worked together, they laughed together, they talked and they played together, and on the surface nothing was different. But to Dallas the air seemed clearer, the sun brighter, every moment separate and special, as though it were being wrapped in a shimmering plastic film to be stored as a memory against hard times. They never talked about the future, and with a concentrated effort on both their parts, rarely thought about it. Their time together was limited and though they knew it, they consciously refused to acknowledge it to each other, or even to themselves. Every moment together was as precious, and their time was meant to be savored, not shadowed with truths from the future.

Yet there was now a new intensity to everything they did, everything they shared, and very few hours were spent apart as they subconsciously tried to fortify themselves against the times ahead. And at night their lovemaking was intense, expansive and endless.

Perhaps somewhere deep in the back of her mind Dallas had thought—even hoped—that once she knew Daniel as a lover, her fascination with him would decrease, her appetite be assuaged, her need for him lessened. In fact, the opposite was true. The more she knew of him, the more she wanted him, and it seemed that she could never have him close enough, often enough, long enough. With every hour he grew more important to her, he filled more of her life, and she felt as though this were only a beginning. A lifetime with Daniel wouldn't be enough for her, and she did not think about the fact that they didn't have a lifetime. She simply couldn't.

But both of them knew it was true. The days were growing cooler, the leaves were beginning to drift through the air, a thin film of ice formed on the water in the rain barrel every night. Daniel pointed out to her the thicker coats on the squirrels and the rabbits, and they watched flocks of birds fly overhead, pointed south. They never said anything, but they both knew.

And then one morning Daniel went to work alone in the woods; when he returned for lunch, he was strangely subdued. Keeping his eyes carefully neutral and his tone nonchalant, he told Dallas that the bridge was finished.

"Oh." After that simple word there was nothing more to say. Dallas set the butter on the table, pulled out her chair and sat down across from him. She tried to smile, but inside her stomach something knotted and twisted, and it felt like the dull edge of a knife.

Home. She was going home. Traffic sounds and chocolate-chip cookies. Running water and bathroom carpeting. Teletype and data screens, restaurants with wine lists, and noisy taverns filled with life. Home. At last, she was going home.

But she didn't have to go right away. Maybe a few more days...a few weeks, a month, a year. What did she think, that she could stay here indefinitely? Forever? She had a job waiting for her—an entirely different life in an entirely different world, a life filled with purpose and meaning and activity. She had people depending on her, things that needed to be done. Winter was coming on. The snows would come, and she would be trapped. She couldn't spend the winter here. She'd go crazy. But maybe just a few more days.

Daniel was looking at her. She smiled weakly; she picked up her fork. They were having soup, and she put the fork down. She said, "Simon was going to send the camera crew down on the fifteenth. It must be near that now. I have to tell him not to bother."

Daniel nodded and broke off a piece of bread from the loaf.

Dallas picked up her spoon. "I have to get a new car."

He smiled. "Be more careful with this one, okay?" His tone was light; his eyes carefully masked his emotions. He was trying to help her. Neither of them wanted to make it more difficult than it had to be.

She laughed, falsely. "Yeah. Right."

"We knew it wasn't going to be easy," Daniel said gently. "We knew it was going to hurt."

She nodded, and put down her spoon. Her throat was tight. She looked at him helplessly. "I *do* have a job to do, Daniel."

He nodded. "So do I," he said quietly.

And that was it.

Dallas wasn't stupid. She knew this was how it must end; she had known it from the beginning. An interlude—the most precious, life-changing interlude of her life—but it was over. There was no choice. She would get over him. It might take a while, and she would never forget the things he had taught her or the person she had come to be because of him, but eventually she would get over him. She had no choice.

Dallas picked up her spoon again; she stared sightlessly into her bowl of soup. She kept her tone normal, almost casual. "So. Tomorrow morning, then?"

"Sure. I'll go down with you. We'll get an early start."

Good. At least she would have one more day with him. At least she wouldn't have to turn her back on him and walk down that moutain alone. One more day, a few more hours. The relief of that knowledge was almost overwhelming.

They shared smiles that were brief and brave, and they each turned to their meal. But neither of them ate very much, and they couldn't find the courage to look at each other again.

That night their lovemaking was greedy and uncontrolled, a narrow outlet for the intensity of desperation that knew no balm. Barely had they reached satiation before they were turning silently to each other again, arousing banked fires, grasping for comfort, seeking reassurance, vainly trying to hold on to what had never been theirs to keep.

With their bodies exhausted and their souls still aching and unfulfilled, they lay together, their hands linked but every other part of them separate, thinking private thoughts, making their own adjustments in their own ways. *It can't be any other way,* Dallas told herself. *It never could have been. We both knew that from the beginning. I was just a visitor in his life, and he in mine, and when I've gone, life will go on, for me and for him. We've both had lovers before. We know how it is.*

There was an entire world out there, for each of them, and each had crucial parts to play in its endless struggles. The needs and wants of two lovers seemed very small and unimportant when placed against the concerns of social disintegration and ecological imbalance. *Life goes on,* she thought firmly. *We loved each other, and it was good, but it has to end now. People say goodbye every day, thousands of them, all over the world, and they survive. So will we. No big deal.*

She moved her arms around him; instinctively he reciprocated the embrace, burying his face in her hair. She whispered, "Come with me—"

"Stay with me," he whispered at the same time. Neither one of them answered. They simply tightened their arms around each other, and held each other close, through the night.

## Chapter Fourteen

Dallas went back to Detroit. The sounds of traffic hurt her ears; the smells of tarmac and jet exhaust at the airport were nauseating. There was light and color everywhere, but to Dallas the impression was like a time-lapse photograph, streaks across a dark canvas that made no sense whatsoever. The cabbie talked non-stop; the doorman welcomed her home effusively. She overtipped both.

For weeks she had dreamed of the sensual thrill of sinking her bare feet into plush carpet; it felt like nylon, nothing more. Her apartment looked sterile and smelled musty. She turned on the television set and turned it off immediately. She pulled back the draperies and looked out over the night skyline, but all she could see was quiet, rolling mountains, fading into the sky. She drew a hot, scented bubble bath and sank into its luxury up to her chin. She closed her eyes and released an extravagant sigh, telling herself how glad she was to be home. Then she started to cry.

They had said good-bye in front of the general store. Cal had kept her rented car, just as he had promised; it had a few extra miles on it, but no actual damage. Dallas had paid him generously for his trouble, and he had pretended reluctance before he accepted. The three of them stood around for a while, talking, then Dallas got into the driver's seat and Daniel stood beside the open door, and they said good-bye. She didn't ask him to come visit her in Detroit; she knew he wouldn't. He didn't ask her to come to the mountain again; he knew she wouldn't. They did not promise to write. They smiled at each other like two awkward strangers, Daniel wished her a good trip; she wished him luck in court. Daniel closed the car door, and she drove away. She didn't look back, but she knew that if she did, he wouldn't be looking at her. It was over. It was better that way.

Dallas went to the studio. She told Simon there would be no story on Daniel Masters. He didn't seem to mind; he had had his hands full since she had been gone, and he was simply glad she was back. He told her she looked great, which only proved that Simon's powers of observation had not improved any in her absence—her eyes were red and puffy, her lips were cracked, and she wore no makeup. Everyone else in the office looked at her a little askance, but Simon was too anxious to get her to her desk, show her the assignment board, dump several stacks of mail in her lap, and pour out his troubles into her ear. It was lunchtime before he finally looked at her, peered more closely, seemed disconcerted and said, "You look different. New shade of lipstick?"

She went home early that day and cried some more.

She bought a new car, a sleek grey Celica with all the options and a few custom extravagances she didn't need and certainly couldn't afford. That lifted her spirits a little. She didn't bother to check with the police station about the criminals who had gotten rid of her last car. It hardly mattered at this point, and she was insured.

She waded through telephone messages, answering some of them and ignoring most. She looked at her mail. She halfheartedly glanced over some material about a possible day-care center scandal. She felt out of step, out of place, as though she were walking in somebody else's body and living somebody else's life. She went to the bookstore and bought every one of Daniel's books, and she spent her nights at home alone, reading and rereading every word he had written.

It soon became apparent to everyone that something was wrong with Dallas. One day Simon stopped by her desk and demanded, "Are you pregnant?"

She stared at him. "No."

He nodded curtly and strode away. "That's all I wanted to know."

She went shopping, spent an exhorbitant amount of plastic money on things she didn't need, and felt better. But when the salesclerk tried to tempt her with a gorgeous natural-fox jacket, Dallas turned away. That was when she knew something was wrong with her. The old Dallas McCabe would have considered that the foxes had given their lives gallantly for a creation as gorgeous as that. The new Dallas only felt slightly sick to her stomach.

At work, she looked at reports; she viewed pieces of film; she read letters. All the flotsam and jetsam of a troubled world eventually landed on Dallas McCabe's desk, and it was overwhelming. *It never stops, Daniel,* she thought in weary amazement. *The crime, the corruption, the disease and the disintegration; it just goes on and on. It doesn't stop when I'm gone. It*

*won't stop when I'm dead. There's nothing I can do
about it. So why am I here?*

She thought about it then. She thought about just
emptying out her desk, walking out of the office,
going home to Daniel. Her heart speeded with the very
possibility of it, and she even picked up the telephone
and dialed the first three digits of the airline. But then
she replaced the receiver slowly. She wasn't going back
to the mountain. She wasn't going to give up Coca-
Cola and Kleenex and toothpaste from a tube. She
wasn't going to chop wood to keep warm and live the
rest of her life without sirloin and read a newspaper
once every five years. She would be miserable. She
would make Daniel miserable.

Like it or not, this was where she belonged. And this
was where she must stay.

A week passed, and two. She went to work; she
came home; she went to work. She lost weight. Frozen dinners had lost their appeal. Work was crazy—all
the noise and the confusion, everyone demanding instant decisions and creating instant crises—and Dallas, for the life of her, couldn't understand what all
the excitement was about. She wondered how she ever
could have found this rat race so appealing. Everybody wanted a piece of her, and they wanted it now—
and what was the point of it all? So a stupefied
America could sit glassy-eyed before its television sets
one more Sunday night and listen to one more person
tell them what was wrong with the world?

Sometimes, to keep herself from going completely
mad, Dallas thought about the things she missed: the
smell of pine and fresh earth; the sound of the creek;
the way the rays of the sun were diffused over the blue-
green curve of the mountain in the mornings; the taste

of dew; apple pie; the sizzle of candlewax; real honey. Daniel.

One day there came across her desk an update of the Senate investigation into the union. It looked good. Two of her own sources had volunteered to testify. It looked, in fact, great. She read the report, made a few phone calls; she was pleased. It was the system at its best, working for the people. And Dallas had a part in it.

Curiously, Dallas called the detective in charge of the investigation of the firebombing of her car. With a great deal of throat-clearing, apologizing, and evasions, he could only report that, no, there didn't seem to be much progress. They had been awfully busy, she must understand, and it was hard to pinpoint the perpetrators.

That made Dallas angry. No, it made her furious. She grabbed her coat and strode out of the studio for the office of the chief of police, her color high, her eyes narrowed in a relentless quest for justice. Around the room a collective sigh arose, relieved grins were shared and several thumbs went up. Dallas McCabe was going to be okay.

WEEKS PASSED. The snow started to blow, and Dallas worried about whether Daniel was warm enough. How high did the snow get up there? What about blizzards? She thought about him trudging back and forth in the snow, carrying buckets of water for drinking and washing and cooking, and she couldn't work. What about Lenore? Did the bird stay inside during the winter, or had she already flown south? What if a storm came, and a tree crashed on the cabin? What if he became ill?

*He's made it through five winters without you, Dallas. He'll survive one more.*

She began seriously investigating reports of abuse in day-care centers, and it was developing into quite a complicated—and appalling—story. Simultaneously, she did a report on a drug scandal within a major-league baseball team. One of the players asked her out, and she went. He was incredibly good-looking, and they had a great time, and at the end of the evening he took her back to his apartment and offered her some cocaine. Dallas smiled at him and took out the mini-tape recorder she had hidden in her pocket with the recording button turned on. She blew him a kiss, said, "Good night, sucker," and left him staring after her in speechless incredulity and rage. Such was the extent of Dallas's scintillating social life.

Thanksgiving came, and all Dallas could think about was the sound wild turkeys made, and how it echoed through the mountain at dusk. But the day-care story was really heating up, and she didn't take time off for Thanksgiving dinner. She worked four-teen hours a day and sometimes well into the night. Often she was too tired even to read from one of Daniel's books before she went to bed.

Christmas came, and the city was alive with lights and color, bustle and madness. For the first time since she had come back, Dallas was mugged. The thief got away with thirty-two dollars, an initialed cigarette lighter and a gold tiepin she had bought for Simon. She just stood on the street corner and laughed out loud as the perpetrator, shooting her covert glances and flashing a pen knife, scuttled down an alleyway. She felt as though she had come home.

Everyone wanted to have Dallas over for a holiday dinner. She gained five pounds. She wondered what Daniel was doing for Christmas, and if he were alone. And she learned that the owner of a large midtown child-care center had been arrested three times for sex offences and had gone free on each count.

On New Year's Eve she went to four parties, and she vaguely remembered agreeing to fly to Monte Carlo with a tall, dark-haired man in a black turtleneck. She awoke the next morning vowing to give up smoking, drinking and eating. Permanently.

On January fifteenth, Dallas, her face grim and her eyes fiery, taped the final segment of the show that would result in the closing of two day-care centers and the arrests of three people. On Sunday night, two weeks later, all America welcomed back the crusading Dallas McCabe they had grown to know and love, and with her, the return of justice, truth, and hope for the future.

That night Dallas, Simon and the crew went to Darien's to celebrate, and for the first time in three months and twenty-one days, Dallas didn't think of Daniel Masters once.

It was March, cold and blustery. Dallas had just finished doing a story on the counterfeiting of generic pharmaceuticals, and, as usual after such an intense investigation, she was both exhausted and exhilarated. She was torn between the adrenaline-charged need to get right on another story, and half-serious daydreams about the Bahamas. Or Hawaii. Yes, Hawaii was just what she needed: mai tais and half-naked Polynesian men, rolling surf, tropical sun. Lots of sun.

At nine o'clock on a Tuesday evening, she was sitting cross-legged on the sofa, wearing a flannel nightshirt and red-and-yellow striped socks, watching television and reading the paper. A bowl of butter-rum ice cream was in her lap and an open package of chocolate-chip cookies was on the floor. The answering machine was picking up her calls, and her dinner, leftover Chinese takeout from the night before, was warming in the microwave oven.

Dallas divided her attention between the television detective show and the news columns of the paper. She was really only interested in the travel section, but trained in diligence, she dutifully scanned every article of news before turning the page. "Five Injured in Freeway Pile-Up." "New Hope for Arthritis Victims." Dallas ignored her spoon and used a cookie to scoop up ice cream, making an open-faced sandwich. She crunched on it happily. "Doctor Indicted on Four Counts of Fraud." "Brothers United After Twenty-Year Search." "FAA Cites Pilot Error in Fatal Crash." Dallas reached to the floor for another cookie. "Land Dispute Tested in Court."

She bit down on the cookie but did not swallow it. She tried to make her hand turn the page, but it wouldn't. With a will of their own, her eyes scanned the article:

Noted author and naturalist Daniel Masters will challenge the Department of Interior in Federal Court in a hearing that begins tomorrow in Greenville, South Carolina....

The oven timer went off. Dallas swallowed the gooey cookie.

Absently, she reached for a spoonful of ice cream, but didn't bring it to her mouth until half of it dripped onto her shirt. *Tomorrow. South Carolina.*

It would be foolish to go, of course. She had no business there. There were a half-dozen stories waiting on her desk, and if she wanted a vacation, she would go to Hawaii.

A lot of press would be there. This could turn into a real media event. Simon would give her the time, and she could always write off the trip as a business expense.

No, that was silly. If Daniel wanted to see her, she wasn't all that hard to find, and she really had much more important things to do.

Thus decided, she folded the paper and went into the kitchen to get her dinner. She was proud of herself. It felt good to have met the crisis and passed over it so easily, with firmness, decision and practicality— just like the old Dallas McCabe. It only proved what she had always known: a lover is just a lover—out of sight, out of mind. She was completely over him. She was back to her old self, confident, self-reliant, in control. Daniel Masters meant nothing to her anymore, and she was doing fine. Just fine.

She was very proud of herself.

DALLAS ARRIVED AT THE FEDERAL COURTHOUSE, in Greenville on Thursday afternoon, near the conclusion of the second day of testimony. She had checked into the hotel around noon, and she couldn't believe that she was actually here. She spent over an hour trying to decide what to wear, and she couldn't believe what she was doing. She started to pick up her suitcase and march right back out. She changed clothes three times. Obviously, she had lost her mind. This was the most absurd thing she had even done in her life.

Even as she slipped silently into the courtroom and took the seat closest to the door, she still couldn't believe she was doing this. Then she saw Daniel sitting at the front table, and her heart started to pound, and she didn't think of anything else.

God, she had missed him. It had been so long, and the fuzzy pictures she held of him in her mind seemed so far away, like a daydream, a figment of her imagination. But now he was sitting there, as real as life itself, and it was like a miracle.

He was wearing a jacket, and his hair had been trimmed a little for the occasion. Dallas sat there and studied the broad lines of his back, the shape of his head, the angle of his bearded jaw when he turned in profile to consult briefly with his attorney, and she heard little, if anything, of the evidence that was being presented. Her attention was fixed upon him so intently, so unpreventably, that she was certain the magnetic force of it would telegraph her presence, drawing his gaze around to meet hers. She couldn't help it. She couldn't take her eyes off him.

She had often wondered, back on the mountain, what he would look like among the normal trappings of a modern society. Even sitting, he was head and shoulders above the rest. Even in suit and tie, his strong individuality showed forth with raw and unchecked power. Even among the hallowed vestiges of one of civilization's oldest institutions, his quiet authority and dominance radiated like a beacon. Or perhaps it was only Dallas's imagination.

*My God,* she thought, and something within her crumpled in despair, even as another, stronger part soared to the very heights of ecstasy. *He hasn't changed a bit.*

Worse, neither had she.

The last of the evidence was presented by four o'clock. The judge announced that he would render a decision in ten days and court was adjourned.

There were, as Dallas had suspected, a great many members of the press present. They gathered in the lobby, their mumblings and shufflings echoing off the high walls, and waited for their quarry to come out. Dallas lingered at the back of the crowd, trying to remain unobtrusive, but she was recognized by a few reporters and a renewed ripple of excitement went through the crowd. If "Spotlight" was covering this event, then it must be a very big deal indeed, and with visions of bigger bylines in their heads, the reporters increased their jostling for positions at the front of the crowd.

Dallas had not intended to stay. She knew now that it would be a huge mistake to stay. Perhaps she had held on to some half-forlorn hope that she would see Daniel again, and there would be nothing, absolutely nothing, and she could walk away calm in the confidence that she was *really* over him. But she had seen him, and even now her skin was tingling with the awareness of his presence, and he wasn't even in the same room. She couldn't stay.

Daniel came through the swinging doors from the courtroom just then, and Dallas knew she couldn't leave.

"Mr. Masters, just a moment, please—"

"Mr. Masters, how do you feel about the case against you?"

"Mr. Masters—"

Microphones were shoved into his face, fresh-faced reporters pushed forward with pens poised above pads, and the clamor of voices in the room was deafening. Daniel looked dismayed. He turned to murmur something to his attorney, who nodded and moved on through the crowd. Daniel held up his hand and said, "No interviews, please." He kept walking.

"Mr. Masters, do you plan on an appeal if—"

"What about your next book? Will any of this—"

"Mr. Masters." Dallas's voice rose clearly and coolly above the crowd. Daniel stopped. She thought she saw his face tighten, perhaps even a faint loss of color, and his eyes searched the room. Her heart was throbbing in her throat; Dallas was surprised that she could even speak. "Will you be returning to the mountain while the court deliberates?"

He saw her, and the slow widening of disbelieving joy in his eyes caught directly in the center of Dallas's chest and seemed to expand outward, so that she could hardly breathe. Yet, he kept his face neutral, and his voice was even as he replied. "No. I'll be staying here."

He never took his eyes off her. He started to move slowly toward her, brushing aside bodies and questions like harmless and pesky insects, and Dallas was drawn toward him as though from nothing more than the power of the electric charge that had been generated when their eyes met. She shouldn't do this. She should turn away. She should *run* away. *Dallas, you're crazy if you let this happen*.

They stood facing each other, only inches apart. It would have been an absurdity to say that the crowd of demanding reporters parted to make room for them, faded away before the force of the chemistry that flared between them, but that was the way it seemed to Dallas. And, in truth, after a moment or two of having their questions completely ignored, all but the most stalwart of the press drifted away, muttering disgruntedly and casting suspicious looks at the two of them. It seemed to Dallas and Daniel that they were the only two people in the world.

Daniel said softly, "Hi." His eyes were mirror-bright.

"Hi." Dallas felt as though she were glowing.

Daniel's eyes moved over her from head to foot, lightening and darkening with each new vista of appreciation, absorbing her hungrily. The pale-pink silk blouse. The long, full-cut gray jacket. The calf-length dirndl skirt of soft, winter-white wool, the pale gray stockings, the classic pumps. The delicately made-up face, the casually, perfectly styled hair. Cool, feminine, stylish. Dallas felt beautiful when he looked at her, and she was glad, so glad, she had taken so much time with her appearance.

His voice sounded a little hoarse when he said, "You look great. Really."

"So do you." She couldn't seem to find her voice. His brown-tweed sport coat, his tie loosened at his throat, his wool slacks, his beige shirt straining over his strong chest, his deep brown eyes. Good? He looked incredible. It was hard to breathe, looking at him. She tried to smile. "Civilized."

The sexual chemistry was palpable, the awareness intense, the need soul-penetrating. It was generated between them like electricity spinning in ever-widening arcs, sealing the world out, pushing them closer together. *Dear God,* Dallas thought. *It hasn't changed. It's still there, stronger than ever.*

"How's everything on the mountain?" Dallas asked.

"Great." He didn't seem to be aware of speaking, and Dallas hardly heard what he said. "Cold."

"How's Emily?"

"Doing good. She asks about you."

"And Lenore?"

"She spent the winter inside. She thinks she's a parakeet."

Dallas cleared her throat. It was hard to breathe. "I stopped smoking."

"Oh, yeah?"

"Yeah." It was hardly a whisper. "For two whole days this time."

"I saw your show the other night," Daniel said. Their eyes were locked together, unable to break away. His said, *My God, I need you.* Hers said, *I don't know how I thought I could stay away from you.* "I was impressed."

Again Dallas smiled. "I told you I was good."

His eyes said hungrily, *Yes.*

Her heart was pounding so forcefully that she thought the movement of it must surely be visible through her blouse. But Daniel didn't look. He couldn't seem to move his eyes away from her face.

They were standing so close, that the material of her skirt brushed against his slacks. Second by second they were moving closer, without even being aware of it. She could almost feel his breath upon her cheek. His warmth penetrated every cell of her skin. She had to part her lips slightly to breathe. His eyes rested upon them.

He said, "I started to write you—"

"Yes," Dallas agreed quickly, almost too quickly. "Many times."

They looked at each other, were absorbed by each other. It went on forever.

Finally Dallas said with a very great effort, "It looks like it's going well."

Daniel's lips moved automatically. His eyes did not. "Yes. My lawyers introduced the Indian Treaty. Yesterday. They think we have an airtight case."

"Good." It was almost a whisper. She wanted to touch him so badly that she ached, but her limbs seemed wooden. His lips were very close. She thought if she tilted her head just a little...

Daniel said softly, "Will you have dinner with me?"

Dallas whispered, "I thought you'd never ask."

His eyes scanned her face, avidly, intensely. His lips were only inches away now. "We could have room service."

"Better," she whispered, returning every invisible caress with her eyes, her face, the imperceptible movements of her body.

"We could skip dinner."

Dallas breathed, "I thought you'd never ask."

# Chapter Fifteen

If ever Dallas had allowed her aching imagination to go this far, she might have expected a moment of awkwardness between two strangers meeting again after such a long time. There was none. Inside Daniel's hotel room, the draperies were drawn, the door was locked, and he took her in his arms. For a moment they were so overwhelmed by the onslaught of emotions that they could not even kiss; they simply held each other and clung to each other, wrapping their arms around each other and letting their closeness fill them. His breath was ragged against her neck and Dallas's head was spinning in counterpoint to the beat of her heart. Then Daniel's mouth covered hers, fiercely, greedily, and every coherent thought and need and response Dallas had ever had dissolved into the flame of desire.

This time there was no long and languorous love-making, no skillful giving and receiving of pleasure, no passion hazed, no timeless explorations. They were lying on the bed, clothing half discarded, tangled in each other's arms and legs, taking of each other with surges of hunger and moments of wonder, listening only to the dictates of their bodies and their hearts.

Once they were distracted, and that was when Daniel murmured breathlessly, "Why, Dallas, you're wearing a bra."

"I do...sometimes." She gasped as his hand, closed over the sheer scrap of lace and embroidery.

"Silk?"

Dallas shook her head against the pillow, biting her lips against the threads of pleasured agony his fingers were sending through her. "Nylon," she managed.

"Feels like heaven," he muttered, and his mouth replaced his hand; a rush of heat and moisture then penetrated the material and made Dallas moan out loud with need for him. In only moments the material was pushed away and his lips and tongue and breath were upon her bare skin. And in moments after that, he was inside her, filling her, answering her desperate demands, bringing them both to a quick, fevered, driving climax in which time disintegrated and space was shattered, and the known world heaved upon its axis and then dissolved into a thousand ephermeral pieces, leaving only the two of them, breaths and bodies and heartbeats intertwined, drifting amidst the wonder of it.

"I feel born again," Dallas whispered, letting her hands drift in aimless delight over the length of his perspiration-dampened arm, testing the strength of it, the texture of the smooth hairs along its surface, its shape and its warmth. She could do that forever.

"My heart just started beating for the first time in four months," he murmured.

"There was never anyone else, in all this time—"

"Not even in my thoughts."

"God, I've missed you."

"I couldn't get away from you."

Suddenly energized with a surge of joy so intense that its bright-white color practically filled the room, Dallas laughed out loud. She rolled over on top of him, her legs stretched out over his, her breasts tantalizing his chest, her fingers spread through his hair. Her eyes danced seductively. "Let me show you how we do it in the big city, fella."

His eyes sparked back at her. "Witch." But, already, one strong hand had circled her neck, bringing her lips down to his, the other hand silpped around her hips, guiding her toward him. "I've been looking forward to this," he murmured against her mouth, just before, with one strong thrust, the depth of his penetration took Dallas's breath away, and they once again were caught up in the cataclysm that threatened to consume them both.

WITHIN TWO DAYS, the intense electric colors of their joyful reunion had settled into a warm glow; a comfortable certainty replaced the urgent edge of passion, and they began to relax. They even dressed and went out to dinner.

Daniel was fascinated by the way the drape bodice of her emerald-green silk dress clung to the shape of her breasts; Dallas couldn't get over how handsome Daniel looked in a tie. *I can't believe I'm doing this,* she thought a little hazily. *I can't believe I'm sitting across from him in a real restaurant, eating coquilles St. Jacques and sipping white wine and watching the way the candlelight plays in his eyes.* She had thought the illusion would fade when brought into the world of reality. She had thought his power over her would disappear when he was transplanted from his natural habitat into hers. But the magical connection they had discovered upon the mountain had bound them through months of time and miles of separation, and it held as strongly now as it ever had. Perhaps even more strongly, as though nothing could ever break it.

*Dangerous ground there, Dallas.*

Dallas put down her fork and sipped her wine. Then she replaced her wineglass, folded her hands in her lap and looked at him. "Daniel," she said quietly, "I think we have to get a few things straight."

He touched his napkin to his lips and sat back, his attention immediately hers.

She looked at him steadily. "You broke my heart, you know."

The corner of his lips turned in a small, half-pained smile. His voice was husky. "You didn't do a hell of a lot of good for mine either, lady."

She took a breath, tightening her hands in her lap. "It's not going to happen again," she told him firmly. "We're grown-up people; we can handle this thing. We know it's not going to last forever. But we're together now because we enjoy each other—"

"And because you're the most enchanting woman I've ever met," he interrupted softly.

Her eyes were caught in his, even as a playful dimple formed at the edge of her mouth. "And because you're the best lover I've ever had."

"And because you take my breath away."

"And you make me remember what life is all about." Dallas felt herself becoming lost in the depth of his eyes, the wonder of his presence. She took another steadying breath. "But it's nothing permanent."

He nodded. "Right."

"We'll have a good time while we can; we'll say good-bye; we won't be sorry."

"Right."

"It just can't work."

"No chance."

"We both know that."

He looked at her soberly. "I'm going to love you forever."

Dallas's hand came out and wrapped around his. Helplessness stole over her. "Me, too," she whispered.

THEY HAD A LITTLE OVER A WEEK together, and they crammed into that time everything they possibly could. They went to the movies and ate tons of buttered popcorn. Dallas introduced Daniel to the delights of scented bubble bath. They walked through the city in the March wind and listened to the traffic sounds and held hands and window shopped; they laughed and they talked, and a cautious hope began to bloom within Dallas. She was on home ground now, in the world of traffic lights and taxicabs, fast-food restaurants and sidewalk joggers; she was carefree and unfettered and in control. And Daniel was with her. He could learn to love her world. Already he seemed to belong here. He was happy, she knew he was. He could write anywhere, couldn't he? Maybe, there was a chance.

Dallas said expansively, "Let's go to New York. Yes, that's exactly what we should do. You said you missed the theater. We'll fly up there and see a show, have dinner—a couple of dinners—go shopping—"

He laughed and put his arm around her waist, hugging her to him. A car whizzed by with a blare of its horn, and the wind chapped their cheeks. "So that's what we should do, hm?"

She nodded enthusiastically. "But first you should let me show you Detroit."

"The very garden spot of the country in March."

"The river at night is spectacular, Daniel. Do you like ethnic food? There's the best Hungarian place…"

The remainder of her words were lost in the creak and groan of a garbage truck as it lumbered by, but already an absent, pensive look had come over Daniel's face.

That night as she came from the bathroom, dressed for bed in a newly purchased negligee of sapphire-blue, she noticed the same look upon Daniel's face as he lay propped up against the pillows, his eyes focused on the flickering television set but not watching it.

She knelt upon the bed beside him and was silent for a moment. He smiled at her, but the haunted look did not completely disappear from his eyes.

"What's wrong?" she inquired softly.

"Nothing." He leaned forward to turn off the television set, and the blankets fell away from his waist, revealing a momentary glimpse of strong flank and thigh. He sat back, drawing her instincitvely into the circle of his arms, his hands playing over the silky fabric of her nightgown. "Hm. Love it. What kind of material is this?"

"Acetate. Melted plastic."

His hand cupped her breast, his fingers massaging the slippery fabric over her flesh. "At least, technology has made one meaningful contribution to the world. You wouldn't believe how erotic this feels."

"Hm…yes, I would." She lifted her face and brushed his lips lightly, but when he would have taken more, she brought her hand to his face, stroking his beard. She probed, "What were you thinking about, before? When I came in?"

His hand slid down her side, explored the feel of gliding material against the curve of her waist and her hip, and that far away look was in his eyes again. His hand rested upon her waist. "Just that the crocus will be coming up soon on the mountain. Maybe this week. You should see them, Dallas, when they first pop up beneath the snow, purple and red and brilliant yellow, like a rainbow through the clouds, a piece of heaven. There's nothing more beautiful in the world." Then he smiled down at her, eyes crinkling with affection, hand tightening on her waist. "Except maybe you."

Dallas let her hand slide down to his shoulder, and she rested her face against his chest so that he couldn't see the desolation that had come into her eyes. Already he was slipping away from her. Already a part of him was back there, just as a part of her would be forever centered in Detroit, with the stories that had to be told, the wrongs had to be righted, the lights and the cameras and the movement. Like the giant Antaeus, Daniel could not survive long away from his own patch of earth, and though Dallas might go mad when torn away from her natural habitat, Daniel would, quite simply, die.

That night she did not fall asleep easily in his arms. She was thinking of how soon it would be that those arms would no longer hold her, and she was too sad to sleep.

ON MARCH TWENTIETH the court rendered its decision—in Daniel's favor. The ecstatic relief in Daniel's eyes was more exciting to Dallas than any award she had ever won, any triumph she had ever claimed, for his victory was hers, and nothing that had ever happened in her life was as exciting or as fulfilling as the look on her lover's face when he walked out of the courtroom, free to live his life as he chose.

They went out, they drank far too much champagne, they laughed, and they toasted each other and the United States Government and the federal justice system and the world in general. Only dimly did Dallas wonder why she was celebrating. Only dimly did she realize that the victory meant that there was no more reason for Daniel to stay here, and their idyll was at an end.

They made love most of the night, and when they awoke the next morning, they looked at each other and knew it was time to say good-bye again.

There was no point in fighting it. They both knew it must come.

Daniel drove Dallas to the airport in the dusty Jeep he had borrowed from Cal. As soon as he left her, he would be turning toward home. The lump that had been in Dallas's chest for the past twenty-four hours only intensified as he took her suitcase and walked with her into the small terminal. She didn't know how she was going to do it. She didn't know how she was going to find the courage to walk away from him again.

*We're both grown up people. We knew this was coming.*

She turned to him inside the terminal, forcing a bright smile. "Well, congratulations again. I'm happy for you, Daniel," she said sincerely, but the smile had begun to waver. "I really am."

Daniel said nothing. His face looked lined and grim. Dallas felt the tears start to restrict her throat. Determinedly she swallowed them back. *Damn it, there's no choice. For either of us.*

She said, haltingly, "I—I'll write you."

"No." His voice was calm and matter-of-fact, but he had to shift his gaze away. "It's better if we don't."

She swallowed again and nodded. Yes, better to end it now. They couldn't keep dragging out the goodbyes. They couldn't keep reaching for what they could never have. Her eyes were bleak as she took her suitcase from him.

"This is killing me," Daniel said quietly.

Dallas could only look at him, everything inside her slowly breaking into tiny, irredeemable pieces. The loud-speaker blared overhead, announcing her flight.

Daniel brought his hands to her shoulders; they tightened there almost painfully. "Damn it," he said lowly, fiercely, "why did it have to be you?"

He pulled her to him, and she said thickly, almost angrily, into his neck, "Why did it have to be *you*?"

The embrace was too brief, the separation too final. The sorrow and the emptiness in his face were as large as a desert, and his voice was as tired as he said, "We just weren't made to fit the mold, Dallas. The two of us are just too unconventional for our own good, I suppose. It simply can't be."

She looked one last time into that adored face, now touched with agony and streaked with loss, and all the light went out of her world as he turned and walked toward the door.

Dallas trudged toward the gate, gripping her suitcase firmly, her head held high, her eyes empty. So be it. Life had its great highs, its deep lows, its victories and defeats. It was over. There was nothing she could do.

*You can't live without him.*

What was she supposed to do? Give up her life for the sake of his? Ask him to do the same for her? Daniel was right; they were simply too individual, too dedicated to their own separate purposes to fit the conventions with which people committed themselves to each other—marriage, children, even living together. None of that was possible for them. It would have been different if he were a mechanic and she were a bank teller. It would have been different if so much did not depend upon them doing their own separate work and answering their own calls in their own way. It would have been different if *they* had been different.

*So you're going to let the only man you ever loved walk out the door? You're going to spend the rest of your life only half-alive, knowing he's doing the same?*

But there was nothing she could do. There was nothing either of them could do. It was out of their control.

"Like hell it is." The words were muttered out loud, and a look of fierce determination came over her face. She dropped her suitcase, swung around abruptly—and was face-to-face with Daniel, who was reaching out to touch her.

"Look," he said quickly, "I know this is going to sound crazy but—"

"I have six weeks leave accumulated."

"There's not much that needs my attention on the mountain during the summer."

"No one says I have to work every minute of every day. Hell, I'm a star. I can pick my own hours."

"A couple of weeks here, a couple of weeks there—"

"We can work it out."

They were breathless, excited, their eyes shooting sparks, their faces glowing with determination. They tumbled into each other's arms, laughing. "We can do it!" Dallas cried, hugging him hard.

Daniel pushed himself a little away, but just a little, so that he could look down at her. His eyes were brilliant, radiating joy. "This is going to be one hell of a crazy relationship," he warned her, loving it.

"It always was." Dallas laughed and tightened her arms around him, pressing her face into his chest. "But we're going to make it work. We're going to be okay."

"We always were," Daniel answered her softly, and closed his eyes, holding her.

After a long moment, they moved apart. Daniel bent to pick up her suitcase, and they turned and walked through the door together.

# Take 4 books & a surprise gift FREE

---

## SPECIAL LIMITED-TIME OFFER

Mail to    **Harlequin Reader Service**®

In the U.S.
2504 West Southern Ave.
Tempe, AZ 85282

In Canada
P.O. Box 2800, Station "A"
5170 Yonge Street
Willowdale, Ontario M2N 6J3

**YES!** Please send me 4 free Harlequin American Romance® novels and my free surprise gift. Then send me 4 brand-new novels as they come off the presses. Bill me at the low price of $2.25 each —a 11% saving off the retail price. There are no shipping, handling or other hidden costs. There is no minimum number of books I must purchase. I can always return a shipment and cancel at any time. Even if I never buy another book from Harlequin, the 4 free novels and the surprise gift are mine to keep forever.

---

Name _____ (PLEASE PRINT)

---

Address _____ Apt. No. _____

---

City _____ State/Prov. _____ Zip/Postal Code _____

This offer is limited to one order per household and not valid to present subscribers. Price is subject to change.

DOAR—SUB-1

# Readers rave about
# Harlequin American Romance!

"...the best series of modern romances
I have read...great, exciting, stupendous,
wonderful."
—S.E.*, Coweta, Oklahoma

"...they are absolutely fantastic...going to be
a smash hit and hard to keep on the
bookshelves."
—P.D., Easton, Pennsylvania

"The American line is great. I've enjoyed
every one I've read so far."
—W.M.K., Lansing, Illinois

"...the best stories I have read in a long
time."
—R.H., Northport, New York

*Names available on request.

H·A·R·L·E·Q·U·I·N

# FIRST·CLASS
*Sweepstakes*

## OFFICIAL RULES

1. NO PURCHASE NECESSARY. To enter, complete the official entry/order form. Be sure to indicate whether or not you wish to take advantage of our subscription offer.

2. Entry blanks have been preselected for the prizes offered. Your response will be checked to see if you are a winner. In the event that these preselected responses are not claimed, a random drawing will be held from all entries received to award not less than $150,000 in prizes. This is in addition to any free, surprise or mystery gifts which might be offered. Versions of this sweepstakes with different prizes will appear in Preview Service Mailings by Harlequin Books and their affiliates. Winners selected will receive the prize offered in their sweepstakes brochure.

3. This promotion is being conducted under the supervision of Marden-Kane, an independent judging organization. By entering the sweepstakes, each entrant accepts and agrees to be bound by these rules and the decisions of the judges, which shall be final and binding. Odds of winning in the random drawing are dependent upon the total number of entries received. Taxes, if any, are the sole responsibility of the prize winners. Prizes are nontransferable. All entries must be received by August 31, 1986.

4. The following prizes will be awarded:

   (1) Grand Prize: Rolls-Royce™ *or* $100,000 Cash!
   (Rolls-Royce being offered by permission of Rolls-Royce Motors Inc.)

   (1) Second Prize: A trip for two to Paris for 7 days/6 nights. Trip includes air transportation on the Concorde, hotel accommodations...PLUS...$5,000 spending money!

   (1) Third Prize: A luxurious Mink Coat!

5. This offer is open to residents of the U.S. and Canada, 18 years or older, except employees of Harlequin Books, its affiliates, subsidiaries, Marden-Kane and all other agencies and persons connected with conducting this sweepstakes. All Federal, State and local laws apply. Void in the province of Quebec and wherever prohibited or restricted by law. Winners will be notified by mail and may be required to execute an affidavit of eligibility and release, which must be returned within 14 days after notification. Canadian winners will be required to answer a skill-testing question. Winners consent to the use of their name, photograph and/or likeness for advertising and publicity purposes in conjunction with this and similar promotions without additional compensation. One prize per family or household.

6. For a list of our most current prize winners, send a stamped, self-addressed envelope to: WINNERS LIST, c/o Marden-Kane, P.O. Box 10404, Long Island City, New York 11101